***The Door Was Thrown Open with
a Crash, and Rogan Entered Like
a Sudden Storm on a Peaceful Day . . .***

"You have gone too far, woman," he bellowed at Liana. "You have not my permission to dismiss my servants."

Liana turned in the tub to look at him. He wore only his big white shirt that hung to the top of his thighs, a wide leather belt about his waist . . . His sleeves were rolled up at the elbows, exposing thickly muscled forearms.

Liana could feel perspiration breaking out on her forehead. She stood in the tub, her slim, firm, full-breasted body rosy and warm from the hot water. "Would you please hand me that drying cloth?" she asked softly in the silence, for Rogan had ceased shouting.

Rogan could only gape at her. She won't be able to use her body to make me forget what she has done today, he thought, but his feet took a step toward her and one hand reached out to touch the curve of her breast.

Liana told herself not to lose her head. She wanted this man, oh yes, but she wanted him for more than a few minutes. She put her hand out and untied the strings of his shirt at the throat, then touched his skin with her fingertips. "The water is still hot," she said softly. "Perhaps you'd allow me to wash you . . ."

Books by Jude Deveraux

The Velvet Promise
Highland Velvet
Velvet Song
Velvet Angel
Sweetbriar
Counterfeit Lady
Lost Lady
River Lady
Twin of Ice
Twin of Fire
The Temptress
The Raider
The Princess
The Awakening
The Maiden
The Taming
The Conquest
A Knight in Shining Armor
Wishes
Mountain Laurel
The Duchess
Eternity
Sweet Liar

Published by POCKET BOOKS

Most Pocket Books are available at special quantity discounts for bulk purchases for sales promotions, premiums or fund raising. Special books or book excerpts can also be created to fit special needs.

For details write the office of the Vice President of Special Markets, Pocket Books, 1230 Avenue of the Americas, New York, New York, 10020.

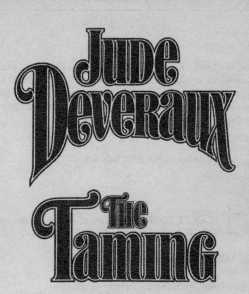

JUDE DEVERAUX

THE TAMING

POCKET BOOKS

New York   London   Toronto   Sydney   Tokyo   Singapore

This book is a work of historical fiction. Names, characters, places and incidents relating to non-historical figures are either the product of the author's imagination or are used fictitiously. Any resemblance of such non-historical incidents, places or figures to actual events or locales or persons, living or dead, is entirely coincidental.

An *Original* Publication of POCKET BOOKS

POCKET BOOKS, a division of Simon & Schuster Inc.
1230 Avenue of the Americas, New York, NY 10020

Copyright © 1989 by Deveraux Inc.

ISBN: 0-671-74383-X

First Pocket Books printing May 1989

14   13   12   11   10   9   8   7

POCKET and colophon are registered trademarks of Simon & Schuster Inc.

Cover art by Lisa Falkenstern
Cover photo by Paccione Photography Inc.

Printed in the U.S.A.

The Taming

CHAPTER ONE

England
1445

*E*ither your daughter goes or I do," Helen Neville said sternly, hands on hips as she looked down at her husband, Gilbert. He was stretched out on a cushioned window seat, the sun streaming in through the old stone window past blue-painted wooden shutters. He was rubbing the ears of his favorite hound while eating tasty little bits of ground meat.

As usual, Gilbert didn't make any response to Helen's demand, and she clenched her fists in anger. He was twelve years older than she and lazy beyond anything she'd ever known. In spite of the fact that he spent most of his time on a horse following a soaring hawk, his belly was large and growing bigger by the day. She had married him for his money, of course, married him for his gold plate, for his thousands of hectares of land, for his eight castles (two of which he'd never seen), for his horses, his army of men, for the beautiful clothes he could give her and her two children. She had read a list of Gilbert Neville's possessions and said yes to the marriage proposal without even asking to see the man.

Now, a year after their marriage, Helen asked herself, If she had met Gilbert and seen his slothfulness, would she have wondered who ran his estates? Did he have a superior steward? She knew he had only one legitimate child, a pale, shy-looking girl who said not a word to Helen before the marriage, but perhaps Gilbert had an illegitimate son who ran his estates.

After they were married and Helen knew she had a husband who was as lazy in bed as he was out of it, she found out who ran the Neville lands.

Liana! Helen wished she'd never heard the name. That sweet-looking, shy-seeming daughter of Gilbert's was a devil in disguise. Liana, like her mother before her, ran everything. Liana sat at the steward's table while the peasants paid their yearly rents. Liana rode through the countryside and saw to fields and ordered broken roofs repaired. Liana decided when a castle had become too dirty and the crops depleted and told the retainers it was time to move. Three times in the last year Helen had first heard that they were moving when she saw a maid packing her bedding.

It had done no good to explain to Gilbert or Liana that she, Helen, was now the lady of the manor and that Liana should relinquish her power to her stepmother. Both of them had merely looked at Helen curiously, as if one of the stone heads of the gutters had begun to speak, then Liana had gone back to ruling and Gilbert had returned to doing nothing.

Helen had tried to take charge on her own, and for a while she thought she was succeeding—until she found out that each servant was asking Liana for verification before carrying out her order.

At first, Helen's complaints to Gilbert had been mild, and usually after she had pleased him in bed.

Gilbert had paid her little mind. "Let Liana do what she likes. You can't stop her. You could no more stop Liana or her mother than you could stop the fall of a boulder. It was and is best to get out of their way." He'd turned over and gone to sleep, but Helen had lain awake all night, her body hot with rage.

By morning she was ready to be a boulder, too. She was older than Liana and, if need be, much more cunning. After her first husband had died and his younger brother had inherited the estates, Helen and her two little girls had been pushed aside by her sister-in-law. Helen had had to stand by and watch as duties that had once been hers were taken over by a younger, much less competent woman. When Gilbert Neville's proposal came, she leaped at the chance to once again have her own household, her own home. But now her place was being usurped by a small, pale girl who should have been married and sent away from her father's house years ago.

Helen had tried to talk to Liana, had tried to tell her of the pleasures of having her own husband, her own children, her own household.

Liana had blinked at her with those big blue eyes of hers, looking as meek as an angel on the chapel ceiling. "But who will take care of my father's estates?" she'd asked simply.

Helen gritted her teeth. "*I* am your father's wife. *I* will do what needs to be done."

Liana's eyes twinkled as she looked at Helen's sumptuous velvet dress with a train in back, at the low V neck in front and in back that exposed a great deal of her beautiful shoulders, at the heavily embroidered, padded headdress, and smiled. "The sun would burn you in that."

Helen found herself defending her words. "I would dress suitably to ride a horse. I'm sure I can ride as

3

well as you can. Liana, it's not proper that you remain in your father's house. You are nearly twenty years old. You should have your own home, your own—"

"Yes, yes," Liana said. "I'm sure you're right, but I must go now. There was a fire in the village last night and I must see to the damage."

Helen had stood there, her face red, her temper black. What good did it do her to be married to one of the richest men in England, to live in one castle after another where the riches were more than she'd ever believed possible? Thick, colorful tapestries hung from every wall, every ceiling was painted with biblical scenes, every bed, table, and chair was covered with an embroidered cloth. Liana kept a roomful of women who did nothing but bend over tapestry frames and ply their needles. The food was divine, as Liana enticed cooks with excellent wages and fur-trimmed gowns for their wives. The latrines, the moat, the stables, the courtyards were always clean, as Liana liked cleanliness.

Liana, Liana, Liana, Helen thought, putting her fists to her temples. With the servants, it was always what Lady Liana wanted, what Lady Liana had ordered, or even what Gilbert's first wife had established. Helen might not have existed for all the power she had in the running of the Neville properties.

It was when Helen's two little girls had begun to quote Liana that Helen's anger came to the boiling point. Young Elizabeth had wanted a pony of her own, and Helen had smiled and said she could have it. Elizabeth had merely blinked at her mother, then said, "I'll ask Liana," and run off.

It was that incident that had caused Helen to now give her husband an ultimatum. "I am less than nothing in this house," she said to Gilbert. She didn't bother to keep her voice down, even though she was well aware of the listening servants around them. They were Liana's servants, well-trained, obedient men and women who knew their young mistress's generosity as well as her wrath and who would, upon request, have laid down their lives for her.

"Either your daughter goes or I do," Helen repeated.

Gilbert looked over the tray of meats that were molded into shapes of the twelve apostles. He chose St. Paul and popped him into his mouth. "And what am I to do with her?" he asked lazily. There wasn't much on earth that could excite Gilbert Neville. Comfort, a good hawk, a good hound, good food, and peace were all he asked in life. He had no idea what his first wife had done to increase the wealth his father had left him and the huge dowry she had brought to the marriage, nor did he know what his daughter did. To his mind, the estates ran themselves. The peasants farmed; the nobility hawked; the king made laws. And it also seemed that women quarreled.

He had seen the beautiful young widow Helen Peverill as she rode across her dead husband's land. Her dark hair had been streaming down her back, her large breasts were nearly coming out of her gown, and the wind plastered her skirts to strong, healthy thighs. Gilbert had experienced a rare moment of lust and had told her brother-in-law he'd like to marry Helen. Gilbert hadn't done much after that until Liana told him it was time for the wedding. After one lusty wedding night, Gilbert was satisfied with Helen and expected her to go off and do whatever women did all day. But she hadn't. Instead, she had begun to nag and nag—about Liana, of all things. Liana was such a sweet, pretty child, always seeing that the musicians played songs that Gilbert liked, telling the maids to bring him food and, on long winter evenings, telling stories to entertain him. He could not understand why Helen wanted Liana to go away. Liana was so quiet, one hardly knew she was around.

"I guess Liana can have a husband if she wants one," Gilbert said, yawning. He believed in people doing what they wanted to. He thought the men worked in the fields from daylight to dark because they wanted to.

Helen tried to calm herself. "Of course Liana doesn't want a husband. Whyever should she want a man to tell her what to do when she has absolute freedom—and absolute power—here? If I had had such power in my dead husband's home, I would never have left." She threw up her hands in a gesture of helpless anger. "To have power and no man to cater to! Liana has heaven on earth. She will *never* leave here."

Even though Gilbert didn't understand Helen's complaints, her screeching was beginning to bother him. "I will speak to Liana and see if there is a husband she wants."

"You have to command her to take a husband," Helen said. "You have to choose a man for her and tell her she is to marry him."

Gilbert looked down at his hound and smiled in memory. "I crossed Liana's mother once and only once. I am not about to make the same error again and cross her daughter."

"If you do not get your daughter out of my house, you will regret crossing *me,*" Helen said before turning on her heel and leaving the room.

Gilbert scratched his hound's ears. This new wife was as a kitten to a lion compared to his first wife. He really couldn't understand what Helen was angry about. It had never crossed his mind that a person would actually *want* responsibility. He picked up a molded St. Mark and ate it thoughtfully. Vaguely, he remembered someone warning him against having two women in the same household. Perhaps he would talk to Liana and see what she thought of this idea of getting a husband. If Helen carried out her threat and moved to another estate, he'd miss her in his bed. But if Liana did marry, perhaps she would marry someone with good breeding hawks.

"So," Liana said softly, "my esteemed stepmother wants to throw me out of my own home, out of the home my mother worked to increase and I have managed for three years."

Gilbert thought perhaps his head was beginning to hurt. Helen had ranted at him for hours on end last night. It seems Liana had given some order for new cottages to be built in the walled town at the foot of the castle. Helen was horrified that Liana planned to use Neville money to pay for these cottages rather than let the peasants pay for them themselves. Helen had been so angry and screeched so loudly that all six of Gilbert's hawks had flown from their perches into the rafters. They had been hooded to keep them calm and the blind, panicked flight had caused one bird to break its neck. Gilbert knew that something had to be done; he couldn't bear losing more of his beloved hawks.

His first thought was to fit the two women with armor and let them joust for who remained and who left, but women had weapons harder than steel: They had words.

"I think Helen believes you'll be, well, happier in

7

your own home. With your own husband and a few brats." Gilbert couldn't imagine being happier than on the Neville lands, but who knew about women?

Liana walked to the window and looked out across the inner courtyard, across the thick castle walls and below to the walled town. This was just one of the estates her family owned, only one of the many she managed. Her mother had spent long years training Liana how to treat the people, how to check the steward's records, and how to bring in a profit every year that would be used to buy more land.

Liana had been angry when her father said he was going to marry a pretty young widow. She didn't like the idea of another woman's trying to take her mother's place and she had a premonition of trouble, but Gilbert Neville had his own stubborn streak and sincerely believed he should be allowed to do whatever he wanted whenever he wanted. For the most part, Liana was pleased he wasn't one of those men who thought of nothing but war and weapons. He stayed with his hounds and his hawks and left the more important matters first to his wife, then to his daughter.

Until now. Now he'd married the vain Helen, whose foremost thought was profit so that she could buy more and richer clothes. Helen kept five women working long hours sewing on her gowns. There was one woman who did nothing but sew on seed pearls. Last month alone, Helen had purchased twenty-four pelts of fur, and the month before that she had bought a basketful of ermine pelts, thinking no more of the expense than if she'd purchased a basket of corn. Liana knew that if she turned over the running of the estates to Helen, she'd bleed the peasants dry just so she could have a belt of gold and diamonds.

"Well?" Gilbert asked from behind Liana. Women!

he thought. He was going to miss the day's hunting if he didn't get an answer from his daughter. The way Helen was acting, she might climb on a horse and follow him just so she could continue to berate him.

Liana turned to her father. "Tell my stepmother I will marry if I find a *suitable* man."

Gilbert looked relieved. "That seems fair enough. I'll tell her, and she'll be happy." He started out the door, then paused and put his hand on his daughter's shoulder in a rare display of affection. Gilbert wasn't a man to look at the past, but at this moment he wished he'd never seen Helen, never married her. He hadn't realized how comfortable he'd been with his daughter to look after his simple needs and a maid now and then to care for his baser needs. He shrugged. There was no use regretting what couldn't be changed. "We'll find you a lusty young man who'll give you a dozen brats to fret over." He left the room.

Liana sat down hard on the feather mattress of her bed and waved her maid out of the room. Liana held her hands up and saw how they were shaking. She'd once faced a crowd of peasants armed with sickles and axes alone, with three terrified maids behind her, yet she'd kept her head and turned the rabble away by giving them what food she carried with her and jobs on her land. She'd dealt with drunken soldiers; she had once escaped a rape by an overzealous suitor. She had been able to deflect one disaster after another with calmness, assurance, and peace of mind.

But the idea of marriage terrified her. Not just frightened her, but deep-down, inside-her-soul terrified her. Two years ago she had seen her cousin Margaret married off to a man chosen by the girl's father. Before the marriage the man had written love sonnets to Margaret's beauty. Margaret used to talk about how her forthcoming marriage was a love match and she so looked forward to a life with this beloved man.

After the marriage, the man showed his true self. He sold most of Margaret's immense dowry to pay his huge debts. He left Margaret in an old, decaying, cold castle with but a few retainers, then went to court, where he spent most of the rest of her dowry on jewels for his many high-born whores.

Liana knew how fortunate she was to have the power of running her father's estates. She knew that no woman had any power unless it was granted to her by a man. Men had been asking for her hand in marriage since she was four years old. She had been betrothed once, when she was eight, but the young man had died before she was ten. Her father had never bothered to accept any offers after that and so Liana had quietly been able to escape marriage. When some suitor had pressed his petition, all Liana had had to do was remind Gilbert of what chaos her marriage would cause and Gilbert refused the offer.

But now this greedy Helen was interfering. Liana considered turning all power of running the estates over to her stepmother and retiring to their estate in Wales. Yes, that would be remote enough. She could live there in privacy, and soon both Helen and her father would forget about her.

Liana stood up, her fists clenched at her side, her simple, unornamented velvet gown sweeping the tile floor. Helen would never allow her to live in peace. Helen would pursue her to the ends of the earth to make sure her stepdaughter was as miserable as all women seemed to be in marriage.

Liana picked up her hand mirror from a little table by the window and stared at her reflection. In spite of all the love poems eager young men who wanted to marry her had written, in spite of the songs the traveling singers who were paid by her had sung, she could not see that she was a beauty. She was too pale, too blonde, too . . . too innocent-looking to be a beauty. Helen was beautiful, with her snapping dark eyes that let everyone know she had secrets, with her sultry way of looking at men. Liana sometimes thought the reason she could control the servants so well was because she was sexless. When Helen walked across the courtyard, men stopped what they were doing and looked at her. Men tugged their forelocks in respect to Liana, but they didn't stand gaping or guffaw and punch each other when she passed.

She moved to the window and looked down into the courtyard. A pretty milkmaid was being teased by an assistant farrier, the boy's hands reaching for the girl's round, shapely body.

Liana turned away, for the sight was too painful for her to bear. Never could she hope for some young man to chase her around a well. She could never find out if some young man *wanted* to chase her. Her father's people would always treat her with the respect of her station and address her as "my lady." Her suitors would do anything to win her hand because they wanted her dowry. It wouldn't matter if she were a hunchback with three eyes; she would still receive flowery compliments and glowing praise of her beauty. Once, a man had sent her a poem about the beauty of her feet. As if he'd ever seen them!

"My lady."

Liana looked up to see her maid, Joice, standing in the doorway. Joice was the closest thing to a friend that Liana had. Being only ten years older than Liana, Joice was almost like a sister. Liana's mother had hired Joice to care for Liana when Liana was just a baby and Joice had been little more than a child herself. Liana's mother had taught her daughter to run estates, but when Liana had had a bad dream, it was Joice who'd comforted her. It was Joice who'd stayed up with her through childhood illnesses and Joice who'd taught her about things other than estate management. Joice had explained how babies were made and what the man who'd tried to rape her had wanted.

"My lady," Joice said, always careful to show respect to her young charge. Liana could afford to be friendly, but Joice was always aware of her place, always aware that tomorrow she could be without a roof over her head or food on the table. She did not volunteer advice that might not be wanted. "There is a dispute in the kitchen and—"

"You are fond of your husband, Joice?"

The maid hesitated before answering. The entire castle knew what Lady Helen was demanding, and the people were of the belief that if Liana left, the Neville estates would be dust in six years. "Aye, my lady, I am."

"Did you choose him or was he chosen for you?"

"Your mother chose him, but I believe she wanted to please me, so I was married to a young and healthy man and I have come to love him."

Liana's head came up. "Have you?"

"Oh yes, my lady, that often happens." Joice felt she was on safe ground here. All women were afraid before their marriage. "When one spends long winter nights together, love often follows."

Liana turned away. *If* one could spend time together, she thought. *If* your greedy husband didn't send you away. She looked back at her maid. "Am I pretty, Joice? I mean actually pretty enough so that a man might be interested in me and not in all this?" She moved her arm to indicate the silk-hung bed, the tapestry on the north wall, the silver-gilt ewer, the carved oak furniture.

"Oh yes, my lady," Joice answered glibly. "You are *very* pretty, beautiful actually. There is no man high or low who could resist you. Your hair——"

Liana put up her hand for the woman to stop. "Let's see to the kitchen dispute." She could not keep the heaviness out of her voice.

CHAPTER TWO

Six months!" Helen screamed at her husband. "For six months that daughter of yours has been finding fault with men! Not one of them is 'suitable.' I tell you, if she is not out of here in another month, I shall take this child of yours that I carry and never return."

Gilbert looked out the window at the rain and cursed God for sending two weeks of foul weather and for creating women. He watched Helen ease herself into a chair with the help of two maids. From the way she complained, it would seem that no woman had ever carried a child before, but what amazed him was how pleased he was at the prospect of another child and a chance to have a son at last. Helen's words and tone grated on him, but he was inclined to do anything she wanted—at least until his son was safely delivered.

"I shall speak to her," Gilbert said heavily, dreading another scene with his daughter. But now he realized that one of the women had to go, and since

14

Helen was able to produce sons, it had to be Liana who left.

A servant found Liana, and Gilbert met her in one of the guest rooms off the solar. He hoped the rain would clear soon and he could go hawking again and not have to deal with this unpleasant business further.

"Yes, Father?" Liana asked from the doorway.

Gilbert looked at her and hesitated for a moment. She was so like her mother, and at all costs he didn't want to offend her. "Many men have come to visit us since your mother—"

"Stepmother," Liana corrected. "Since my stepmother announced to the world that I was ready to be sold, that I was a bitch in heat and needed stud service. Yes, many men have come here to look at our horses, our gold, our land and also, as an afterthought, at the plain-faced Neville daughter."

Gilbert sat down. He prayed that in heaven there would be no women. The only female allowed would be the kestrel hawk. He wouldn't even allow mares or female dogs. "Liana," he said tiredly, "you're as pretty as your mother, and if I have to sit through one more dinner with men telling you, at length, of your beauty, I shall go off food forever. Tomorrow I may have my table set up in the stables. At least the horses will not regale me with how white my daughter's skin is, how radiant her eyes, how golden her hair, how rose-red her lips."

There was no answering smile from Liana. "So I am to choose one of these liars? I am to live like Cousin Margaret while my husband spends my dowry?"

"The man Margaret married was a fool. I could have told her that. He canceled a day's hawking to diddle with some man's wife."

"So I am to marry a man who likes hawking best? Is

that the solution? Perhaps we should hold a hawking tournament and the man with the hawk with the biggest kill wins me as a prize. It makes as much sense as anything else."

Gilbert rather liked that idea, but wisely didn't say so. "Now see here, Liana. I've liked some of the men who've been here to visit. What about that William Aye? Good-looking fellow he is."

"Every one of my maids thought so, too. Father, the man is stupid. I tried to talk to him about the bloodlines of the horses in his stables and he had no idea what they were."

Gilbert was taken aback at that. A man should know about his horses. "What about Sir Robert Fitzwaren? He seemed smart enough."

"He told everyone he was smart. He also said he was strong and brave and fearless. According to him, he's won every tournament he's ever entered."

"But I heard he was unseated four times last year at— Oh, I see what you mean. Bragging men can become tiresome."

Gilbert's eyes lit up. "What about Lord Stephen, Whitington's boy? Now there's a man for you. Good looking. Rich. Healthy. Smart, too. And the boy knows how to handle a horse and a hawk." Gilbert smiled. "I'd guess he knows something about women. I even saw him *reading* to you." Reading, in Gilbert's opinion, was an unnecessary burden for a person to carry.

Liana remembered Lord Stephen's dark blond hair, his laughing blue eyes, his skill with a lute, the way he controlled an unruly horse, how he'd read from Plato to her. He was charming to everyone he met, and everyone in the household adored him. He'd not only told Liana she was lovely, but one evening in a dark corridor he'd grabbed her and kissed her until she was breathless, then whispered, "I'd love to take you to bed with me."

Lord Stephen was perfect. Flawless. Yet something . . . Maybe it was the way he glanced at the gold vessels lined up on the mantelpiece in the solar or the way he'd looked so hard at Helen's diamond necklace. There was something about him that she didn't trust, but she couldn't say what. It wasn't wrong, exactly, for him to take note of the Neville wealth, but she wished she saw a bit more lust in his eyes for her person and not her wealth.

"Well?" Gilbert prompted. "Is there anything wrong with young Stephen?"

"Nothing, really," Liana said. "He's—"

"Good, then it's done. I shall tell Helen, and she can start planning the wedding. This should make her happy."

Gilbert left Liana alone, and she sat down on the bed as if her body were made of lead. It was settled. She was to *marry* Lord Stephen Whitington. To spend the rest of her life with a man she didn't know yet who would have absolute power over her. He could beat her, imprison her, impoverish her, and he'd have a perfect, and legal, right.

"My lady," Joice said from the doorway, "the steward asks to see you."

Liana looked up, blinking without seeing for a moment.

"My lady?"

"Have my horse saddled," Liana said, and damn the steward, she thought. She wanted a good long run, with the horse pounding beneath her. Perhaps enough exercise would help her forget what awaited her.

Rogan, the oldest of what was left of the Peregrine family, squatted on his heels and stared at the castle on the horizon. His dark eyes were full of his thoughts —and his fears. He would rather face a battle than what he faced today.

"Putting it off won't make it any easier," his brother Severn said from behind him. Both men were tall and broad-shouldered like their father, but Rogan had inherited a sheen of red to his dark hair from their father, while Severn, who had a different mother, had more delicate facial features and hair streaked with gold. Severn was also quicker to be impatient, and now he was impatient with his older brother's immobility.

"She won't be like Jeanne," Severn said, and behind him the twenty knights stopped moving and held their breath. Even Severn stopped breathing for a moment, fearing that he'd overstepped himself.

Rogan heard his brother, but he didn't betray the emotion that went through him at the mention of Jeanne's name. He did not fear war; he did not fear charging animals; he did not fear death, but the thought of marriage made him hesitate.

Below them ran a deep stream, and Rogan could almost feel the cold water on his body. He stood and went to his horse. "I will return," he said to his brother.

"Wait a minute!" Severn said, grabbing the reins. "Are we to just sit here and wait for you while you decide whether or not you have courage enough to visit a slip of a girl?"

Rogan didn't bother to answer but looked at his brother with hard eyes.

Severn released the reins. Sometimes Severn thought Rogan could tumble stone walls with those eyes of his. Even though he'd lived all his life with this older brother, Severn felt he knew very little about him; Rogan was not a man to reveal much about himself. As a boy, when that bitch Jeanne had betrayed him so publicly, Rogan had withdrawn into himself, and in the ten years since, no one had penetrated his outer shell of hardness.

"We will wait," Severn said, stepping out of the way and allowing Rogan to pass.

When Rogan was gone, one of the knights behind Severn grunted. "Sometimes a woman changes a man," he said.

"Not my brother," Severn answered quickly. "No woman anywhere is strong enough to change my brother." There was pride in his voice. The world around them might change from day to day, but Rogan knew what he wanted and how to go about getting it. "A woman alter *my* brother?" he said derisively.

The men smiled at the impossibility of such an idea.

Rogan rode down the hill, then along the stream for a while. He wasn't sure what he wanted to do, just put off the time when he had to go to the Neville heiress. What a man had to do for money disgusted him. When he had heard the heiress was being put up for sale, so to speak, he had told Severn to go and get her and bring her back with her wagonloads of portable wealth and the deeds to some of her father's estates. Or, better yet, return with the gold and papers alone and leave the woman behind. Severn had said that a man as rich as Gilbert Neville would want only the oldest Peregrine, the man who would become duke as soon as the Peregrines wiped the Howards off the face of the earth.

As usual, Rogan's body tightened with hatred when he thought of the Howards. The Howards were the cause of everything bad that had happened to the Peregrines for three generations. They were the reason he was now having to marry some old-maid heiress, the reason he wasn't at home now—in the *real* Peregrine home, the place the Howards had stolen. They had stolen his birthright, his home, and even his wife.

And marrying this heiress, he reminded himself, would bring him one step closer to regaining what was rightfully his.

There was a clearing in the trees and the stream spread out to catch in a beautiful rock-edged pool. On impulse, Rogan dismounted, then began to shed his clothes, undressing down to the loincloth tied about his waist. He stepped into the icy pool and began to swim as hard and as fast as he could. What he needed was a good long hunt to expend the pent-up energy in his body, but swimming might do as well.

He swam for nearly an hour, then stepped out of the pool, his sides heaving with exertion. Stretching out on a patch of sweet green grass in the sun, he was soon sound asleep.

He slept so soundly that he did not hear the quiet gasp of the woman as she came to the pool for water. Nor was he aware that the young woman stepped back into the trees and watched him.

Liana rode hard and fast, outdistancing her father's knight who tried to keep up with her. Her father's men ate rather than trained and she knew the trails of the land better than they did; it was easy to escape them. Once she was alone, she headed for the pool north of the castle. She'd be alone there and she'd be able to think about her forthcoming marriage.

She was still some distance away from the pool when she saw a bit of faded red through the trees. Someone was there. She cursed her luck, then cursed her foolishness at having left her guard behind. She halted her horse, tied him to a tree, then crept quietly toward the pool.

The red was the dress of one of the farmers' wives who lived in town and had three small fields outside the walls. Liana saw that the woman was standing absolutely still and was so absorbed in what she was looking at that she didn't hear Liana approach. Curious, Liana started to move softly forward.

"My lady!" the young woman gasped. "I . . . I came to get some w-water."

Her nervousness increased Liana's curiosity. "What were you looking at?"

"Nothing of any importance. I must go. My children will need me."

"You're leaving the pool with an empty water jug?" Liana pushed past her and looked through the bushes and immediately saw what had held the woman's attention. Lying on the grass in a patch of sunlight was a splendid-looking man: tall, broad-shouldered, slim-hipped, heavily muscled, with a strong-jawed face shadowed with dark whiskers and long, dark hair that glinted red in the sunlight. Liana looked from his feet to the top of his head, wide-eyed with interest as she gazed at the honey-colored skin of his nearly nude body. She'd had no idea a man could be so beautiful.

"Who is he?" she whispered to the farm wife.

"He's a stranger," the woman whispered back.

Near the man was a pile of clothes of coarse wool. With the sumptuary laws, it was often possible to guess a person's income and station in life by his clothes. This man wore no fur of any kind, not even the lowly rabbit allowed the lower classes. He had no musical instrument nearby, so he was no traveling musician.

"Perhaps he is a huntsman," the farm wife whispered. "Sometimes they come to trap game for your father. With your wedding, more game will be needed."

Liana shot the woman a quick look. Did everyone know of her life? Her wedding was what she'd come here to contemplate. She looked back at the man on the grass. He looked like a young Hercules, power and muscle now asleep, merely waiting to be awakened. If only Lord Stephen looked like this man, she wouldn't mind marriage so much. But even asleep, this man radiated more strength than Lord Stephen had when clad in full armor. For a moment she smiled as she pictured telling Helen she'd decided to marry a lowly huntsman, but then her smile left her because she doubted that this man would want her if she weren't endowed with wagonloads of silver and gold. For just one day she'd like to be a peasant girl, to see if she were woman enough to interest a handsome man.

She turned to the farmer's wife. "Take off your dress."

"My lady!"

"Take off your dress and give it to me, then return to the castle. Find my maid, Joice, and tell her no one is to search for me."

The woman paled. "Your maid will never talk to the likes of me."

Liana tugged an emerald ring from her finger and handed it to the woman. "Nearby is a knight, probably searching for me. Give him this and he will take you to Joice."

The woman's expression changed from fearfulness to slyness. "He is a handsome man, isn't he?"

Liana narrowed her eyes at the woman. "If I hear one word of this in the village, you'll regret it. Now, get out of here." She sent the woman away wearing only a coarse linen undergarment, as Liana wasn't about to allow the woman's filthy body to touch the velvet of her gown.

The peasant dress Liana put on was very different from her high-waisted, full-skirted gown. The scratchy wool was one piece that clung to her body from her neck to below her hips, showing the slim curves of her body. The wool was crude and dirty and it stank, but it was revealing. She rolled the sleeves, stiff with years of grease, back to her elbows. The skirt reached only to her ankles and the shortness made her feel free to walk or even run through the ferns.

With this dress on, Liana felt she was ready to face what lay ahead. She peeped through the branches to look at the man again. Every time she'd ever seen the peasants laughing and chasing one another through the fields came back to her. She'd once seen a boy give a flower to a girl. Would this divinely handsome man offer her flowers? Perhaps he'd weave a garland for her hair as one knight had done for her a few months ago—except this time it would be for *real*. This time the man would present her with flowers because of her person and not for her father's wealth.

Her heavy headdress removed and hidden in the bushes, her long pale hair streaming down her back, Liana stepped forward into the clearing and toward the man. He did not awaken even when she stumbled over a pile of rocks.

She moved closer to him, but he didn't stir. He was indeed a beautiful man, made the way God intended a man to look. She could hardly wait for him to see her. She'd been told that her hair was like spun gold. Would he think so?

His clothes were in a heap not too far from him, and she went to them and lifted his shirt, holding it at arm's length, putting her hands out to the wide edges of the broad shoulders. The wool was thickly spun, and she thought what a better job her women did at spinning.

As she looked at the shirt she saw something odd, then leaned forward for a closer look. Lice! The shirt was crawling with lice.

With a little squeal of disgust, she threw the shirt from her.

One moment the man was asleep on the ground and the next he was standing before her in all his nude glory. He was indeed magnificent: tall, powerfully muscled, not an ounce of fat. His thick shoulder-length hair was dark, but it looked almost red in the sunlight, and there was a reddish stubble on his heavy jaw. His eyes were dark green and alive with emotion.

"How do you do?" Liana said, holding out her hand to him, palm downward. Would he sink to one knee before her?

"You threw my shirt in a bog," he said angrily, looking down at the pretty blue-eyed blonde.

Liana withdrew her hand. "It was crawling with lice." What did one say to a huntsman when one was his equal? Lovely day, isn't it? Would you like to fill my water jug for me? There, that seemed ordinary enough.

He gave her an odd look. "You can get my shirt out of the bog and wash it. I have to go somewhere today."

He had a very pleasant voice, but she didn't like what he was saying. "It's good the shirt sank. I told you it was covered with lice. Perhaps you'd like to pick blackberries. I'm sure we could find—" To her consternation, the man grabbed her shoulders and turned her toward the pool, then gave her a shove.

"Get my shirt out of the bog and wash it."

How dare he touch her without permission! Liana thought. Wash his shirt, indeed! She'd leave now and go back to her own clothes and her horse and the safety of her father's castle. She turned away, but he caught her forearm.

"Can't you hear well, girl?" he said, spinning her about. "Either you get the shirt out or I throw you in after it."

"Throw me in?" she asked. She was on the verge of telling him who she was and just what she would or would not do when she looked into his eyes. Handsome eyes, yes, but also dangerous eyes. If she told him she was Lady Liana, daughter of one of the richest men in England, would he perhaps hold her for ransom?

"I . . . I have to get back to my husband and . . . and children. Lots of children," she said haltingly. She had liked this man's aura of power when he was asleep, but when he was holding her arm, she didn't like it nearly as much.

"Good," he said, "then, with lots of brats, you'll know how to wash a shirt."

Liana looked toward the oozy black bog where only his shirtsleeve could be seen. She had no idea how to wash a shirt, and the idea of touching the lice-infested thing repulsed her.

"My . . . my sister-in-law does my laundry," she said, and was pleased with herself for having thought of such a good idea. "I'll go back and send her to you. She'll be glad to wash it."

The man didn't say a word but pointed at the bog.

She realized he was not going to allow her to leave. Grimacing, Liana walked toward the bog and leaned forward to reach the edge of the sleeve. She couldn't reach it, so she stretched further—then further.

She fell face forward into the rich, thick ooze of mud, her arms sinking to her elbows, her face covered. For a moment she struggled to get out of the bog, but there was nothing to hold on to. Then an arm swooped down and pulled her up to dry land. She stood there sputtering for a moment, then the man pushed her backward into the pond.

Face forward into a bog, then backward into ice-cold water.

She managed to get to her feet and started out of the pond. "I am going home," she muttered, feeling close to tears. "Joice will make me a hot posset and build me a fire, and I'll—"

The man caught her arm. "Where do you think you're going? My shirt is still buried."

She looked up into his cold green eyes and all fear of him left her. Who did he think he was? He had no right to order her about even if he thought she was the lowliest field gleaner. So he thought he was her master, did he?

She was wet through and freezing, but anger was keeping her warm. She smiled what she hoped was an ingratiating smile at him. "Your wish is my command," she murmured, and managed to keep a calm face when he grunted with satisfaction, as if that was the answer she was supposed to give.

She turned her back to him and got a long stick from under a tree, then went back to the bog. She fished the shirt out, held it on the end of the stick for a moment, then with all her might, she sent it flying to hit him cold and hard smack across the face and chest.

While he was peeling the shirt from his body, Liana began to run. She knew the woods better than any stranger ever could, and she went straight to a hollow tree and disappeared inside it.

She heard him crashing through the woods nearby and she smiled to herself at his inability to find her. She'd wait until he was gone, then go to her horse on the other side of the pond and make her way home. If he was a huntsman, tomorrow she'd greet him in her father's house and have the satisfaction of hearing his apology for his conduct today. Perhaps she'd borrow one of Helen's gowns, something covered in furs, with a jeweled headdress. She'd sparkle so brightly he'd have to shield his eyes from the glare.

"You might as well come out," he said from just outside the dead tree.

Liana held her breath.

"You want me to come in after you? Or shall I chop the tree down around your ears?"

Liana couldn't believe he really knew where she was. Surely he was bluffing. She didn't move.

His big arm came into the tree, caught her waist, and pulled her out—and against his hard chest. His face was smeared with black mud, but those eyes of his burned, and for a moment Liana thought he might kiss her. Her heart began to pound in her breast.

"Hungry, are you?" he said, his eyes laughing at her. "Well, I haven't got time. I have another wench waiting for me." He pushed her from him and back toward the pond.

Liana decided that merely appearing before him in a radiant gown would not be enough. "I shall make him crawl," she muttered.

"Will you, now?" he said, overhearing her.

She whirled to face him. "Yes," she said through clenched teeth. "I will make you crawl. I will make you regret treating me like this."

He didn't smile, in fact his face seemed made of marble, but his eyes showed amusement. "You'll have

27

to wait for that day, because now I intend to make you wash my clothes."

"I'd sooner—" She broke off.

"Yes? Name your price, and I'll see if I can manage it."

Liana turned away from him. It was better to just get it over with, to get his clothes washed and get away from him. Today he had the power, but tomorrow she would be the one who held the reins—and the whip and the chains, she thought with a smile.

At the pond's edge she stopped, refusing to obey him with any semblance of acquiescence. Her attitude seemed to amuse him further. He picked up his muddy shirt and slammed it against her chest so that, by instinct, she caught it.

"Might as well do these too," he said, and heaped her arms full of his other lice-infested clothing, then knelt down and washed the mud off his face.

Liana gasped and dropped the load to the ground.

"Get busy," he said. "I need those clothes for courting."

Liana realized that the sooner she got this over with, the sooner she could get away from him. She grabbed a fist full of shirt, dunked it into the water, then slammed it against a rock. "She won't have you," Liana said. "She might like the look of you, but if she has any sense, she'll jump from the town wall before she'll agree to marry you."

He was stretched out on the grass in the sun, his head propped on his hands as he watched her. "Oh, she'll have me, all right. It's a matter of whether I'll want her. I'll marry no shrews. I'll take her only if she's biddable and soft-spoken."

"And stupid," Liana said. She wanted to kill the lice, so she picked up a small rock and began pounding the clothes. Then, as she turned the shirt over, she saw the tiny holes the rock was making. Her eyes widened in horror, then she smiled. She'd clean his clothes for him all right, but they'd look like a fisherman's net when she finished. "Only a stupid woman would have you," she said loudly, hoping to distract him from what she was doing.

"Stupid women are best," he answered. "I want no clever woman. Clever women cause a man trouble. Are you done with those yet?"

"They are filthy and need a lot of work," she said as sweetly as she could manage. Thinking of his appearing at a girl's door in clothes filled with holes pleased her. "And I guess women have given you a great deal of trouble in your life," she said. His vanity was overwhelming.

"Very little trouble." He was watching her.

Liana didn't like the way he was looking at her. In spite of her wet clothes, he was making her feel very warm. He seemed lazy and quiet now, but she'd seen his anger and felt the violence just under his skin.

"How many children did you say you have?" he asked softly.

"Nine," she said loudly. "Nine little boys, all of them big and strong like their father. And their uncles," she added nervously. "My husband has six huge brothers, strong as oxen, and tempers! I never saw such tempers. Only last week—"

"What a liar you are," he said calmly, putting his head back down on the ground and not looking at her. "You've never had a man."

She stopped pounding the clothes. "I've had a hundred men," she said, then stopped. "I mean, I've had my husband hundreds of times and—" She was making a fool of herself. "Here are your clothes. I hope they itch you to death. You *deserve* a body covered with lice."

She stood over him, then dropped the wet clothes on his hard, flat belly. He didn't flinch from the cold but stared up at her with eyes that seemed warm and compelling. She wanted to leave him and she knew she was now free, but somehow she just stood there, her eyes locked with his.

"Such good work must be rewarded. Bend to me, woman."

Liana felt herself sinking to her knees before him while he came up to meet her. He put his big hand behind her head, his fingers entwined in her hair, and pulled her lips to his.

A few men had tried to kiss Liana, but they had never been so expert as this. His lips, so unlike his manner, were soft and warm and she closed her eyes to the sensation.

The kiss was all she'd hoped a kiss could be and her arms moved to encircle his neck as she pressed her body to his, feeling his sun-warmed skin through her cold clothes. He moved his lips on hers, opening his mouth slightly, and she followed his lead. Her hands moved to his hair. It was clean from his swim and so warm she thought she could feel the redness of it.

When he broke the kiss and moved away from her, she kept her eyes closed and leaned toward him, wanting more of him.

"There, that's enough," he said with amusement in his voice. "A virginal kiss for a virgin. Now, go along home to whoever should have been protecting you and don't go chasing after men again."

Liana's eyes flew open. "Chasing after men? I was not—"

He gave her a quick kiss, a twinkle in his eyes, before rising. "Spying on me from the bushes. You ought to learn what lust is before you try to inspire it. Now, off you go before I change my mind and give you what you've asked for. I've got more important business to tend to today than some hungry virgin."

It didn't take Liana long to recover herself. She was on her feet in seconds. "I will freeze in hell before I am hungry for the likes of you."

He paused as he started to put a leg into a pair of wet braies. "I'm tempted to make you eat those words. No," he said and began moving again, "I have other things to do. Perhaps later, after I'm married, you might come to me. I'll see if I have time for you then."

There were no curse words vile enough to describe what Liana was feeling. "You will see me again," she managed to say. "Oh yes, you will, but I do not think you will be so arrogant when we meet again. Pray for your life, peasant." She stormed past him.

"I do every day," he called after her. "And I'm not—"

She didn't hear any more as, once in the trees, she pulled her gown and headdress from their hiding place and ran toward her horse. The animal waited quietly while Liana tore the woolen dress from her body. She flung it to the ground, then stamped on it, grinding it into the dirt.

"Disgusting!" she said. "Filthy, dirty people," she muttered. And she had thought the peasants' lives romantic. They were so *free!* "They have no one to protect them," she said to her horse. "If my guard had been here, he'd have skewered that swine. If Lord Stephen had been here, he'd have made him crawl. I would have laughed to see that red-haired devil kiss Lord Stephen's shoe. What shall I do with him, Belle?" she asked the horse. "The rack? Drawing and quartering? Disembowelment? Burning at the stake? Yes, I like that. I'll have him burned. I shall serve dinner, and his burning shall be the entertainment."

Dressed in her own clothes once again, she mounted her horse and gave a glance of hatred in the direction of the pond. She tried to imagine the man's violent death, but then she remembered his kiss. She shook her head as if to clear away those thoughts. Again she tried to think of his burning, but she couldn't get past imagining his beautiful form tied to the pole.

"Damn him!" she cursed, and kicked her horse forward.

She had not gone but a short distance when she came to fifty of her father's knights, suited in heavy armor as if going to war. *Now* they decide to look for me near the pond, she thought. Why didn't they come when he was tossing her in the water or making her wash his clothes . . . or when he was kissing her?

"My lady!" the lead knight exclaimed. "We have been searching for you. Have you been harmed?"

"Actually, I have," she said angrily. "In the forest on the east side of the pond is—" She stopped. She didn't know why, but suddenly fifty men against one unarmed peasant seemed very unfair.

"Is what, my lady? We will kill it."

"Is the largest flock of the prettiest butterflies I have ever seen," she said, giving the man her most dazzling smile. "I lost track of time. I am so sorry if I worried anyone. Shall we return?" She turned her horse and rode ahead of the men, greatly puzzled by what she'd done. It would be better, of course, to wait and tell her father what had happened and how that awful man had treated her. Yes, that was it. She was just being sensible. Her father would know how to deal with him. Perhaps seal him inside a nail-studded barrel. Yes, that sounded like a good idea.

CHAPTER
THREE

$\sim\cdot\!\!\!\!\!\!\!\!\ast\cdot\sim$

Rogan watched the girl go and regretted the fact that he hadn't had time for her. He would have liked to touch that pale skin of hers—and that hair! It was the color of the mane of a horse he'd owned as a boy.

A horse killed in battle by the Howards, he remembered with bitterness, and pulled hard on the knitted, footed stockings.

His big toe came through a hole just below the knee. Without thought, he pulled the hose over his toe then yanked on the braies again. His little toe stuck at the ankle. This time his clothing got his attention. He held the braies up to the sunlight and saw the hundreds of tiny holes. Now the stockings were holding together out of habit, but in a matter of days they'd start unraveling. He grabbed his shirt and saw that it too was full of holes, as was his woolen overtunic.

Damn the presumptuous snippet of a girl, he thought with anger. Here he was to marry the Neville heiress and his clothes were falling off his body. If he ever saw that wench again, he'd—

Rogan stopped his thoughts and looked at the shirt again. She'd not wanted to wash his clothes. What she'd wanted was a good tumble in the grass. When she didn't get it, she'd had her revenge on him, and revenge was something Rogan understood very well.

In spite of his anger, in spite of the fact that he was now going to have to go to the expense of new clothes, he looked at the sunlight shining through the holes in his shirt and he did something he rarely did: He smiled. Saucy wench, she wasn't afraid of him. She had risked a well-deserved beating when she'd pounded holes in his clothes. If he'd caught her, he would have . . . He would probably have given her the tumble she wanted, he thought, still smiling.

He tossed the shirt into the air, caught it, then began to dress. He felt better now about marrying the Neville heiress. Perhaps after his marriage he'd find the blonde beauty and see if he could give her what she wanted. Maybe he'd take her with him and maybe he'd fill her belly with the nine brats she claimed to have.

Once dressed, he mounted his horse and rode up the bank to where his brother and his men waited.

"We've waited long enough," Severn said. "Have you built your courage now? Can you face the girl?"

Rogan's humor left his face. "If you want to keep that tongue of yours, you'll hold it still. Mount and ride. I go to marry a woman."

Severn went to his waiting horse, and as he put his foot in the stirrup, something blue in the grass caught his attention. He picked it up and saw that it was a piece of yarn. He dropped it again and gave it no more thought as he rode after his hardheaded brother.

"My lady," Joice said again, then waited. But Liana made no response. "My lady!" she said louder, but still no response. Joice looked at Liana staring out the window, her mind far away. She had been this way since yesterday, when she'd returned from her ride. Perhaps it was her impending marriage—the messenger had been sent to Lord Stephen this morning—or perhaps it was something else altogether. Whatever it was, Liana was not telling anyone. Joice eased out of the room and closed the heavy oak door.

Liana hadn't slept during the night and she'd given up all attempts at work. She just sat on the window seat in her room and stared at the village below. She watched people scurrying, laughing, cursing.

The door opened with a bang. "Liana!"

There was no possibility of ignoring the angry, hate-filled voice of her stepmother. Liana turned cool eyes to her. "What do you want?" She couldn't look at Helen's beauty without seeing Lord Stephen's smiling face, his eyes shifting to the gold salver on the mantel.

"Your father wants you to come to the Hall. He has guests."

There was a bitterness in Helen's voice that piqued Liana's curiosity. "Guests?"

Helen turned away. "Liana, I don't think you should go down. Your father will forgive you; he forgives you everything. Tell him you have seen this man and do not want him. Tell him you have given your heart to Lord Stephen and want no one else."

Now Liana was indeed interested. "What man?"

Helen turned back to look at her stepdaughter. "It's one of those dreadful Peregrines," she said. "You probably don't know of them, but my former husband's land was near theirs. For all their long line of ancestors, they are poor as a honey-wagon driver—and about as clean."

"So what do these Peregrines have to do with me?"

"Two of them arrived last night and the oldest one says he has come to marry you." Helen threw up her hands. "It's like them. They don't ask for your hand—they announce that one of the filthy beasts is here to marry you."

Liana remembered another filthy man, a man who had kissed her and teased her. "I am pledged to Lord Stephen. The acceptance to his proposal has already been sent."

Helen sat down on the bed and weariness made her shoulders droop. "That's what I've told your father, but he won't listen. These men brought two huge hawks as gifts for him, two big peregrine falcons like their name, and Gilbert has spent all night with them recounting one hawking story after another. He is convinced they are the best of men. He doesn't notice the stench of them, the poverty of them. He ignores the stories of their brutality. Their father wore out four wives."

Liana looked steadily at her stepmother. "Why do you care who I marry? Isn't one man as good as another? What you want is for me to get out of your house, so what difference does it make who I marry?"

Helen put her hand on her growing belly. "You will never understand," she said tiredly. "I merely want to be mistress in my own house."

"While I must leave and go to some man who—"

Helen put up her hand. "It was a mistake for me to try to talk to you. Go to your father, then. Let him marry you off to this man, who will probably beat you, a man who will take every penny you have and leave you without so much as the clothes on your back. Clothes! Clothes are nothing to these men. The oldest one dresses worse than the kitchen boys. When he moves, you can see holes in his filthy garments." She heaved herself off the bed. "Hate me if you must, but I pray that you do not ruin your life merely to do what I say you should not." She left the room.

Liana wasn't much interested in this new man who had announced he planned to marry her. Men like him had been coming night and day for months now. For her part, she couldn't see a great deal of difference in them. Some were old, some were young, some had brains, some did not. What they had in common was a desire for the Neville money. What they wanted was—

"Holes in his clothes?" Liana said aloud, her eyes wide. "Holes in his clothes?"

Joice came into the room, "My lady, your father—"

Liana pushed past her maid and ran down the steep spiral stairs. She had to see this man, had to see him before he saw her. At the bottom of the stairs she ran out the door and through the courtyard, past knights lounging about, past horses waiting for riders, past spitcock boys resting in the sun, and into the kitchen. The enormous open fireplaces made the rabbit warren of rooms feverishly hot, but Liana kept running. She pulled open a little door near the slophole and went up the steep stone stairs to the musicians' gallery. She put her finger to her lips to silence the fiddle player as he started to address her.

The musicians' gallery was a wooden balcony at one end of the Great Hall, with a waist-high wooden rail blocking the musicians from view. Liana stood in one corner of the gallery and looked down into the Hall.

It was *him*.

The man she'd seen yesterday, the man who had kissed her, sat at her father's right hand, an enormous falcon on a perch between them. Sunlight streaming through the windows seemed to make the red in his hair catch fire.

Liana leaned back against the wall, her heart pounding. He wasn't a peasant. He had said he was off to do some courting, and he'd meant her. He had come to *marry* her.

"My lady, are you all right?"

Liana waved the harpist away and looked back at the men below, not sure of what she'd seen. There were two men with her father, but to her eyes, she could see only one of them. The dark man seemed to dominate the hall with his sprawling way of sitting and the intensity with which he spoke and listened. Her father laughed and the blond man laughed, but her man did not.

Her man? Her eyes widened at the thought.

"What is his name?" she whispered to the harpist.

"Who, my lady?"

"The dark man," she said impatiently. "There, that one. Below."

"Lord Rogan," the musician answered. "And his brother is—"

"Rogan," she murmured, not caring about the blond man. "Rogan. It suits him." Her head came up. "Helen," she said, then flung open the door and started running again. Down again through the kitchens, past a dog fight the men were laying odds on, across the cobbled yard to the south tower, then up the stairs, nearly knocking over two maids who had their arms full of laundry, and into the solar. Helen sat before a tapestry frame and barely glanced up when Liana came rushing in.

"Tell me about him," Liana demanded, panting from her run.

Helen was still smarting from Liana's remarks of an

39

hour before. "I know nothing about any man. I am merely a servant in my own home."

Liana grabbed a stool from against the wall and went to sit before Helen. "Tell me all you know about this Rogan. Is he the one who has asked for me? Reddish hair? Big, dark? Green eyes?"

Every person in the solar came to a standstill. Lady Liana had never shown the least interest in a man before.

Helen looked at her stepdaughter with concern. "Yes, he is a beautiful man, but can you not see more than his beauty?"

"Yes, yes, I know, his clothes are crawling with lice. Or they were until I— Tell me what you know of him," Liana demanded.

Helen did not understand this young woman at all, but she'd never seen her so alive, so flushed, so pretty. A feeling of dread was spreading over her. Sensible, sane, mature Liana could not possibly fall for a man's beauty. There had been hundreds of handsome men here in the last months and not one of them—

"Tell me!"

Helen sighed. "I don't know a lot about them. Their family is old. It's said their ancestors fought with King Arthur, but a few generations ago the eldest Peregrine gave the dukedom, the family seat, and the money to the family of his second wife. He had his eldest children declared illegitimate. After he was dead, the wife married a cousin of hers and the son of Peregrine became a Howard. Now the Howards own the title and the lands that once belonged to the Peregrines. That's all I know. The king declared all the Peregrines bastards and they were left with two decaying old castles, a minor earldom, and nothing else."

Helen leaned toward Liana. "I have seen where they

live. It is hideous. The roof has fallen in places. It's filthy beyond belief, and those Peregrines care nothing for dirt or lice or meat covered with maggots. They live for only one thing and that is to revenge themselves on the Howards. This man Rogan doesn't want a wife. He wants the Neville money so he can wage war on the Howards."

Helen took a breath. "The Peregrines are horrible men. They care only for war and death. When I was a child there were six sons, but four of them have been killed. Maybe only these two are left, or perhaps the men breed sons like rabbits."

On impulse, Helen took Liana's hand. "Please do not consider this man. He would eat you alive for breakfast."

Liana's head was reeling. "I am made of stronger stuff than you think," she whispered.

Helen drew back. "No," she whispered. "Do not think of it. You cannot consider marriage to the man."

Liana looked away from her stepmother. Perhaps there was some other reason Helen wanted to keep her away from Rogan. Perhaps she wanted him for herself. Perhaps they had been lovers when she'd lived near him, while her first husband was alive.

Liana was about to say as much when Joice entered the room.

"My lady," she said to Liana. "Sir Robert Butler has arrived. He asks for your hand in marriage."

"Accept him," Helen said instantly. "Accept him. I know his father. An excellent family."

Liana looked from Joice to Helen and knew she could take no more. She pushed past the two women and hurried down the stairs, Helen and Joice following her as fast as they could.

In the courtyard below stood eleven men, all splendidly dressed, their velvet tunics trimmed in gold, their caps fashionably arranged in the latest extravagance, jewels on their fingers sparkling in the sunlight.

Liana tried to pass them to reach the stables in the outer courtyard. A hard ride might clear her head. But Helen stopped her by grabbing her elbow.

"Sir Robert?" Helen said.

Reluctantly, Liana turned to look at the man. He was young, handsome, with dark brown hair and eyes. He was beautifully dressed and he smiled at her sweetly.

She hated him at first sight.

"This is my stepdaughter, Lady Liana," Helen said. "How is your father?"

Liana stood there stiffly, listening to the two of them exchange pleasantries and wanting desperately to get away. She had to go somewhere and think, for she had the decision of her life to make. Should she marry a man who smirked at her, who made her wash his clothes?

"I'm sure Liana would love to go with you. Wouldn't you, Liana?" Helen asked.

"What?"

"Sir Robert has agreed to accompany you on your ride. He will protect you from any harm as well as your own father would, won't you, Sir Robert?"

Liana hated the way Helen smiled at the man. Was she actually sleeping with men besides her husband? "And who will protect me from him?" Liana said sweetly, looking at Helen. "But then I wear no jewels, so perhaps I'll be safe."

Helen gave Liana a quelling look. "My stepdaughter is indeed amusing." She glared at Liana. "But not *too* amusing, I hope." She pushed Liana forward. "Go with him," she hissed.

Hesitantly, Liana walked through to the outer courtyard, where her horse was stabled.

"I had hoped to win your hand because of your father's lands," Sir Robert said in a pleasant voice, "but now that I have seen you, you are a prize in yourself."

"Oh?" She stopped and turned to face him. "Are my eyes like emeralds or sapphires?"

His eyes widened in surprise. "I would say sapphires."

"My skin is like ivory or the finest satin?"

He gave her a little smile. "I would say the petals of the whitest rose."

Her eyes hardened. "And my hair?"

His smile widened. "Your hair is hidden."

She jerked off her headdress. "Gold?" she asked angrily.

"Sunlight on gold."

She turned away from him angrily and missed seeing Sir Robert's repressed laughter.

"Would you allow me to escort you on a ride?" he asked politely. "I swear on my mother's soul that I will not compliment one part of your lovely form. I will call you a hag if you so wish."

She didn't look back at him as she went toward her horse, which the stableboy was already saddling. She didn't find anything humorous in what he was saying. Of course he'd tell her she was a hag. He'd say anything she wanted him to.

She ignored him as she rode through the outer gate, across the drawbridge, and toward the nearby forest. She didn't think about where she was going, but she headed for the pond. Behind her, she knew Sir Robert was having a difficult time keeping up with her, but she didn't slow down for him.

When she halted near the edge of the pond, she sat still on her horse for a moment, remembering yesterday, when she'd seen Rogan lying there. She smiled in memory of the look on his face when she'd slammed the muddy clothes into his chest.

"My lady is as good a rider as she is beautiful," Sir Robert said as he reined his horse near hers. When Liana started to dismount, he protested that he must help her.

She spent two hours with him at the pond and found him to be an utterly perfect man. He was kind, considerate, pleasant, and learned, and he treated her as if she were a fragile flower that might break at any second. He talked to her about love songs and fashions and assumed she'd be wildly interested in what was going on at King Henry's court. Three times Liana tried to direct the talk to land management and the price of wool, but Sir Robert would hear none of it.

All the time she was with him she kept thinking about the time she'd spent with Lord Rogan. He was a dreadful man, of course. He was dirty, demanding, and arrogant. He'd ordered her about as if she were his slave. Of course she had been dressed as a peasant and he had known he was an earl—or if what Helen had said was true, then perhaps he was actually a duke. But there was something about him, something strong and magnetic that made her able to think of little else except him.

"Perhaps I can teach you the new dance. Lady Liana?"

"Yes, oh certainly." They were walking side by side down a wide wagon path through the forest. Twice he'd offered to take her arm, but she'd refused him. "How does a man want a wife to act?" she asked.

She wasn't aware of how Sir Robert's chest swelled

with pride as her words raised his hopes. "Wives were meant to give a man comfort and support, to make a home for him, to bear his children. Wives are to give a man love."

She raised one eyebrow at him. "And as much land as her father can afford?"

Sir Robert chuckled. "That helps, of course."

Liana was frowning as she remembered Rogan's words: "I'll marry no shrews. I'll take her only if she's biddable and soft-spoken."

"I guess all men like soft, obedient women," she said.

Sir Robert looked at her with lust in his eyes, lust for her beautiful person as well as for the wealth that came with her. For his part she could be a vixen, in fact he rather liked her spitefulness, but he would never tell a woman that. It was better to tell them to be obedient and hope for the best.

They walked in silence, but Liana's head was reeling. Why would she even consider marriage to someone like Lord Rogan? There was nothing to recommend him. He had treated her with every discourtesy, but then he'd thought she was a peasant. He'd probably have kissed her hand and murmured pleasant phrases about the perfume of her skin if he'd known who she was. And would lice crawl up her arm? she wondered.

She looked at Sir Robert and gave him a weak smile. He was clean and pleasant and boring—oh so very, very boring. "Would you kiss me?" she asked on impulse.

Sir Robert didn't have to be asked twice. Gently, he took her in his arms and pressed his lips against hers.

Liana could have fallen asleep. She stepped back and looked at Sir Robert in surprise. So *that* was why she considered marrying Lord Rogan. She desired him. When he kissed her, her toes curled. When he stood before her with almost no clothing on, her own body grew hot. Right now Sir Robert could remove every stitch of his clothing and she knew she'd feel nothing.

"Liana," he whispered, and took a step toward her.

Liana turned away so quickly, his hair ruffled in the breeze she caused. "I have to return. I have to tell my father I agree to the marriage."

Sir Robert was so stunned he stood still for a moment, unable to move. Then he ran after Liana, grabbed her into his arms, and began kissing her neck and throat. "Oh my darling, you have made me the happiest man on earth. You don't know what this means to me. We've been plagued with fires for the last year. I had nearly lost hope of being able to rebuild."

She pulled away from him. "I thought it was my golden hair and my sapphire eyes you desired."

"That, too, of course." He took both her hands in his and began kissing them enthusiastically.

She snatched her hands away and hurried toward her horse. "You'll have to find someone else to rebuild for you. I've decided to marry the oldest Peregrine."

Sir Robert let out a yelp of genuine horror as he ran after her and caught her arm. "You cannot possibly consider any of them. They are—"

She put her hand up to stop him. "It is not for you to decide. Now, I'm going to return to my house and you may remain here or go with me. When you do return, I suggest you take your men and leave the Neville lands and go in search of another heiress to repair your damaged estates. And next time, perhaps you'll take better care of your properties and prevent the fires before they start." She went to her horse and mounted.

Sir Robert looked after her for a moment, his disappointment leaving him. Perhaps he was better off without this termagant. Marriage to a woman like her could be hell. Perhaps he'd rather lose a bit of land than saddle himself with this woman for the rest of his life.

Like hell he would, he thought. Damn those Peregrines! Women seemed to like them in spite of their dirt and their lifelong battle for lands and titles that weren't theirs. If Liana marries one of those Peregrines, within three years she'll be old and worn out from being used harder than a plow horse, he thought with some satisfaction.

He mounted his horse and followed her. It would be better to take his men and leave right away. He couldn't bear to see the betrothal ceremony of the lovely Lady Liana and one of those Peregrines. He shrugged his shoulders. It was no longer any concern of his.

Liana stood before her father and stepmother in the solar and made the announcement that she was going to marry Lord Rogan.

"Wise choice, girl," Gilbert said. "Best falconer in all of England."

Helen's face was slowly turning purple. "Do not do this," she said, gasping. "You are trying to spite me."

"I have done what you wanted and chosen a husband," Liana said coolly. "I would think you'd be pleased with me."

Helen tried to calm herself, then she sank down heavily in her chair and threw her hands up in surrender. "You win. You may stay here. You may run the estates and the servants. You may have it all, for all I care. When I go to meet my God, I will not have it on my head that I forced my husband's daughter to this living death. You win, Liana. Does this give you pleasure? Go now. Go from my sight. At least leave me this one room, where neither you nor your dead mother still rule."

Liana was puzzled by her stepmother's speech and she thought about it as she turned to leave the room. She was nearly to the door when she realized what Helen was saying. She turned back quickly.

"No," she said with some urgency in her voice, "I *want* to marry this man. You see, I met him before. Yesterday. We were alone for a while and . . ." She looked down at her hands, her face red.

"Oh dear God, he has raped her," Helen said. "Gilbert, you must hang him."

"No!" Gilbert and Liana said in unison.

"The hawks—" Gilbert began.

"He didn't—" Liana began.

Helen put up her hands for silence, then clutched her belly. Her child would no doubt be born with cloven feet after the hell her stepdaughter had put her through during her pregnancy. "Liana, what has the beast done to you?"

Made me wash his clothes, she thought. Kissed me. "Nothing," she said. "He has not touched me." She meant to say penance at mass for that lie. "Yesterday while I was riding, I met him and I . . ." She what? Liked him? Loved him? Hated him? Probably all of them. Whatever she felt for him, it was strong. "And I want to accept his offer of marriage," she finished.

"Good choice," Gilbert said. "The boy is a man if ever I saw one."

"You're a fool, Liana," Helen whispered, her face pale. "Rarely does a girl have such a doting father that he will let her choose her own husband, and now I understand why. I would never have guessed you to be so stupid." She sighed. "All right. It's on your head now. When he beats you—if you're still alive—you may return here and have your wounds dressed. Go now. I can't bear the sight of you."

Liana didn't move from where she was. "I do not want to meet him before the ceremony," she said.

"At last, some wisdom," Helen said sarcastically. "Stay away from him as long as you can."

Gilbert was eating grapes. "He hasn't asked to see you. I guess yesterday was enough, eh?" He grinned and winked at his daughter. He didn't know when a woman had pleased him so much. The Peregrine boys might be a little rough around the edges, but that was because they were *men,* not popinjays ruled by women.

"I guess so," Liana said. She was afraid that if he saw her and realized she was the woman who'd tossed the clothes at him, he'd refuse to marry her. He didn't like shrews, and if Rogan wanted a soft-spoken wife, then she was going to *be* a soft-spoken wife.

"Well, it's easy enough to arrange," Gilbert said. "I'll say you have the pox and he can exchange rings with a proxy. We'll set the wedding for . . ." He looked at Helen, but she was stony and silent. "Three months. Is that all right with you, daughter?"

Liana looked at Helen, and instead of hating her stepmother, she remembered the way Helen was ready to allow Liana to remain as a spinster in the Neville household. Perhaps Helen didn't hate her after all. "I will need gowns," Liana said softly. "And I will need household goods. Do you think you could help me choose what I need?"

Helen looked bleak. "I cannot make you change your mind?"

"No," Liana said. "You cannot."

"Then I will help you," Helen said. "If you died, I would help lay out your body for burial, so I will ready you for this."

"Thank you," Liana said, smiling, and left the room feeling wonderfully light and happy. She had a great deal to do in the next three months.

The Peregrine banner of a rampant white falcon on a red background with three horses' skulls in a diagonal band across the falcon's belly flew over the campsite. Some of the men slept in tents or under the baggage wagons, but Rogan and Severn lay on blankets on the ground, their bodies surrounded by weapons.

"I don't understand why she agreed to marry you," Severn said once again. It was something he'd been puzzling on since Gilbert Neville had said his daughter had agreed to the marriage. Rogan had merely shrugged, then started negotiating what was to be included in the dowry. Neither Rogan nor Gilbert seemed to think it was odd that the young woman, after refusing most of England, should take Rogan sight unseen.

"She turned down everyone else," Severn said. "Not that I approve of allowing a girl to choose her own husband, but why would she say no to a man like Stephen Whitington?"

Rogan turned onto his side, away from his brother, and grunted. "The girl has a head on her shoulders. She made the right choice."

It was Severn's turn to grunt. "There's more to it than you're telling me. You didn't seduce the girl in private, did you?"

"I never laid eyes on her. I was too busy trying to seduce Neville out of his gold. Maybe he beat the girl and told her who she was to marry, just as he should have done in the first place."

"Perhaps," Severn said. "But I still think you—"

Angrily, Rogan looked across the night at his brother. "I never met the girl, I told you. I was with Neville from morning till night."

"Except when you went off alone before we went to Neville's castle."

"I didn't—" Rogan began, then stopped and remembered the girl who'd complained about his clothes. He had forgotten about her until this moment. He'd have to remember to look for her when he returned in three months' time for his wedding. "I didn't see the heiress," Rogan said softly. "Her father must have arranged the marriage. He's a fool of a man and I could buy his soul for a dozen or so hawks."

"I doubt if you'd have to pay that much," Severn scoffed, then paused a moment. "Weren't you curious about the woman? I'd want to see a woman I was to marry before I married her. She could be fat and old for all you know."

"What do I care about a wife? It's her lands I want. Now go to sleep, little brother, for tomorrow's Wednesday and Wednesday takes a lot of energy."

Severn smiled in the darkness. Tomorrow he'd see Iolanthe and everything would be the same. But in three months' time Lady Liana Neville would enter their lives and things would still remain the same, for if she was anything like her father, she was a cowardly little thing.

CHAPTER
FOUR

N o, no, no, my lady, good wives do not screech. Good wives *obey* their husbands," Joice said. She was tired and exasperated. Lady Liana had asked her to teach her how to be a good wife, but Liana had had too much control for too long and it was almost impossible to make her understand how a wife was supposed to behave.

"Even when he is a fool?" Liana asked.

"Especially when he is a fool," Joice answered. "Men like to believe they know everything, that they are always right, and they want absolute loyalty from their women. No matter how wrong your husband is, he will expect you to stand by him."

Liana listened to this carefully. This is not what her mother thought of marriage, nor did Helen. And neither of them had been beloved wives, she thought with a grimace. In the last month she'd come to realize how different she wanted her marriage to be from the two she'd seen. She didn't want to live in hatred for the rest of her life. Her mother hadn't seemed to mind the fact that she despised her husband, nor did Helen, but Liana wanted her life to be different. She'd seen a love match once of a couple who, after years of marriage, still gave one another long looks and sat for hours talking to each other. Liana wanted *that* kind of marriage.

"And he'd rather have obedience than honesty?" Liana asked. "If he is wrong, I am not to tell him so?"

"Most certainly not. Men like to think their wives believe them to be next to God in everything. Take care of his house, bear him sons, and when he asks your opinion, tell him that he knows much more about such matters than you do, that you are merely a woman."

"Merely a . . ." Liana said, trying to understand this. The only man she'd ever really known was her father, and she hated to think what the Neville lands would be like if her mother had refused to govern them. "But my father—"

"Your father is not like most men," Joice said as tactfully as possible. She had been stunned when Lady Liana had asked for her advice about men, but she thought it was high time. Liana had better learn what men were actually like before she tied herself to someone like those Peregrines. "Lord Rogan will not allow you such freedom as your father has."

"No, I guess not," Liana said softly. "He has said he will marry no shrew."

"No man wants a shrew. He wants a woman who will praise him, who will see to his comfort, and who will be eager in bed."

Liana thought she could handle two of those points easily. "I'm not sure Lord Rogan believes in comfort. His clothes are dirty and I believe he does not bathe often."

"Ah, now there is where a wife can have power. All

men like comfort. They like a certain dish for eating, a certain cup for their favorite drink, and whether your Lord Rogan knows it or not, he likes an orderly, quiet household. His wife should take care of the servants' quarrels, she should see that his table is loaded with delicious food. You can replace his scratchy, dirty clothing with soft new ones. These are ways to a man's heart."

"And if his lands are in a muddle, then I—"

"Then that is his business. It is not a woman's concern," Joice said sharply.

Liana thought it might be easier to run a hundred estates than to please one man. She wasn't sure she could remember all the rules of what a man did and did not like. "You are sure of all this? Staying in the solar and tending merely to household business will win my husband's heart?"

"I am sure of it, my lady. Now, will you try on this new gown?"

For three months Liana tried on new gowns. She ordered furs, Italian brocades, jewels. She set every woman who could hold a needle to embroidering. Not only did she order her own wardrobe, but she had a splendid set of clothing made for Lord Rogan. The only time her father took any notice of the proceedings was to remark that the bridegroom should dress himself. Liana took no notice of him.

When she wasn't with Helen working on her new wardrobe, Liana was supervising the packing of her dowry. All the Neville wealth that was not in land was in portable goods. Gold plates and ewers were packed in straw and put into wagons, as were precious glass vessels. She took tapestries, linens, pieces of carved-oak furniture, candles, feather pillows and mattresses.

There were carts full of rich fabrics, furs, a fat iron-bound chest full of jewels and another of silver groats.

"You will need everything," Helen said. "Those men have not one comfort in their lives."

Liana smiled at that because perhaps the comfort she brought would help her husband love her.

Helen saw Liana's lovesick smile and groaned, but she didn't try to talk to Liana again, as she'd seen how impossible it was to attempt to reason with her. Helen just helped to denude the Neville castle of its riches, and she gave Liana no more advice.

The wedding was to be a small one, as the Nevilles were not favorites among the aristocracy and royalty of the land, for Gilbert's father had purchased his earldom from the king only a few years before he died. There were still many people who could remember when the Nevilles were merely rich, ruthless merchants charging five times what they paid for an item. Liana was glad for the excuse to save the expense of an enormous wedding celebration so she'd have more to take with her to the Peregrine castle.

Liana didn't sleep much the night before her wedding. She kept going over in her mind the things she had learned about pleasing a husband, and she kept trying to visualize her new life. She tried to imagine lying in bed with the handsome Lord Rogan. She thought about his touching her and caressing her and saying tender words to her. She had decided not to be "married in her hair," but to wear a jeweled headdress because she knew her long flaxen hair was her best feature and she wanted to share it with him and him alone on their wedding night. She imagined long walks together, as they laughed and held hands. She imagined sitting before the fire on a cold winter evening and reading aloud to him, or playing a game of draughts. Perhaps they'd play for kisses.

She smiled in the darkness at the thought of what he would say when he discovered he'd married the woman by the pool. Of course *that* woman had been a shrew, but Rogan's wife would be the demure, quiet, loving Lady Liana. She imagined his gratitude when she changed those dirty, rough clothes of his for fine silks and wools. She closed her eyes for a moment and imagined how incredibly handsome he would be dressed in dark velvet, green perhaps, with a jeweled chain extending from one broad shoulder to the other.

She would introduce him to the pleasures of bathing with rose-scented oil in the tub. Perhaps afterward he'd rub oil into her skin, even between her toes, she thought with a sigh of heavenly pleasure. She imagined lying on a clean, soft featherbed and laughing together over their first meeting—how childish they'd been not to have known at first sight that they were the love of each other's lives.

Just before dawn she dozed off, a smile on her lips, only to be awakened moments later by an unearthly clatter in the courtyard below. By the sound of the shouts of men and the clank of steel, they were being attacked. Who had left the drawbridge down?

"Oh Lord, don't let me die before I marry him," Liana prayed as she leaped out of bed and began running.

In the hall, Helen was also running, as was half the household, it seemed.

Liana made her way through the chaos to her stepmother. "What is it? What has happened?" she shouted above the noise.

"Your bridegroom has at last arrived," Helen said angrily. "And he and all his men are drunk. Now someone who doesn't value his life will have to get this Red Falcon of yours off his horse, bathed, dressed, and sober enough to say his vows to you." She paused and gave Liana a look of sympathy. "You vow away your life today, Liana," she said softly. "May God have mercy on your soul." Helen turned and started down the stairs to the solar.

"My lady," Joice said from behind Liana. "You must return to your room. You cannot be seen on your wedding day."

Liana went back to her room and she even allowed Joice to coax her into bed, but she could not sleep. Once again Rogan was under the same roof as she was and soon . . . soon he'd be here in bed with her. Just the two of them. Alone and quiet and intimate. What would they talk about, she wondered. They knew so little about each other. Perhaps they'd talk about first learning to ride a horse or maybe he'd tell her about where he lived. This Peregrine castle would be Liana's new home and she longed to know about it. She had to plan where her mother's tapestries would be hung, where her gold plates would be set to best display them.

She was so happy in her thoughts that she dozed off for a while until Joice came to wake her and four giggling maids began to dress her in red brocade with a cloth-of-gold underskirt. Her double-horned head-dress was red, embroidered with gold wire, and strung with hundreds of tiny pearls. A long transparent silk veil hung down her back.

"Beautiful, my lady," Joice said, tears in her eyes. "No man will be able to take his eyes from you."

Liana hoped so. She hoped she was as physically appealing to her husband as he was to her.

She rode sidesaddle on a white horse to the church

and she was so nervous she barely saw the crowds of people lining the sides of the road and yelling their wishes that she bear many children. Her eyes were straining ahead to see the man standing by the church door. Her palms were wet as she drew nearer to him. Would he take one look at her, see that she was the woman who hit him with a mud-soaked garment, and refuse to marry her?

When she was close enough to see him, she smiled with pride that he looked as good as she'd imagined in the green velvet tunic that she'd had made for him. The tunic barely reached the tops of his thighs and his powerful, muscular legs were tightly encased in dark knitted hose. On his head he wore a short-brimmed fur hat with a large ruby twinkling on the band.

She swelled so in pride at the look of him that her ribs ached against the steel bones in her corset. Then she held her breath as he stepped down from the church steps and started toward her. Was he going to lift her from her horse himself and not wait for her father, who rode ahead of her, to do it?

Her horse moved maddeningly slowly. Perhaps he could see she was the woman from the pond and he was pleased. Perhaps she had haunted his thoughts for the past three months as he had hers.

But Rogan did not come to her horse. In fact, as far as she saw, he did not so much as glance her way. Instead, he went to her father's horse and caught the bridle. The entire procession halted as Liana watched Rogan talk earnestly to her father. Liana watched in puzzlement until Helen moved her horse forward to stand beside her stepdaughter.

"What is that red devil up to now?" Helen spat out. "Those two are wrong if they think we will wait while they talk of hawks."

"Since he is to be my husband, I assume we must wait," Liana said coolly. She'd had enough of Helen's complaints about Rogan.

Helen kicked her horse's ribs and went to stand on the far side of her husband. Liana could not hear what was being said over the noise of the crowd, but she could see Helen's anger. Gilbert remained impassive and even leaned back in the saddle while Helen talked angrily to Rogan, but Rogan merely looked across at her with unseeing eyes.

Liana hoped he would never look at her like that. After a moment Rogan looked about him, as if seeing the crowd for the first time, and as an afterthought he looked at Liana sitting quietly on her horse. Liana held her breath as his cool eyes scanned her from toe to head. She did not see any recognition in his eyes and she was glad, because she didn't want to risk his refusing to marry her. When his eyes rose to meet hers, Liana lowered her lashes, hoping to seem modest and obedient.

After a moment, she looked up to see Rogan returning to the church steps and Helen riding toward her.

"That man you plan to marry," Helen said with a sneer, "was asking for twelve more knights' fees. He was saying he would walk away now and leave you here if he didn't get them."

Liana's eyes widened in alarm. "Did my father agree?"

Helen closed her eyes for a moment. "He agreed. Now, let's get this over with." She kicked her horse forward to ride behind Liana.

Gilbert helped his daughter from her horse, and she walked up the stairs to meet her husband. The ceremony was brief, the vows no different from what they had been for centuries. Liana kept her eyes lowered throughout, but when she vowed to be "meek and obedient in bed and at board," the crowd cheered her. Twice she stole looks at Rogan, but he merely seemed impatient to be away—as she was, she thought with a smile.

When they were pronounced man and wife, again the crowd cheered and the bride and groom, their family and guests went inside to mass, for the wedding was of the state and therefore outside the church, but mass was of God. The priest blessed their marriage and began the mass.

Liana sat quietly beside her new husband and listened to the Latin incantations for what seemed to be hours. Rogan did not look at her, did not touch her. He yawned a few times, scratched a few times, and sprawled his long legs in the aisle. At one point she thought she heard a snore coming from him, but his brother punched him and Rogan sat up straighter on the hard bench.

After mass, the wedding group rode back to the castle while the peasants threw grains at them and shouted, "Plenty! Plenty!" For three days and nights every man, woman, and child would have all the food and drink they could hold.

Once over the drawbridge and into the inner courtyard, Liana sat on her horse and waited for her husband to lift her down. Instead, she watched as Rogan and his brother Severn dismounted and went to the wagons loaded and waiting along the stone wall.

"He cares more for your goods than for you," Helen said as a groom helped Liana from her horse.

"You have had your say," Liana snapped. "You do not know all there is. Perhaps he has reasons for his actions."

"Yes, such as not being human," Helen said.

"There's no use reminding you of what you've done. It's too late now. Shall we go in and eat? It is my experience that men always come home when they're hungry."

But Helen was wrong, because neither Rogan nor his men came in to the feast Liana had spent weeks organizing. Instead, they stayed outside, going through the wagons that were packed with her dowry. She sat alone at her father's right side, the groom's place next to her empty. All around she could feel the tittering of the guests as they looked at her with sympathetic eyes. She kept her chin up and refused to let them see she was hurt. She told herself it was good that her husband was interested in his property. A man who was so concerned about his estates wasn't likely to gamble them away.

After a couple of hours, when most people had finished eating, Rogan and his men came into the Hall. Liana smiled, for now, surely, he'd come to her and apologize and explain what had kept him. Instead, he stopped beside Gilbert's chair, reached between Gilbert and Helen, and picked up a two-pound piece of roasted beef and began to gnaw on it.

"Three wagons are full of feather mattresses and dress goods. I want them filled with gold," Rogan said, his mouth full.

Gilbert had had nothing to do with the packing of the wagons and so could not answer Rogan's complaint. He opened his mouth to speak, but nothing came out.

Helen had no such problem. "The mattresses are for my daughter's comfort. I don't imagine that place of yours has even the barest comforts."

Rogan turned cold, hard eyes on her and Helen almost backed down. "When I want a woman's opinion, I will ask for it." He looked back at Gilbert. "I am having an accounting made now. You will regret it if you have cheated me." He stepped away from the table, the meat eaten, and wiped his greasy hands on the beautiful velvet tunic Liana had had made for him. "You can keep your feathers."

Helen was on her feet instantly as she confronted Rogan. He was much taller than she and overpoweringly large, but she held herself rigid before him. Her anger gave her courage. "Your own wife, the wife you have chosen to ignore, supervised the loading of those wagons and she has not cheated you. As for the household goods, either they go with her or she remains here in her father's house. Choose now, Peregrine, or I'll have the marriage annulled. No daughter of mine goes from my house naked."

The entire room was silent. Only a dog snuffling in a corner could be heard and it, too, soon quietened. Guests, acrobats, singers, musicians, jesters all paused in what they were doing and looked at the tall, handsome man and the elegant woman confronting each other.

For a moment Rogan did not seem to know what to say. "The marriage has been performed."

"And not consummated," Helen flashed back at him. "It will be easy to have it annulled."

The anger in Rogan's eyes increased. "You do not threaten me, woman. The girl's goods are mine and I will take what I want." He took a step backward and grabbed Liana's arm, pulling her out of her chair. "If the girl's virginity is a problem, I'll take it now."

This statement made the half-drunk crowd laugh, and their laughter increased as Rogan pulled Liana up the stairs and out of sight.

"My room . . ." Liana said nervously, not exactly sure of what was going on. She was aware only that at last she was going to be alone with this magnificent man.

Rogan flung open a door to a guest room that was being used by the Earl of Arundel and his wife. The countess's maid was folding clothes. "Out," Rogan commanded the girl, and she scurried to obey him.

"But my room is—" Liana began. This was not the way things were supposed to happen. She was to be undressed by her maids and to be put nude between pure clean sheets and he was to come to her and kiss her and caress her.

"This room is good enough," he said, and pushed her back onto the bed, then grabbed her skirt hem and flung it over her head.

Liana fought her way out from under several heavy layers of cloth, then gasped as Rogan's considerable weight covered her. The next moment she cried out in pain as he entered her. She was unprepared for such pain and she pushed away from him, but he didn't seem to notice as he began to make quick, long strokes. Liana gritted her teeth to keep from crying and she clenched her fists against the pain.

Within minutes he was finished and he collapsed on her, limp and relaxed. It took Liana a moment to recover from the onslaught of pain, but when she opened her eyes she could see Rogan's dark hair, could feel the softness of it against her cheek. His face was turned away from her, but his thick, clean hair covered her cheek and forehead. How heavy yet how light he felt. His broad shoulders covered her small body, yet his hips didn't seem as wide as hers.

She lifted her hand and touched his hair, put her fingers into it, then her nose, and inhaled the fragrance of him.

Slowly, he turned to face her, his lids heavy with fatigue. "I slept for a moment," he said softly.

She smiled at his closed eyes and stroked the hair at his temple. His lashes were thick, his nose finely cut, his skin dark and warm and as finely pored as a baby's. His cheeks were stained dark with unshaven whiskers, but they didn't take away from the relaxed softness of his mouth.

Her finger moved from his temple and down his cheek to his lips. When she touched his lower lip, his eyes sprang open and the greenness of them was startling. Now he will kiss me, she thought, and for a moment she held her breath as he looked at her.

"A blonde," he murmured.

Liana smiled at him since her hair color seemed to please him. She put up her hand to pull off her headdress and all three feet of her hair cascaded out. "I wanted to save it for you," she whispered. "I hoped you would like it."

He picked up a strand of the fine, golden hair and curled it about his fingers. "It's—"

He halted in mid-sentence and all softness left his face. Immediately he got off of her and stood, glaring down at her. "Cover yourself and go to that hellion of a stepmother of yours and tell her the marriage is consummated. Tell her there will be no annulment. And you can ready yourself, for we leave here to-night."

Liana pushed her skirts down over her bare legs and sat up on the bed. "Tonight? But the marriage celebra-tion goes on for two more days. Tomorrow I have planned dancing and—"

Rogan hastily straightened his clothes. "I have no time for dancing, and I have no time for back-talking wives. If this is how you plan to start, then you can stay here with your father and I will take the goods with me. My men and I leave in three hours' time. Be there or not, it doesn't matter to me." He turned and left the room, closing the door loudly behind him.

Liana sat where she was, too stunned to move. He would leave her behind!

There was a soft knock on the door, then Joice entered. "My lady?" she said.

Liana looked up at her maid, all her puzzlement showing in her eyes. "He leaves here in three hours and he says I may go with him or not. He doesn't care one way or the other."

Joice sat down on the bed and took Liana's hand. "He thinks he does not need a wife. All men think that. It is up to you to prove to him that he does need a wife by his side."

Liana pulled away from her maid, and when she moved her legs, she felt pain. "He hurt me."

"It's always like that the first time."

Liana stood and anger began to race through her. "I have *never* been treated like this before. He did not bother to even come to his own wedding feast. I had to sit there and endure the stares and smiles from the people. And this!" She glanced down at her skirt. "I may as well have been raped. I'll let him know who he's dealing with." She had her hand on the door latch when Joice's words stopped her.

"And he will look at you with hatred as he looked at Lady Helen."

Liana turned back.

"You saw how he despised her," Joice continued, and suddenly felt very powerful. Her young charge might be beautiful and rich, but she was listening to and obeying Joice. "Believe me, I know what men like Lord Rogan want. He will hate you just as he does her if you defy him."

Liana rubbed the fingers of her right hand together.

She could still feel his hair against her skin and she remembered that, for a moment, there had been softness in his eyes. She did not want to take that away. "What do I do?" she whispered.

"Obey him," Joice said firmly. "Be ready in three hours. Lady Helen will no doubt protest your leaving, but stand with your husband against her. I have told you how men want loyalty from their wives."

"*Blind* loyalty?" Liana asked. "Even now, when he is wrong?"

"Most especially when he is wrong."

Liana listened to this, but still she didn't understand.

Seeing that her young mistress was still confused, Joice continued. "Swallow your anger. All married women feed on anger that they keep to themselves. You will see. You will learn to swallow so much anger that it will become a way of living to you."

Liana started to say something, but Joice cut her off.

"Go and get ready now or he will leave you."

Feeling very confused, Liana hurried out of the room. She was going to do whatever she could to prove to this man that she could be a good wife, and if it meant repressing her rage, then so be it. She'd show him that she could be the most loyal of wives.

As Lord Rogan went down the stone steps, a frown on his handsome face, the first person he met was Lady Helen. "The deed is done," he said to her. "There will be no annulment. If there is anything to be added to the wagons, then do it, for we leave in three hours' time." He started past her, but Helen put herself in front of him.

"You will take my stepdaughter away from her own wedding feast?"

Rogan didn't understand what these women were making such a fuss about. If it was food they wanted, they could take plenty with them. "I will not starve the girl," he said, making an effort to take the hatred from Helen's eyes. He was not used to women hating him. For the most part they were like that girl he'd married: adoring and soft-eyed.

"You *will* starve her," Helen said, "as your father starved his wives of warmth and companionship." Her voice lowered. "As you starved Jeanne Howard."

Helen stepped back when she saw the look on Rogan's face. His eyes hardened and he looked at her with such rage that she began to tremble.

"Never come near me again, woman," he said coldly, in a low undertone. He then stalked past her, ignored the calls of the guests to come and join them in a drink, and went outside to the courtyard.

Jeanne Howard, he thought. He could wring that woman's neck for mentioning Jeanne to him, but it made him remind himself to be careful with this new wife, not to allow pretty blue eyes and blonde hair to sway him.

"You look ready to run someone through," Severn said jovially. His face was flushed from too much food and drink.

"Are you ready to leave?" Rogan growled at him. "Or have you been too busy bedding the wenches to tend to the business at hand?"

Severn was used to his brother's constant anger and he'd had too much wine to let it bother him now. "I have anticipated you, brother, and filled a wagon full of food. Do we leave the feather pillows or take them?"

"Leave them," Rogan snapped, then hesitated. In his mind he heard Helen Neville saying, "As you starved Jeanne Howard," and felt a knife twisting in his gut. The girl he'd married—what was her name? —seemed simple enough. "Let her have her feather mattresses," he growled to Severn, and went to check on his men.

Severn watched his brother walk away and wondered what his pretty little sister-in-law was like.

CHAPTER
FIVE

*L*iana hurried to dress herself, to make sure all her new clothes were packed, and to direct her maids to pack her personal articles. Three hours was such a short time to ready herself for her new life.

All the while that she was rushing about, Joice lectured her.

"Do not complain," Joice said. "Men hate women who complain. You are to take whatever he gives you and never say a word in protest. Tell him you are *glad* to be leaving your wedding feast, glad to have three hours to prepare yourself. Men like their women to be smiling and cheerful."

"He hasn't liked me yet," Liana said. "He hasn't taken any notice of me yet except to abolish the risk of an annulment," she said with some bitterness.

"It will take years," Joice said. "Men do not give their hearts easily, but if you persevere, love will come to you."

And that's what she wanted, Liana thought. She

wanted her beautiful husband to love her and to need her. If swallowing a little anger now and then would make him love her, then so be it.

She was ready before the three hours were up, and she went downstairs to say goodbye to her father and stepmother. Gilbert was drunk and talking of hawks with some men and barely had a word of farewell to say to his only child, but Helen hugged her tightly and wished her all the best in the world.

Outside, with the Peregrine knights mounted and waiting to ride, the big white falcon banner before them, Liana felt a momentary terror. She was leaving all that she knew behind and trusting her fate to these strangers. She stood frozen where she was and looked for her husband.

Rogan, atop a big roan stallion, came riding in front of her, so close she put up her arm to shield her face from flying gravel. "Mount and ride, woman," he said, and moved to the head of his men.

Liana hid her clenched fists in the folds of her skirt. Swallow anger, she thought, and tried to calm herself at his rudeness.

Out of the dust came Rogan's brother, Severn, and he smiled at her. "May I help you mount, my lady?" he asked.

Liana relaxed and smiled at this handsome man. He was as ill dressed as Rogan had been and his dark golden hair was too long and ragged at the edges, but at least he was smiling at her. She put her hand on his extended arm. "I would be honored," she said, and walked with him toward her waiting horse.

Liana was just mounted when Rogan rode back to them. He did not look at her, but he scowled at his brother.

"If you are through playing lady's maid, come with me," Rogan demanded.

"Perhaps your wife would like to ride in front with us," Severn said pointedly over Liana's head.

"I want no women," Rogan snapped, still not glancing at Liana.

"I don't think—" Severn began, but Liana cut him off.

Even she knew that she would not please her husband by being the cause of an argument with his brother. "I would rather stay here," she said loudly. "I will feel safer surrounded by the men, and you, sir," she said to Severn, "are needed by . . . by my husband."

Severn frowned for a moment as he looked at her. "As you wish," he said, and with a little bow he rode away from her, to position himself beside his brother at the head of the line.

"Oh excellent, my lady," Joice said as she came to ride beside her mistress. "You have pleased him now. Lord Rogan will like an obedient wife."

As they rode through the courtyard, across the drawbridge, and onto the dusty road, Liana sneezed at the dust. "I have been the obedient wife, but now I must ride behind ten men on horses and half a dozen wagons," she muttered.

"You will win in the end, though," Joice said. "You will see. Once he sees that you are obedient and loyal, he will love you."

Liana coughed at the dust and rubbed her nose. It was difficult to think of love and loyalty when one had a mouthful of dirt.

They rode for hours, Liana remaining where she was in the middle of the procession, none of her husband's men talking to her. The only voice she heard was Joice's, lecturing her on obedience and duty, and when Severn asked her if she was comfortable, Joice answered for her mistress, saying that if

Lord Rogan wanted his wife here, then of course Lady
Liana was happy where she was.

Liana gave Severn a weak smile and choked on a
cloud of dust.

"That one shows far too much interest in you,"
Joice said when Severn was gone. "You had better let
him know his place right away."

"He is only being kind," Liana said.

"If you accept his kindness, you will cause problems
between the brothers. Your husband will wonder
where your loyalties lie."

"I am not sure my husband has yet looked at me,"
Liana mumbled to herself.

Joice smiled through the cloud of dust that
surrounded them. With each day she was feeling more
and more powerful. As a child, Lady Liana had never
listened to her and several times Joice had been
punished because Liana had escaped her rule and
gotten into some mischief. But at long last here was
something she knew which her mistress didn't.

They rode well into the night and Liana knew Joice
and her other six maids were drooping with exhaustion, but she did not dare ask her husband to stop.
Besides, Liana was too excited to rest. Tonight would
be her wedding night. Tonight she would lie all night
in her husband's arms. Tonight he would caress her,
touch her hair, kiss her. A day spent riding in a little
dust was worth such a nightly reward.

By the time they did stop to make camp, her senses
were alive with anticipation. One of the knights
perfunctorily helped her dismount, and Liana told
Joice to see to the other women. Liana looked about
for her husband and saw him disappearing into the
trees.

Behind her, Liana was vaguely aware of the complaints of her women, who weren't used to riding

horses such a distance, but she had no time for them. Taking her time, and trying to act casually, she followed her husband into the woods.

Rogan answered a call of nature in the woods, then walked deep into the still darkness toward the little stream. With every step he took, his muscles tightened harder. It had taken longer to get here than when he traveled without wagonloads of goods, and now the darkness was so complete he had to feel his way along the bank.

It was a while before he found the cairn, the six-foot-high pile of stones that he'd built to mark where his eldest brother, Rowland, had fallen to a Howard blade. He stood for a moment, his eyes adjusting to the faint moonlight on the gray stones, and heard the sounds of battle once again in his head. Rowland and his brothers had been hunting and Rowland, feeling safe since they were two days' ride from the Howards' land—the Peregrine land, in truth—had walked away from the protection of his men and sat by the river to drink a jug of beer alone.

Rogan knew why his older brother wanted to be alone and why he so often drank himself into a stupor each night. He was haunted by the deaths of three brothers and their father—all at the hands of the Howards.

Rogan had watched his beloved brother walk off into the darkness and he hadn't tried to stop him, but he'd signaled a knight to follow and keep watch over his brother, to protect him while he lay in drunken oblivion.

Rogan looked at the stones and remembered, and once again cursed himself for having fallen asleep that night. Some small sound woke him, or maybe it wasn't a sound but a premonition. He jumped from his pallet on the ground, grabbed his sword, and started running. But he was too late. Rowland lay beside the stream, a Howard sword through his throat, pinning him to the ground. The knight who guarded him was also dead, his throat slashed.

Rogan had thrown his head back and given a long, loud, piercing cry of agony.

His men and Severn were beside him instantly and they tore the woods apart looking for the Howard attackers. They found two of the men, distant cousins of Oliver Howard's, and Rogan made sure their deaths were long and slow. He ended one man's life when the man mentioned Jeanne.

The demise of the two Howards did nothing to bring back his brother, nor did it lessen Rogan's sense of responsibility now that he was the eldest of the Peregrines. Now it was his job to protect Severn and young Zared. He had to protect them, provide for them, and most of all, he had to get the Peregrine lands back, the lands the Howards had stolen from his grandfather.

His senses were dulled with memory, but at a snapping branch he whirled and put his sword to the throat of the person behind him. It was a girl, and for a moment he couldn't remember who she was. Yes, the one he'd married that morning. "What do you want?" he snapped. He wanted to be alone with his thoughts and his memories of his brother.

Liana looked down at the sword pointed at her throat and swallowed. "Is that a grave?" she asked hesitantly, remembering every word Helen had said about the violence of these men. He could kill her now that he had her dowry, and all he had to do was say he'd found her with another man and he would escape unpunished.

"No," Rogan said curtly, having no intention of telling her about his brother, or anything else for that matter. "Go back to the camp and stay there."

It was on the tip of Liana's tongue to tell him she'd go where she pleased, but Joice's warning to be obedient echoed in her head. "Yes, of course I'll return," she said meekly. "Will you return with me?"

Rogan wanted to stay where he was, but at the same time he didn't want her walking in the woods alone. For all that he couldn't remember her name, she was a Peregrine now and therefore an enemy of the Howards. They would no doubt love to hold another Peregrine woman captive. "All right," he said reluctantly. "I'll return with you."

Liana felt a little thrill of pleasure run through her body. Joice was right, she thought. She had meekly obeyed her husband and he was walking her back to the camp. She waited for him to offer her his arm, but he didn't. Instead, he turned his back on her and started walking. Liana ran after him for a few steps, but then her gown caught on a fallen log. "Wait!" she called. "I'm caught."

Rogan came back to her and, as always, Liana's heart seemed to beat a little faster when he was near.

"Move your hands," he said.

Liana looked into his eyes, saw the way the moonlight made them sparkle, and was aware of nothing else—until he brought his sword down on the log and hacked away a big piece of her skirt. She gaped at the hole and was utterly speechless. That embroidered silk had cost her quarterly rents from six farms!

"Now, come on," he commanded, and turned his back on her again.

Swallow! she commanded herself. Fight the anger down and do not display it. A woman is always loving and kind. A woman does not point out her husband's faults. Fighting her anger, she began to follow him and wondered if he was looking forward to their wedding night with as much anticipation as she was.

With every step he took, Rogan remembered ever more vividly his brother's death. Two years' time had done very little to dull the memory. Here he and Rowland had talked of buying horses. Here he and Rowland had talked of James and Basil's deaths eight years before. Here Rowland had spoken of protecting Zared. Here—

"Could you tell me something of your castle? I'll need to know where to hang my tapestries."

Rogan had forgotten the girl was with him. William, who had been three years older than Rogan, died as a boy of eighteen. His dying words were to get the Peregrine lands back and that would make sense of his death.

"Is it a large place?" the girl asked.

"No," he answered gruffly. "It is very small. It's the discards of the Howard bitch." He halted at the edge of the forest and gaped at the campsite. Before him was a sea of big feather mattresses on the ground. They might as well set up torches and blow trumpets to announce their whereabouts to the Howards.

Angrily, he strode across the campsite to reach his brother, who was talking and smiling at one of the Neville maids. He punched his brother's shoulder to turn him around.

"What stupidity is this?" he demanded. "Why not invite the Howards down on our heads?"

Severn pushed Rogan's shoulder. "We're well guarded, and there are only a few mattresses for the women."

Rogan punched Severn's chest. "I want them out of

sight. The women can sleep on the ground or they can go back to Neville."

Severn doubled his fist and planted it in Rogan's chest, but his heavier brother didn't waver. "Some of the men want to sleep with the women."

"All the better that they do not sleep too well. If a Howard comes, we'll be ready—as we were not ready the night Rowland was butchered."

Severn nodded at that and went to tell the men to stow the feather cushions.

At the edge of the forest, Liana stood and watched her husband and brother-in-law punch each other as if they were sworn enemies. She held her breath for fear their fight would erupt into bloodshed, but after a few minutes of low, guttural sentences, they separated, and Liana released her breath. She looked about her and saw some of her women staring, but none of the Peregrine knights seemed to take any notice of their masters' rough exchange. Yet Liana knew that any one of those blows would have felled most men.

At that moment, Joice came running to her, her face contorted with emotion. "My lady, they have no tents. We are to sleep *on the ground.*" She said the last with horror.

Usually when they traveled, Liana, her father and stepmother, and most of the women, if they were not guests of another landowner, slept in sumptuous tents. Since they moved most of their furniture with them from castle to castle, the beds and even tables were set up inside the tents.

"And there is no hot food," Joice continued. "We have only cold meats that were taken from your wedding feast. Two of the women are in tears."

"Then they'll have to dry their tears," Liana snapped. "You have told me that a good wife does not complain. That goes as well for her maids." Liana was much too excited about the prospect of the coming night to worry about cold meats and tents.

At a noise, both turned to see the Peregrine knights removing the feather pallets from the ground and returning them to inside the wagons.

"No!" Joice gasped, and went toward the men.

For the next hour, all was chaos as Liana settled her maids to sleeping on the ground under the stars. She removed bags full of furs from the wagons and had them put on the ground, skin side down, and this helped mollify the tears. A few of the Peregrine knights put their arms around the women and comforted them.

Liana had furs placed outside the camp, in the deep shade of an oak tree, for herself. Joice helped her remove her mutilated gown and put on a clean linen nightshirt, then Liana lay down and waited. And waited. And waited. But Rogan did not come to her. She had not slept the night before, and that and the long journey made her sleep even though she tried to stay awake to greet him. But she went to sleep with a smile on her lips, knowing how her husband would wake her.

Rogan lay down on the coarse woolen blankets near Severn, where he always slept on their journeys.

Sleepily, Severn turned to him. "I thought you had a wife now."

"The Howards attack and I'm thrusting away at some girl," Rogan said sarcastically.

"She's a pretty little thing," Severn said.

"If you like rabbits. The only way I can tell which one she is is by the color of her dress. Is today Thursday?"

"Yes," Severn answered. "And we'll be home Saturday night."

"Ah, then," Rogan said softly. "I'll not have rabbit for dinner on Saturday."

Severn turned away and went to sleep while Rogan lay awake for another hour. His memories in this spot were too strong to allow him to sleep. His mind was filled with plans of what he'd do with the Neville gold now that he had it. There were war machines to build, knights to hire and equip, food to be purchased for the long siege ahead, for he knew that regaining the Peregrine lands was going to take a long, long time of warfare.

Not once did he think of his new wife, who waited for him on the opposite side of the camp.

The next morning Liana's temper was not the best it had ever been. Joice came to her mistress with a stream of complaints from the maids. The Peregrine knights had been harsh in their lovemaking and two of the maids were bruised and sore.

"Better bruised and sore than well and comfortable," Liana snapped. "Bring me the blue gown and headdress and tell the women to stop complaining or I'll give them something to complain about."

Liana saw her husband through the trees and once again choked her anger down. Were all marriages like this? Did all women suffer one injustice after another and have to bite their tongues? Was this truly the way to love?

She wore a blue satin gown with a gold belt set with diamonds. There were also small diamonds on the tall padded headdress she wore. Perhaps today he'd look at her with desire. Perhaps last night he had been shy about lying with her when his men were about. Yes, perhaps there were reasons for his behavior.

He didn't greet her that morning. In fact, he walked past her once and didn't even look at her. It was as if he didn't recognize her.

Liana mounted her horse with the help of a knight and once again rode in the middle of the men, behind the dust and horse manure.

Toward midday she grew restless. She could see Severn and Rogan at the head of the line talking earnestly and she wanted to know what interested them so much. She reined her horse to the side.

"My lady!" Joice said in alarm. "Where are you going?"

"Since my husband does not come to me, I will go to him."

"You cannot," Joice said, eyes wide. "Men do not like forward women. You *must* wait until he comes to you."

Liana hesitated, but her boredom won out. "I will see," she said, and kicked her horse forward until she rode beside her brother-in-law, Rogan next to him. Severn glanced at her; Rogan did not. But neither man gave her a word of greeting.

"We'll need all the grain we can get," Rogan was saying. "We'll have to store it and ready ourselves."

"And what about the fifty hectares along the north road? The peasants say the fields won't produce and the sheep are dying."

"Dying, ha!" Rogan snorted. "The bastards are no doubt selling them to passing merchants and keeping the coin. Send some men to burn a few houses and whip a few farmers and we'll see if their sheep keep dying."

Here was a place where Liana felt at home. Discussions of sheep and peasants were what had occupied her life for years. She didn't think of "obeying" or of keeping her counsel to herself. "Terrorizing peasants never did any good," she said loudly, not looking at either man. "First we must find out if what they say is true. It could be many things: The land could be overused, the water could be bad, or a curse could have been put on the sheep. If it's none of these things and the peasants are cheating us, then we banish them. I've found that banishment works as well as torture, and it's so much less . . . unpleasant. Once we get there, I shall look into it." She turned to smile at the men.

Both of them were staring at her with their mouths open.

Liana didn't understand their expressions at all. "It could also be the seeds," she said. "One year a mold destroyed all our seed and—"

"Back!" Rogan said under his breath. "Get back to the women. If I want an opinion from a woman, I will ask," he said in the same tone as he might say that he'd ask his horse about the grain before he asked a woman.

"I was merely—" Liana began.

"I will tie you inside a wagon if you say more," Rogan said, his eyes hard and angry.

Liana swallowed more anger as she turned her horse and went back to the women.

Severn was the first to speak when they were again alone. "The water? What could be wrong with the water? And a curse. Do you think the Howards put a curse on our sheep? How do we get rid of it?"

Rogan was staring straight ahead. Damned woman, he thought. What was she trying to do, interfere in men's work? Once he'd allowed a woman to interfere. Once he'd listened to a woman, and she had repaid him in treachery. "There is no curse. Merely greedy peasants," Rogan said firmly. "I'll show them whose land they farm."

Severn was thoughtful for a moment. He was not possessed of the same hatred of women that his brother was. There were many things that he discussed with Iolanthe, and he often found her answers were wise and useful. Perhaps there was more to this Neville heiress than he'd thought when he first saw her.

He turned in the saddle and looked back at her. She sat rigid on her horse, her back straight, her eyes glittering with anger. Severn turned and grinned at his brother. "You've offended her now," he said jovially. "Her temper won't be so sweet tonight. I've found that a gift will usually put a woman in a better mood. Or perhaps compliments will work. Tell her that her hair is like gold, tell her that her beauty tempts you from your soul."

"The only thing that tempts me is the gold in the wagons, not in her hair. And I think that tonight you'd better take one of the maids to keep you from thinking of women's hair."

Severn kept smiling. "While you lay with your pretty wife and give her a few sons?"

Sons, Rogan thought. Sons to help him fight the Howards. Sons to live on the Peregrine lands once he took them back. Sons to ride beside him. Sons to teach to fight and ride and hunt. "Yes, I'll give her sons," Rogan said at last.

Liana was convinced Joice was right after her confrontation with Rogan. It was going to take a while to teach herself to be obedient and to listen and to keep her ideas to herself.

That night they camped again, and again Liana put furs under a far tree. But again Rogan did not come to her. He did not speak to her or even look at her.

Liana refused to cry. She refused to remember Helen's words of warning. Instead, she remembered the time at the pool of water when he'd kissed her. He seemed to find her desirable then, but not now. She slept fitfully and woke before dawn, before the rest of the camp was awake. She rose, a hand at her stiff back, and made her way into the woods.

Stooping down to take a drink from a little spring, she became aware of eyes on her and whirled to see a man standing in the shadows. She gasped and put her hand to her throat.

"Do not leave the safety of the camp without a guard," came Rogan's low voice.

She was acutely aware that she wore only her thin silk robe over her nudity, her hair hanging loose down her back, and he wore only his braies, the hose covering him from waist to toe, his broad chest bare. She took a step toward him. "I could not sleep," she said softly. She wished he'd reach for her, take her in his arms. "Did you sleep well?"

He frowned at her. Somehow, she was familiar, as if he'd seen her before. She was tempting enough in the early morning light, but he felt no raging desire for her. "Get back to the camp," he said, then turned away from her.

"Of all the—" she said under her breath but caught herself. Was there some reason this man ignored her? Joice said she'd be able to make herself indispensable to him once she was in his home. There she'd be able to make him comfortable and see to his many needs.

And there they'd share a bed, she thought with pleasure.

She hurried forward to catch up with him. "Do we reach the Peregrine castle today?"

"It's the Moray castle," he said tightly. "The Howards occupy the Peregrine lands."

She was having to rush to keep up with him, her long robe causing her to trip over branches and stones.

"I've heard of them. They stole your lands and title, didn't they? You would be a duke now if it weren't for them."

He halted abruptly in front of her and turned angry eyes on her. "Is that what you hope for, girl? That you have married a duke? Is that why you married me and turned down the others?"

"Why no, I didn't," she said, astonished. "I married you because . . ."

"Yes?" he demanded.

Liana couldn't very well say that she lusted after him, that her heart was pounding in her throat even now at being so close to him, and that she greatly wanted to touch the bare skin of his chest.

"There you are," Severn said from behind them, thus saving Liana from answering. "The men are ready to ride. My lady," he said, nodding to Liana.

His eyes studied her so hard that she blushed, then looked up through the curtain of her hair to see if Rogan saw. He did not. He had started toward the camp, leaving Liana where she was. She made her way back to the camp by herself, following along behind the brothers.

"She's prettier than I first thought," Severn said to his brother as they rode.

"She doesn't interest me at all," Rogan said. "No woman who has 'wife' attached to her interests me."

"I would imagine that you'd fight hard enough if someone tried to take her." Severn was jesting with his brother, but the minute the words were out, he regretted them. Ten years ago someone had indeed tried to take a wife of Rogan's and he'd fought so hard to get her back that two of their brothers had been killed.

"No, I would not fight for her," Rogan said softly. "If you want the woman, take her. She means less than nothing to me. The gold she brought me is all I want of her."

Severn frowned at his brother's words, but he said no more.

CHAPTER
SIX

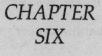

Moray Castle came into sight at midday, and a more depressing sight Liana had never seen. It was the old-style castle, made for protection, and left unchanged for over a hundred and fifty years. The windows were arrow slits, the tower was thick and impenetrable-looking. Men lined the battlements, which were broken in places, looking as if the castle had been attacked and never repaired.

As they drew closer, she could smell the place. Over their own horses and the unwashed bodies of the Peregrine knights came the stench of the castle.

"My lady," Joice whispered.

Liana did not look at her maid, but stared ahead. Helen had told her of the filth of the place, but she was not prepared for this.

They came first to the moat. All the latrines of the castle emptied into this protective body of water and it was thick with excrement as well as kitchen slops of rotting animal carcasses. Liana kept her head high and her eyes forward while, around her, her maids coughed and gagged at the smell.

They rode in single file through a long, low tunnel and overhead Liana saw three openings for heavy, spiked iron gates that could be dropped on intruders. At the end of the tunnel was a single courtyard, half the size of her father's outer bailey, yet there were three times the people here. Her nose already outraged, now it was her ears' turn. Men hammered hot iron on anvils; dogs barked; carpenters hammered; men yelled at each other above the noise.

Liana could hardly believe the noise and the stench of stables and pigsties, which looked as if they'd not been cleaned in years.

To her right a maid squealed and her horse side-stepped into Liana's. Liana looked up to see what had frightened the girl. A urinal from the third story opened into the courtyard and now a heavy waterfall of urine was cascading and splashing down the wall into a deep puddle of filth on the ground below.

After the maid's squeal, neither Liana nor her maids said another word. They were too horrified to be able to speak.

To Liana's right were two stone staircases, one leading to the single tower, the other to the lower two-story slate-roofed building. With this small castle there were no inner and outer courtyards, no separation of lord and retainer, but everyone lived together in this small space.

At the head of the stairs Liana saw two women. They searched the crowd of newcomers until they saw Liana, then one of them pointed at her and they both laughed. Liana could see they were maids, but the filth of the place made it obvious they did no work. She'd soon fix them and teach them not to laugh at their betters.

The girls sauntered down the stairs and as they rounded the short stone wall, Liana saw their figures. They were both short, buxom, small-waisted, big-hipped girls with lots of coarse dirty brown hair hanging in long braids down their backs. Their clothes were tight and revealing and they walked with an insolent, exaggerated sway to their hips. They strutted across the courtyard in a slow way that made their big breasts move under their clothes, and most of the men stopped to watch them.

As a knight helped Liana from her horse, she saw the maids ooze their way toward Rogan. He was yelling at some men about the Neville wagons, but Liana saw him glance down at the girls. One of them turned and gave Liana such a look of triumph that Liana's fingers itched to slap her face.

"Shall we go inside, my lady?" Joice said meekly. "Perhaps inside it's . . . ." Her voice trailed off.

It was obvious that her husband was not going to show her her new home and by now Liana didn't expect him to. Assuming that the staircase the insolent maids had used led to the lord of the manor's quarters, she lifted her skirts and went up them, kicking bones and what looked to be a dead bird out of the way as she ascended.

At the top of the stairs was a large room, the doorway partitioned off by what once must have been a beautiful carved wooden screen, but now axe heads were buried in the wood and nails had been driven into it to hold maces and lances. Through the wide wooden doors of the screen, one of which hung by only one hinge, was a room about forty-five feet long by twenty-five feet wide, with a ceiling as high as the room was wide.

Liana and her maids stepped into this room in silence because no words could express what they saw.

Filthy would not describe it. The floor looked as if every bone from every meal that had been eaten in this room for over a hundred years was still on it. Flies swarmed around the maggot-covered bones, and Liana could see things—she refused to consider what things—crawling about under the thick layer of refuse.

Spider webs with fat occupants hung from the ceiling almost to the floor. The double fireplaces at the east end of the hall had three feet of ashes in them. The only furniture in the room were a thick, heavy table made of a slab of blackened oak and eight scarred, broken chairs, all covered with grease from years of meals.

There were several windows in the room, some of them fifteen feet above the floor, but the glass and the shutters were gone, so the smell of the moat, the courtyard, and this room mingled.

When one of the maids behind her swooned and began to faint, Liana wasn't surprised. "Stand up!" she commanded, "or we'll have to lay you on the floor." The girl uprighted herself immediately.

Taking her courage in her hands, as well as her silk skirt, Liana made her way across the room to the stairs in the northwest corner. These too were covered with bones, straw crushed to powder, and what was possibly a dead rat. "Joice, come with me," she said over her shoulder, "and the rest of you remain here."

Up eight stairs was a room, opening to the left, and a toilet, to the right. Liana just looked into the room but did not enter it. It contained a small round table, two chairs, and hundreds of weapons of war.

Liana continued up the circular stairs, a timid Joice behind her, until she reached the second floor of the tower. Before her was a short, low round-topped hallway, and a few feet along it was a door leading off to the right. This was a bedchamber with a filthy straw-filled mattress on the floor, the straw so old, it was merely two pieces of coarse wool on the floor. A latrine led off this room.

Joice stepped forward and put her hand down as if to touch the two blankets heaped at the foot of the mattress.

"Lice," was all Liana said, and moved on down the hallway.

She entered the solar, a large, spacious room filled with light from the many windows. Along the south wall was a wooden staircase that led up to the third floor. A rustle overhead made Liana look up. Along the carved corbels that held the ceiling beams were wooden perches and here sat hawks, all of them hooded and jessed. There were peregrines, kestrels, merlins, goshawks, and sparrow hawks. The walls were coated with bird droppings, which had dripped down to form hard hills on the floor.

Liana lifted her skirt higher and went across the filthy floor to the east side of the room. Here were three arches, the center one creating a little room, one wooden door barely hanging, the other missing. Set in the stone wall was a little piscina, the basin used by the priest for ablutions after mass.

"It is sacrilege," Joice whispered, for this was a private oratory, a holy place for the saying of mass for the family.

"Ah, but here we have an excellent view of the moat," Liana said, looking out the window and trying to bring some humor into this hideous place. But Joice did not laugh or smile.

"My lady, what shall we do?"

"We shall make my husband comfortable," Liana said with assurance. "First we will prepare two bedrooms for tonight, one for my husband and me," she could not prevent the flush that crept over her face, "then one for you and my maids. Tomorrow we shall start on the rest of the place. Now, stop standing and staring. Go and get those women I saw below. A little work should take the insolence out of them."

Joice was afraid to move about the castle alone, but her mistress's manner gave her courage. She was afraid of what lurked in the shadows and corners of the castle. If something attacked, how long would it be before they found her bones among the others?

In the solar, Liana went to the other arched rooms flanking the oratory. The bird droppings were less in evidence here and she could see that under the dirt the walls had once been painted with scenes. Once they were cleaned she could have them repainted, and there on that far west wall she'd hang a tapestry. For a moment she could almost escape the smells of the room, the ominous sound of birds' wings rustling, and the sound of whatever was moving about under the refuse on the floor.

"They won't come, my lady," said a breathless Joice from the doorway.

Liana came back to reality. "Who won't come? My husband?"

Joice was indignant. "The maids! Lord Rogan's maids won't come. When I told them they were to come and clean, they laughed at me."

"Did they?" Liana said. "Let's see what they say to me." She was ready for a good fight. She'd been so obedient and had swallowed so much anger in the past few days that she wanted an outlet for it, and overdeveloped maids who pointed at her and laughed would be an excellent target.

Liana stormed down the steep stairs, across the lord's chamber, down the outside stairs, and into the loud, dirty courtyard. The two maids she'd seen before were lounging near the well, allowing three young knights to draw buckets of water for them while they brushed their big breasts against the men's arms.

"You!" Liana said to the first one. "Come with me."

Liana turned on her heel and started back toward the castle only to realize that no maids were following her. She looked back to see the two maids smiling at her as if they knew something she did not. Liana had never had a maid disobey her before. Always before, she'd been backed by her father's power.

For a moment, Liana didn't know what to do. She could feel the eyes of the other people in the courtyard on her, and she knew that now was the time to establish her power as mistress of the castle. But she couldn't do that unless they knew she had her husband's backing.

Rogan was near the far wall of the courtyard, directing the unloading of a wagon that contained several suits of armor that were part of Liana's dowry. Angrily, she made her way across the courtyard, sidestepping three fighting dogs, overstepping a pile of rotting sheep entrails.

She knew what she wanted to say, the demands she wanted to make, but when Rogan turned to her, annoyed that she was interrupting him, her confidence faded. She so much wanted to please him, wanted to have his eyes change when he looked at her. Now he seemed to be trying to remember who she was.

"The maids will not obey me," she said quietly.

He looked at her in consternation, as if her problem had nothing to do with him.

"I want the maids to start cleaning, but they won't obey me," she further explained.

That seemed to relieve his puzzlement. He turned

back to the wagons. "They clean what's needed. I thought you brought maids."

She moved between him and the wagon. "Three of my maids are *ladies,* and the others . . . well, there's just too much for them to do."

"Dent that armor and I'll dent your head," Rogan shouted to a laborer who was unloading the wagon. He looked down at Liana. "I have no time for maids. The place is clean enough as it is. Now, go away and let me get these wagons unloaded."

He dismissed her as if she didn't exist, and Liana stood there staring at his back and feeling the eyes of every man and, most of all, those two maids on her. So this was what Helen had warned her about. This was what marriage was like. A man courted you until he got you, then you were less than . . . than a piece of steel to him. Of course, with Rogan, she hadn't even received the courting.

Now she knew that at all costs she must keep her dignity. She didn't look right or left but walked straight ahead toward the stone steps and went up them and into the castle. Behind her she could hear the noise of the courtyard resume with tripled force, and she even heard some high-pitched female laughter.

Liana's heart beat quickly with the humiliation she'd received. Helen had said she'd been spoiled by her power at the Neville estates, but Liana had had no real idea of what she meant. She suspected that few people realized how different other people's lives were from their own. She'd expected her married life to be somewhat different, but this feeling of being powerless, of not existing, was something altogether new to her.

This must have been how Helen felt at the Neville

estates when the servants obeyed Liana and not her. "She felt like this, yet she was still good to me," Liana whispered.

"My lady," Joice said softly.

Liana blinked at her maid and saw the fear on the older woman's face. Liana didn't seem so sure of herself now as she had before the wedding. At the moment she was too tired to think what she was going to do in the future. For now the immediate needs were for food and a place to sleep.

"Send Bess to find the kitchens and bring up supper—I do not want to eat in company tonight. Then get some of my bedding sent up to the solar." She put her hand up to stop Joice from speaking. "I don't know how to accomplish that. It seems that I have no power in my husband's home." She tried to keep the self-pity out of her voice, but she didn't succeed. "And find some shovels. Tonight we will empty two rooms of enough filth to be able to sleep. And tomorrow we'll—" She stopped because she didn't like to think of tomorrow. If she had no power, even in directing a maid, she would be a prisoner just as if she were locked in a dungeon.

"Find out what you can about this place," Liana said as an afterthought. "Where is Lord Severn? Perhaps he could . . . help us." There was little strength in Liana's voice.

"Yes, my lady," Joice said meekly and left the room.

Slowly, Liana made her way up the circular staircase to the solar. The hawks moved on their perches at the sound of her, then settled again. If the whole castle were not littered with the remains of people's living, she might have thought the place deserted. It was so unlike her father's house, with people moving in and out of rooms, people laughing and teasing. Here there were only men, hard-faced, unsmiling men with scars on their bodies and weapons in their hands. There were no children, and no women except for the two bitches who'd laughed at her and refused to obey her.

She looked below at the moat and in the fading light saw the head of a cow bob in the black, thick ooze. This place was to be her home. Here she was to bear children and raise them. And what love she was to have was to come from a husband who didn't seem to recognize her from one hour to the next.

How was she to make him love her? Perhaps if she and her maids cleaned the place, perhaps if she made this castle a fit place to live, he would be glad he married her. He would think of her as more than just the person who came attached to the dowry.

And food, she thought. Perhaps if she hired some good cooks and covered his table with delicious, delectable food. Surely the man who ate well, slept between clean sheets, wore clean clothes, would be pleased with the woman who made this possible.

And then there was the bed. Liana had heard her maids say a woman who pleased a man in bed could control him out of it. She'd get one bedroom clean by tonight and he'd seek her out, for now that they had privacy, he'd want his wife. She smiled for the first time since seeing Moray Castle. She just had to be patient and what she wanted would eventually come to her.

Moments later all seven of her maids came to the solar, their arms loaded with food, pillows, and blankets, and chattering all at once.

It took Liana a while to understand what the women were saying. Lord Severn was with someone called the Lady and wasn't likely to be seen for three or four days. Other than the Lady and her maids, there were only eight women in the whole castle.

"They do no work," Bess said, "and no one would tell me what they do."

"And they're named for the days of the week. Sunday, Monday, Tuesday, and so forth, except one is called Waiting. They didn't seem to have any other names," Alice said.

"And the food is awful. The flour is full of weevils and sand. The baker just bakes it into the bread."

Bess leaned forward. "They used to buy bread from a baker in town, but he filed an order of a feud against the Peregrines for nonpayment and . . ."

"And what?" Liana demanded, trying to eat a piece of meat that could have been used for saddle leather.

"The Peregrine men tore the door off the baker's house and . . . and used his flour bins for a toilet."

Liana put her inedible meat down. The women had cleaned off a seat under one window and now sat there together. Below them they could hear the sounds of steel on steel, of men yelling, of food being eaten with open mouths. It seemed that her husband and his men were eating in the room below, but no one had thought to ask the wife of their lord to join them.

"Did you perhaps hear which bedchamber is Lord Rogan's?" she asked, trying to keep her dignity.

The women looked at each other, pity in their eyes.

"No," Joice murmured. "But surely that one there, the large one, is his room."

Liana nodded. She hadn't yet felt strong enough to mount the wooden stairs of the solar and see what rooms were above—or, more likely, what manner of filth was there. If birds were kept in the solar, were pigs kept in the upper bedrooms?

It took two hours of hard work to shovel out two bedrooms. Liana wanted to help, but Joice refused to allow it and Liana understood. At the moment her maids were almost her equals, as they all felt lost and alone in this strange, foul-smelling place, but Joice did not want her mistress to lose her power over these women. So Liana sat on the window seat in the solar and held a clove-studded orange to her nose to block out the smell of the moat.

When at last her room was ready—not clean, but at least she could walk in it without tripping over bones—a maid persuaded a farrier to bring up two mattresses, and Liana, with Joice's help, undressed and went to bed. She lay awake for a while, waiting for her husband to come to her. But he didn't.

In the morning she awoke to loud noises and hideous smells. What she had thought was a bad dream was reality.

In the morning Rogan walked into the Lord's Chamber to see Severn sitting at the table, his head resting tiredly on his hand, and eating bread and cheese. "I didn't expect to see you for a while. Want to go hunting with me?"

"Yes," Severn answered. "I need the rest after last night with Io. You look well rested. Your wife didn't bother you too much last night?"

"Last night was Saturday," Rogan gave for an answer.

"And you didn't spend it with your wife?"

"Not on Saturday."

Severn scratched his arm. "You'll never get any sons like that."

"Are you ready to go or not? I'll get around to her. Maybe next . . . I don't know when. She's not something to stir a man's blood."

"Where is she now?"

Rogan shrugged. "Upstairs, maybe. Who knows?"

Severn washed the rest of the bread down with sour wine and spit sand onto the floor. What his brother did was none of his business.

For three days Liana and her maids worked at cleaning the solar. And for three days she was afraid to go belowstairs. She couldn't bear to show her face to the people of Moray Castle. They all knew that she had been rejected by her husband, that he not only refused to sleep with her but that he refused to give her power over his servants.

So Liana stayed alone, never seeing her husband, never having any contact with the people of the castle. So far, she thought, not only wasn't she winning her husband's love with her meekness, but he wasn't even noticing her, meek or otherwise.

It was on the afternoon of the fourth day that she dared to venture up the wooden stairs. The upper floor was as dirty as the solar had been, except there were no signs that anyone had been here for years. She wondered where the people of the castle slept and instantly pictured them altogether in a heap.

She walked along the hall and looked into one empty bedroom after another, scaring rats as she went along, creating little dust storms behind her. When she was about to leave to go downstairs again, she thought she heard a spinning wheel. Lifting her skirts, she ran to the far bedroom and pushed open the heavy door.

Sitting in a stream of sunlight was a very pretty older woman with dark hair and brows, working at a flax wheel. The room was clean, there was cushioned furniture here, and the windows had glass in them. This had to be the Lady who Lord Severn visited. Perhaps she was an aunt or some other relative.

"Come in, dear, and close the door before we both choke on the dust."

Liana did as she was bid and smiled. "I didn't know anyone was here. What with the state of everything, that is." She felt very comfortable with this lovely woman, and when she nodded at a chair, Liana took it.

"It is awful, isn't it?" the lady said. "Rogan wouldn't notice the dirt even if it were so deep he had to swim through it."

Liana quit smiling. "He wouldn't notice me if I were drowning in it," she said under her breath to herself, not meaning for the lady to hear.

But she did hear. "Of course he wouldn't notice you. Men never notice the good women who see that their clothes are clean, that their food is well cooked, and who bear their children in silence."

Liana's head came up at this. "What women *do* they notice?"

"Women like Iolanthe." She smiled at Liana. "You haven't met her. She's Severn's greensleeves. Well, not an actual greensleeves. Actually, Io is the wife of a very wealthy, very old, very stupid man. Io spends his money and lives here with Severn, who is neither old nor wealthy and not at all stupid."

"She lives *here?* She chooses to live in this . . . this . . ."

"She has her own apartments over the kitchen, quite the best apartments in the castle. Io would demand the best."

"I demanded help from the servants," Liana said bitterly, "but got nothing."

"There are demands and there are demands," the lady said, spinning her flax into a fine, smooth strand. "Do you love Rogan very much?"

Liana looked away and didn't even question her intimacy with this woman. She was so tired of having only maids to talk to. "I think I could have loved him once. I agreed to marry him because he was the only man who was honest with me. He didn't praise my beauty then look at my father's gold."

"Rogan is always honest. He never pretends to be what he is not, to care about what does not matter to him."

"True, and he does not care about me," Liana said sadly.

"But then you do lie, don't you, dear? The Liana who hides from the laughter of maids is not the Liana who ran her father's estates, the Liana who once faced a mob of angry peasants."

Liana didn't ask how the woman knew these things about her, but she felt tears welling in her eyes. "I don't think a man could love that Liana. Joice says men like—"

"And who is Joice?"

"My maid. Actually, she is somewhat like a mother to me. She says—"

"And she knows all about men, does she? Raised by one, married to one, mother to many?"

"Well, no, actually, she grew up with me. She was an orphan before that and lived in the women's quarters. She is married, though, no children, but then she only sees her husband three times a year so . . . Oh, I see what you mean. Joice has not had a great deal of experience with men."

"No, I thought not. Remember, dear, it isn't the woman who cleans a man's house who has battles fought for her, it is the woman who sometimes wields a whip."

That made Liana laugh. "I can't imagine taking a whip to Lord Rogan."

"Only a muddy shirt," the woman said, eyes smiling, then her head came up. "Someone comes up the stairs. Go, please. I don't want to be disturbed."

"Yes, of course," Liana said and left the room, closing the door behind her. She almost went back into the room to ask how she'd known about the muddy shirt, but Joice came to the head of the stairs and said Liana was needed.

The rest of that day Liana spent in isolation in the solar, only her maids for company, and Liana kept hearing the woman's words. She was so confused about what to do. She thought of going to Rogan and demanding that he make the servants obey her, but the idea was ridiculous to her. He'd merely turn away. She couldn't imagine he would listen to her merely because she shouted at him. Of course she could always draw a sword on him. That idea almost made her giggle. So all she could do was wait. Perhaps someday he'd come to the solar, perhaps to get one of his hawks, and he'd see how clean the place was and he'd want to remain, then he'd turn to her with love in his eyes and—

"My lady?" Joice said. "The hour grows late."

"Yes," Liana said heavily. She'd go to her empty, cold bed once again.

It was hours later that she awoke to an odd sound and a light. "Rogan!" she gasped, and turned over to see not her husband but a tall boy, a very pretty boy, with dirty shoulder-length dark hair and a ragged velvet tunic over baggy knit hose. He was standing by the wall, one leg on a stool, elbow on knee, eating an apple and staring at her in the light of a fat, bright candle.

Liana sat up. "Who are you and what are you doing in my room?"

"Come to have a look at you," he said.

He must be younger than his height indicated because his voice hadn't changed yet, she thought. "You've seen me, now get out of here." She did not have to put up with insolence in the room she'd chosen for her own.

He loudly munched on his apple and made no move to leave. "I guess you've been waiting for my brother for a while now."

"Your brother?" Liana remembered Helen's saying she didn't know how many Peregrine sons were left.

"I'm Zared," the boy said, putting his foot on the floor and throwing the apple core out the window. "I've seen you now. You're just like they said, and Rogan won't be coming tonight." He started out the door.

"Wait just a minute!" Liana said in a voice that made the boy halt and turn back. "What do you mean I'm like they said, and where is my husband that he won't be here tonight?" Liana hoped the boy would say Rogan was on some secret mission for the king, or perhaps had taken a temporary vow of chastity.

"Today's Wednesday," Zared said.

"What has the day of the week to do with my husband?"

"I heard you met them. There're eight of them. One for each day of the week and one for when one of the Days has female trouble. Sometimes two of them at a time have female trouble, then Rogan is hell to live with. Maybe he'll come to you then."

Liana wasn't sure, but she thought she was beginning to understand. "Those maids," she said softly. "Do you mean that my husband sleeps with a different one each night? That they are a . . . a *calendar?*"

"He tried one for each day of the month once, but he said it made for too many women around the place. He's made do with eight. Severn is altogether different. He says Iolanthe is enough for him. Of course, Io is—"

"Where is he?" Anger was beginning to surge through Liana. Anger swallowed from the first time she met Rogan was pumping through her veins. She was regurgitating it, like something as vile as the moat below. "Where *is* he?"

"Rogan? He sleeps somewhere different every night. He goes to the Days' rooms. He says they get jealous if they come to his room. Tonight, this being Wednesday, he'd be on the top floor of the kitchen apartments, first door on the left."

Liana stood. Her entire body was filled with rage. Every muscle was taut.

"You aren't going there, are you? Rogan doesn't like to be bothered at night, and I can tell you, his temper isn't pleasant. One time he—"

"He hasn't seen *my* temper yet," Liana said through clenched teeth. *"No one treats me like this and lives to tell about it. No one!"* She pushed past Zared and went out into the hall, where she grabbed a flaming torch from the wall. She wore her robe and her feet were bare but she didn't notice the bones she stepped on, and when a snarling dog got in her way, she used the torch as a sword and the dog skulked away.

"I heard you were a rabbit," Zared said from behind her, following her in wonder. But this wife didn't look like a rabbit now as she marched down the stairs and through the Lord's Chamber. What was Rogan's wife going to do? Whatever was going to happen, Zared knew Severn must be fetched.

CHAPTER
SEVEN

Liana wasn't sure where the kitchen apartments were, but she seemed to find them by instinct. Instinct was the only thing she had to direct her feet because her brain was taken over by memories of the humiliations she had suffered since her wedding. He hadn't asked to see her before their marriage. He had demanded more money at the church door. He *raped* her after their wedding—and merely to consummate the marriage, not because he'd had any desire for her. For days he had ignored her, dumped her in this cesspit of a castle, and not so much as introduced her to the castle staff as his wife.

She went down the stairs to the courtyard and then up narrow stone stairs to what she guessed was the kitchen, then up a steep spiral stone staircase. Something slimy squished under her foot, but she took no notice. Nor did she notice the people who were beginning to rise from their beds and follow her, looking with interest at this meek and mild rabbit of a woman who their lord had brought home.

Liana went up and up the stairs, kicking once at an overzealous rat that tried to make a meal of one of her toes, until she reached the top floor. She quietly opened the first door on the left and stepped inside the room. There, sprawled on his stomach, his beautiful body bare—the body she had once lusted for—was her husband. And his right arm was thrown across the plump, nude body of one of the maids who'd refused to obey Liana.

Liana didn't think about what she was doing but put the torch to the corner of the mattress—one of the mattresses she had brought with her—then set another corner on fire.

Rogan awoke almost immediately, and he reacted instantly by grabbing the sleeping maid from the fiery bed, then leaping up. The girl awoke and began screaming and kept screaming when Rogan dropped her on the far side of the room. He grabbed the smoldering blanket from the bed and began to beat at the spreading flames. The door burst open and Severn came in and helped his brother put out the fire before it reached the rafters of the wooden ceiling. When the flames were at last out, the two brothers shoved the charred remains of the mattress out the window, where they fell below into the moat.

The maid's screams had stopped, but now she stood huddled into a corner of the room, her eyes alive with terror. She made little whimpering sounds.

"Stop that!" Rogan commanded. "It was just a little fire," he said, then followed the girl's eyes to where Liana stood, still holding the torch. It took Rogan a moment to understand what had happened, and then he didn't believe what he thought to be true. "You set the bed on fire. You tried to kill me," he stated, then turned to Severn. "She's with the Howards. Take her and burn her in the morning."

Before Severn could answer, before any of the many people, including Zared, who were crowding at the doorway could reply, Liana's rage erupted.

"Yes, I tried to kill you," she said, and advanced on him with the flame of the torch toward him, "and I wish I had succeeded. You have humiliated me, dishonored me, ridiculed me—"

"I?" Rogan said, utterly astonished. He could have easily taken the torch away from her, but she looked rather good with all that fair hair and thin robe in the firelight. And her face! Was she the girl he'd thought plain? "I have paid you every respect. I have hardly been near you."

"True!" she hissed at him, taking another step toward him. "You left me alone at my own wedding feast. You left me alone on my wedding night."

Rogan wore the look of a man unjustly accused. "You are no longer a virgin. I saw to that."

"You *raped* me!" she half yelled at him.

Now Rogan was beginning to get angry. In his view, he had never raped a woman in his life. Not because he was morally opposed to it but because with his face and form, he'd never found the act necessary. "I did not," he said under his breath, watching the way her breasts moved under her robe.

"I can see we aren't needed," Severn said loudly, but Rogan and Liana were so intent on each other they didn't hear him. Severn pushed the others out of the room and shut the door behind him.

"But she must be punished," Zared said. "She nearly killed Rogan."

"Interesting wench, that one," Severn said thoughtfully.

"She has my room!" Wednesday wailed, a charred blanket wrapped around her nudity.

Severn smiled. "She may have taken more than

your room. Go sleep with Sunday. And you," he said to Zared, "go to bed."

Inside the room, Liana and Rogan faced each other. Rogan knew he should punish her—after all, she might have killed him—but now that he knew her action was merely a woman's jealous fit, he knew it was nothing to be concerned about. "I should have you flogged."

"You lay a hand on me, and the next time I'll set your *hair* on fire."

"Now, see here—" he said. She was going too far. He was willing to put up with women's little tempers —after all, they were women—but this was too much.

Liana jabbed the torch at him. He seemed utterly unaware that he was wearing not a stitch of clothing. "No, it is *your* turn to listen to me. I have stood by silently and watched as you have ignored me, belittled me. You allow those . . . those Days of yours to laugh at me. Me! The lady of the castle. I am your wife, and I am going to be treated as I deserve. So help me God, you will treat me with courtesy and respect—I do not demand love—or you had better never sleep when I am by, for you will never wake up again."

Rogan was speechless. It was one thing to be threatened by an enemy, but this woman was his *wife!* "No woman threatens me," he said quietly.

Liana jabbed the torch at him and in one swift gesture he took it from her, then caught her waist. He meant to haul her from the room, to take her below and lock her in the cellar, but when her face was close to his, his anger turned to desire. Never had he desired a woman as much as he desired this one. He would die if he could not have her.

He put his hand to her shoulder and started to tear the robe from her.

"No!" she said, pulling back from him.

He was blinded with passion, his brain given over to the wanting of her. He wrapped his hand in her hair and pulled her toward him.

"No," she whispered, her lips against his. "You do not rape me again. You may make love to me all night, but you do not rape me."

Rogan was taken aback by her. Women gave themselves to him, women had seduced him, but he'd never had a woman make demands of him. And suddenly, he wanted to please her. It had never occurred to him before whether he was pleasing a woman or not, but this one he wanted to please.

His hands on her shoulders loosened their grip until his fingers were softly holding her skin. Gently, he pulled her toward him. He didn't usually trouble himself much with kissing the women he bedded because they were always ready and eager for him and it was a waste of time to kiss them. But he wanted to kiss this woman.

Liana leaned her head back and gave herself to his kiss, feeling the softness of his lips, her hands reaching up to touch his hair. His lips moved over hers, enveloping hers, then his tongue tip touched hers and Liana moaned and leaned her body into his.

Rogan could wait no longer for her. His arms tightened about her, then one hand bit into her thigh as he lifted her right leg to wrap it about his waist. Then his other hand lifted her left leg.

Liana, having had so little experience with sex, had no idea what was going on, but she loved the kissing and the feeling of her bare bottom against his skin. She was unprepared for when he slammed her back against the stone wall and entered her with all the force of a man using a battering ram to attack a locked door. She cried out in pain and protest, but her face was buried in the muscle of his chest and she could not be heard.

It seemed that he kept up his deep, hard thrusts for hours, and at first Liana hated the act, the man, everything that was being done to her, but after a while, her eyes opened wider, for she felt a deep inner pleasure that was beginning to spread through her body.

She cried out in surprise, then clutched Rogan's hair in her hands, pulling it hard while she brought her mouth down on his.

Her sudden passion was enough to finish Rogan and with a final thrust, he went limp against her, pushing her back hard against the stones as he leaned against her, his heart pounding.

Liana wanted more. She wasn't sure exactly what she wanted, but what she'd received wasn't enough. Her nails bit into his shoulders.

Rogan drew his head away from her shoulder and looked at her, startled. He could see that he had not pleased her. Instantly, he dropped her legs and stepped away from her and began searching for his braies in the debris on the floor. "You may go now," he murmured, feeling anger rising in himself.

Liana was energized by the too-brief lovemaking. "I have a bedroom off the solar prepared for us."

"Then you can go there and sleep," he said with anger, but when he turned to look at her, his anger vanished. Her eyes were bright and alive and her hair was wild and free about her head. He almost reached for her again, but he forced his hands to remain at his side. Women who were new to him were always exciting, he told himself.

Liana didn't try to repress the anger she felt. The vision of him in bed with another woman was too fresh and too painful. "So that you can go to another woman?" she hissed at him.

"Why, no," he said, surprised. "So that I can sleep. There is no bed in here."

This statement, delivered so solemnly, made Liana smile. "Come with me," she said softly, holding out her hand to him. "I have a clean, fragrant bed ready for us."

Rogan didn't want to take her hand and he knew he shouldn't sleep with her, because he'd learned from experience that when you slept the whole night with women, they began to think they owned you. He'd been "owned" by a woman once and— In spite of his sensible thoughts, he took her hand, and her smile at him deepened.

"Come," she whispered, and he followed her like a little dog on a leash as she led him down the stairs to the kitchen, then out into the courtyard. It was quiet now and she paused to look up at the stars. "They're beautiful, aren't they?"

At first Rogan didn't know what she meant. Stars were to guide you when traveling at night. "I guess they are," he said softly. The moonlight on her hair made it silver.

She stepped back against him, her back against his chest. This was what she'd imagined marriage to be, her husband holding her in the moonlight. But Rogan made no move to put his arms around her, so Liana put her hands about his wrists and guided his arms about her shoulders.

Rogan was startled for a moment. It was such a waste of time to be standing outside in the middle of the night, holding a bit of a girl and looking up at the stars. Tomorrow he had so much to do. But then he put his nose in her hair, smelled the clean, spicy fragrance of it, and he couldn't remember what he had to do tomorrow. "What's your name?" he whispered against her hair. He had trouble with women's names and had years ago assigned them a date as opposed to a name.

Liana didn't let her little lump of anger rise to the surface. "I am Lady Liana, your wife," she said, then turned in his arms and put her face up to be kissed. When he didn't kiss her, she kissed him, her hands caressing the back of his neck as she did so. Then she put her head against his shoulder and snuggled her body close to his.

Rogan found himself holding her, just standing there and holding her close to him. He'd never done this before. Women were for sex, for fetching what a man needed, for doing whatever a man wanted. They were not for standing in the middle of a courtyard and just holding. There was no purpose behind such an action, yet he was powerless to move.

Liana heard the movement behind her, someone who couldn't sleep, perhaps. She was not used to being married and so immediately felt wrong for touching a man so intimately. "Come, let's go before they find us."

Again, Rogan followed her as she led him up the stairs, past the Lord's Chamber and up to the hall that led to the solar. Here was the bedroom that had once belonged to his father and his wives. He hadn't been in it for years. This girl, this Liana, had hung a tapestry on one wall. There were fat, fragrant candles burning. There was a bed against one wall, a holy cross above it.

Rogan took a step backward, but the girl tugged on his hand.

"Come, I have wine, good wine from Italy, and I will pour you a glass."

Rogan wasn't sure how she did it but moments later

he was nude and in her soft, clean bed, a silver goblet of wine in his hand and her pressed to his shoulder, his arm holding her to him, his fingers playing with her hair.

Liana snuggled her body against his as if she were trying to become part of his skin. There were so many questions she wanted to ask him about the castle, about the people. Who was the Lady she'd seen spinning? She wanted to know more about Severn's Iolanthe. And why wasn't Zared fostered to another knight and in training?

But she'd poured out too much emotion tonight and was now too tired to talk. She put her hand on the hair of his chest, felt his big, strong body next to hers and, contentedly, she drifted into sleep.

Rogan heard her soft breathing of sleep and thought that he should go. He should leave her now and go find somewhere else to sleep. He remembered the way she'd set the bed on fire. If he hadn't wakened, he could have burned to death. By rights she should be in the dungeon now and at dawn he should tie her to a stake and burn her—just as she tried to burn him. But he made no movement. Instead, he lifted her hand from his chest and looked at it with curiosity. It was such a small, weak, useless hand, he thought just before he fell asleep, still holding her in his arms.

When he awoke, it was full morning and he could hear the noise of the courtyard below. With the daylight, his senses returned. He was wrapped about the girl as if they were the entwined roots of a tree. He shoved her from him and rolled out of the bed, then started toward the garderobe. There was a urinal in the little hall before the room with the seat and he paused to relieve himself.

Liana awoke and stretched luxuriously in the bed. She had never felt so good in her life. This was what

marriage was supposed to be: standing in the courtyard in the night in your husband's arms and looking
at the stars, sleeping in his arms, waking to know that
he's near you, hearing a man in the garderobe. He
walked out of the latrine, scratching his bare chest and
yawning.

"Good morning," she said, moving her legs about
under the blankets.

Rogan's mind was on the day's work. Now that he
had the Neville gold, he could begin hiring knights to
help him fight the Howards. Of course he'd have to
train them properly. Most men were lazy louts with
the strength of children. And speaking of lazy, he'd
better get Severn out of that witch-woman's bed or
there'd be no strength left in his brother. He left the
room without once looking at, or remembering, his
wife.

Liana sat up in the bed in shock when he walked out
without acknowledging her. She had half a mind to
run after him and— What? she wondered. She lay
back against the pillows and smiled. She had been
quiet and meek and obedient and he had ignored her.
She had tried to burn him to death and he'd spent the
night with her. The lady who'd been spinning had said
men never fought battles for women who were meek
and mild. Would Rogan perhaps fight a battle for a
wife who tried to set him on fire?

"My lady!" Joice said excitedly as she burst into the
room and began chattering.

Liana's thoughts were so occupied with her husband that she did not at first hear Joice's words.
"What? Fire Lady? What are you talking about?"
When Liana began to understand the story, she
laughed. It seemed the story of Liana's lighting
Rogan's bed had traveled all over the village as well as
the castle, and she had been dubbed the Fire Lady.

"Two of the Days have already gone back to their parents in the village," Joice said, "and the others are afraid of you."

There was pride in Joice's voice, and Liana thought it was ironic coming from this woman who had counseled meekness. If she'd continued to follow Joice's advice, last night would never have happened.

"Good!" Liana said firmly, flinging the covers back and getting out of bed. "We shall use the fear while we have it. Perhaps you and the other women should mention poison and . . . snakes—yes, that's good. If a maid doesn't do her work, I might have snakes put in her bed."

"My lady, I don't think—"

Liana whirled on her maid. "You don't think what, Joice? That I should use my own judgment? Do you think that I should continue to rely on your advice?"

Joice knew she'd lost her power over her mistress. "No, my lady," she whispered. "I meant . . ." She couldn't finish.

"Fetch me the green silk, then come and do my hair," Liana said. "Today I begin to clean my house."

The people of Moray Castle found that the Pale Rabbit had indeed turned into the Fire Lady. They were used to working for the Peregrine brothers, who demanded five things at once of each person, but this little woman, in her brilliant green dress, her fat blonde braids down her back, demanded ten times the work of the masters. She took every man and knight from his usual task and set him to hauling trash. Fireplaces were shoveled out. Bucket after bucket was filled with bones and filth and dumped into the now-empty Neville wagons and hauled away. Liana got Zared to find three other boys and the four of them set about killing rats. She sent men to the village to hire women to scour the walls and floors and furniture. She also hired men to use weighted nets to start dragging the moat and when the nets would not sink into the filth but floated on top, she ordered the men to dig a trench and drain the filth away—if it will move, she thought. The men balked at that, fearing Lord Rogan's sword more than they feared her fire.

"My husband will give permission," she said to the two men before her, both of them afraid for their lives.

"But, my lady," one man said, "the moat is for defense and—"

"Defense!" Liana gasped. "An enemy could *walk* across it as it is now." But no matter what she said, the men would not start digging. She gritted her teeth. "Where is my husband, then? I will go to him and we will settle this between us."

"He is beating farmers, my lady."

It took Liana a moment to understand. "What?" she whispered.

"Someone is stealing, and Lord Rogan beats men until someone tells him who the thieves are."

Liana raised her skirts and ran inside the castle walls. While her horse was being saddled, she got directions to where Rogan and his brother were and minutes later she was riding furiously across the countryside, six armed knights close behind her.

The sight that greeted her was one of horror. One man was tied to a tree, his back bloody from whip lashes. Another three men stood together, shaking with terror as a man held his bloody whip aloft. Four women and six children stood by crying, two of the women on their knees and begging Rogan for mercy. Six Peregrine knights stood to one side of Rogan and Severn, who were deep in conversation, seemingly oblivious to what was going on around them.

"Stop!" Liana screamed, and came off her horse while it was still running. She hurled herself before the cringing farmers. "Do not kill them," she said, looking into Rogan's hard green eyes.

Rogan and his men were so shocked, the knight lowered his whip for a second. "Severn, take her," Rogan commanded.

"*I* will find who is stealing from you," she shouted, twisting away before Severn could grab her. "I will deliver the thieves to you and you may punish them, but not these random people."

Her actions and her words effectively silenced everyone, from Rogan down to the children whose father was tied to the tree.

"You?" Rogan said, as much surprised as anything.

"Give me two weeks' time," Liana said breathlessly, "and I will find your thief. Terrorized peasants do not produce good crops."

"Terrorized . . ." Rogan began, then his bewilderment left. "Get her the hell out of here," he commanded his brother.

Severn's big arm caught Liana's waist and pulled her from in front of the three condemned men. Liana thought fast. "I'll lay you odds I can find your thieves in two weeks," she shouted. "I have a chestful of jewels that you have not seen. Emeralds, rubies, diamonds. I'll give them to you if I do not produce the thieves in two short weeks."

Once again, Rogan and the people quietened and stared at her. They were all wondering what manner of woman she was, Rogan wondering most of all.

Severn's grip on her waist loosened, and Liana went to her husband and looked up at him as she put her hand on his chest. "I have found that terror breeds terror. I have dealt with thieves before. Let me do this now. If I am not right, in two weeks' time you may kill all of them and you will have the jewels."

Rogan could only gape at her. She had nearly

burned him to death last night and now she was making a wager with him like a man and interfering in his business. He had half a mind to yet send her to the dungeon.

"I could take the jewels," he heard himself saying as he looked at her and remembered how alive she'd been last night. A sudden wave of desire overtook him, and he turned away before he touched her in front of his men.

"They are well hidden," she said softly and put her hand on his arm. The same desire was also flooding her veins.

Rogan shook her hand away. "Take the thieving bastards," he said gruffly, just wanting to get away from her. "In two weeks I will have the jewels and I will have taught a woman a lesson," he said, trying to make light of the matter and not unman himself before his men. But a glance at his brother and his men showed they were not close to laughing. They were looking at Liana with deep interest.

Rogan cursed under his breath. "We ride," he growled, moving toward his horse.

"Wait," Liana said, running after him. Her heart was pounding in her throat, for she knew that what she was about to say was greatly daring. "What do I get if I win the wager?"

"What?" Rogan said, glaring down at her. "You get the damned thieves. What else do you want?"

"You," she said, hands on hips, smiling at him. "If I win the wager, I want you as my slave for one whole day."

Rogan gaped at her. He was going to have to remove some of this woman's hide and teach her how a wife should act. He didn't say a word but put his foot in the wooden stirrup.

"Wait a minute, brother," Severn said, grinning. He

was recovering from his shock faster than the others. No one, including him, had seen but a few men and even fewer women challenge Rogan. "I think you should take the lady's wager. After all, you can't possibly lose. She'll never find the thieves. We've been looking for months. What do you have to lose?"

Rogan, iron-jawed, cold-eyed, glanced at his knights and then at the peasants. He would win the stupid wager and he'd send her away before she interfered again. "Done," he said, and without another look at Liana, he mounted his horse and started riding hard. His thoughts were black with anger. Damned bitch, she'd made a fool of him before his men!

His anger hadn't subsided when he reached the castle. And once inside the gate, he sat on his horse to stare in disbelief at his men, his laborers, his women, all shoveling manure, sweeping, and scouring.

"I'll be damned," Severn muttered from beside Rogan as he stared at one old knight while he stuck a pitchfork into a four-foot-high pile of manure.

Rogan felt as if his own men were betraying him. He threw back his head and gave a loud, long, hideous war cry—and the people in the courtyard came to a halt. "To work!" he bellowed at his men. "You are not women! Work!"

He didn't wait to see if he was obeyed, but dismounted and strode angrily up the stairs to the Lord's Chamber, then to the private room to one side of it. This room was his and his alone. He slammed the door shut and sat down on the old oak chair that had belonged to the head of the Peregrines for three generations.

He sat, then stood abruptly and glared at the chair. There was a puddle of cold water in the seat, where someone had been scrubbing it. So angry he could barely see, he looked about the room and saw that it was clean. The foot-deep debris was gone from the floor, the spider webs that connected the weapons on the wall were gone, the rats were gone, the grease was gone from the table and chairs.

"I'll kill her," he said from between his teeth. "I'll have her drawn and quartered. I'll teach her who owns the Peregrine lands, who rules the Peregrine men."

But as he put his hand on the door, he noticed a little table against the wall. He remembered seeing Zared's mother use that table, but he hadn't seen it for years. He wondered if it had been in this room all that time and he just hadn't seen it. On top of the table, neatly placed, was a stack of precious, clean, expensive paper, beside it were a silver inkwell and half a dozen quill pens, the points sharp and ready for use. The paper and pens drew Rogan like a moth to a flame. For months he'd had an idea for a trebuchet, a wooden war machine that could throw large stones with great force. He'd been thinking that if it were built with two cranks instead of one, he could make the throwing arm much higher and get more power behind the stones. Several times he'd tried drawing his ideas in the dirt, but he hadn't been able to make a line fine enough.

"The wench can wait," he muttered, and went to the table and slowly and clumsily began to draw his ideas. He wasn't as familiar with a pen as he was with a sword. The sun set, he struck a flint and lit a candle, and kept on laboriously drawing his design for the trebuchet.

CHAPTER
EIGHT

❧

After Rogan left the peasants, it took a while for Liana's heart to calm. She was certainly doing a poor job of pleasing her husband, wasn't she? She could see his dark form, still wearing his wedding clothes, which were becoming greasier by the day, riding toward the castle and she wanted to run after him and apologize. It had hurt her to see the rage in his eyes. Perhaps it was better when he ignored her. Perhaps it was better—

"My lady, thank you."

Liana looked down to see a thin, tired-looking peasant woman, her head bowed beneath her ragged hood as she took the hem of Liana's gown and kissed it.

"Thank you," the woman repeated.

The other peasants came to her and bowed down before her, and their groveling made Liana feel sick. She hated to see people as downtrodden as these. The peasants on her father's land were fat and healthy, while these were gray with fatigue and ill health and fear.

"Get up, all of you," she commanded, then waited while they slowly obeyed her, the fear increasing in their eyes. "I want you to listen to me. You heard my husband: He wants the thieves, and *you* are going to deliver them to him." She saw the way their eyes hardened at her words. There was pride left in these people, a pride that made them protect the thieves from a hard master.

Her voice softened. "But first you are going to eat. You"—she pointed to a man who, if she had not intervened, would have a bloody back now—"go and slaughter the fattest cow on all the Peregrine lands and two sheep, then bring them here and roast them. You shall eat, because you have a great deal of work to do in the coming weeks."

None of the peasants made a move.

"The hour grows late. Go!"

One man went to his knees, his face showing his agony. "My lady, Lord Rogan punishes any person who touches what is his. We cannot kill his animals or eat his grain. He keeps all of it and sells it."

"That was the way it was before I came," Liana said patiently. "Lord Rogan has not as much need for money as he once did. Go and kill the animals. I will take the lord's wrath on my head." She swallowed at that, but she couldn't allow the peasants to see her fear. "Now, where is the baker's shop? The one who has the feud against my husband?"

It took Liana hours to set in motion what she meant to do. Two weeks was so little time. The six knights with her, at first silently standing by and watching with that special expression of amusement that men affect when a woman does something that they cannot, she put to work.

She ordered a wheat field cut, the grain given to the baker, the sheaves to be used to thatch the decayed roofs of the peasants' houses. She ordered a knight to supervise a mass cleaning of the streets, which ran with human and animal excrement. Another knight supervised a washing of the peasants, who were as dirty as the streets. At first she was appalled at the refusal of the merchants to take her word that they would be paid, but remembering the story of what her husband's men had done to the baker, she forgave the merchants and gave them silver coins from the bag she carried on her horse.

It was sundown when she returned to Moray Castle, and she smiled as she saw two knights nodding sleepily in their saddles. Her plan was to make the peasants comfortable enough so that their loyalty would be to the master and not to a few thieves who were probably sharing their booty with the hungry farmers. It was not going to be easy to clean up a village within two weeks, but she was going to try.

The stench of the moat greeted her nostrils as she neared the castle, and she knew she'd have to get Rogan's permission to drain the thing before the men would proceed. But inside the walls, she could see the difference. There was less filth on the ground, less piled up in the stables and around the shallow buildings built along the walls. When she rode up, the workers looked up at her and some men tugged at their forelocks in respect of her. Liana smiled to herself. They were beginning to notice her now.

She mounted the stairs to the Lord's Chamber. Here the women had concentrated their efforts. It wasn't clean yet, not by Liana's standards—the walls would have to be whitewashed anew—but she could walk across the tile floor without tripping over bones.

Inside the room, at the clean table and chairs, sat

Severn and Zared, their heads down on the table. Stretched along the length of the table was a long, three-deep pile of the fattest dead rats Liana had ever seen. They looked as if they were meant to be trophies of war.

"What is this?" she asked sharply, startling Severn and Zared awake.

Zared smiled at her and Liana thought again what a pretty, beardless boy he was.

"We killed them all," Zared announced proudly. "You wouldn't by chance know how to count, would you? Rogan does, but not as high as this many."

Liana didn't want to get near the rats, but Zared was so proud she felt she had to. She pointed and began counting. Each one she counted, Zared threw out the window into the moat below. Liana meant to protest, but a few rats weren't going to make the moat worse than it already was. One of the rats was still alive and Liana jumped back while Zared brought a fist down on the rodent's head. Severn grinned proudly.

Liana counted fifty-eight rats, and when they were gone from the table, she tiredly sat down next to Severn and looked about the room.

"Fifty-eight!" Zared was saying. "Wait until I tell Rogan."

"Someone forgot to throw those bones out," Liana said wearily, looking at the wall over the double fireplace. There were six horses' skulls hanging there. She hadn't noticed them before since they were probably covered with cobwebs, she thought.

She became aware of Severn and Zared gaping at her, looking as if she'd suddenly grown horns. She glanced down at the front of her gown, which was dirty but not hideously so. "Is something wrong?" she asked.

"Those are the Peregrine horses," Zared said in a strained whisper.

Liana had no idea what the boy meant, so she looked to Severn. His handsome face was changing in expression from astonishment to a kind of cold, deep rage that, until now, Liana had thought only Rogan capable of.

Severn's voice was quiet when he spoke. "The Howards laid siege to Bevan Castle and starved our family. My father, Zared's mother, and my brother William died there. My father went to the walls and asked the Howards to allow the woman freedom, but they would not." Severn lowered his voice. "Before they died, they ate the horses." He turned to the skulls hanging on the walls. *"Those* horses." He looked back at her, his eyes burning. "We do not forget, and the skulls will not be removed."

Liana looked at the skulls with horror. To be so hungry that one was reduced to eating horses. It was on the tip of her tongue to say that the Peregrine peasants were condemned to a lifelong siege and would probably be glad of horses to eat, but she refrained.

"Where is my husband?" she asked after a while.

"In his brooding room," Zared said cheerfully, while Severn cast the youngster a warning look.

Liana didn't pursue Zared's words because she understood more than she had at first. Perhaps there were reasons for her husband's anger, for his obsession with money. She stood. "If you will excuse me, I must bathe. Tell my husband I—"

"Bathe?" Zared said, sounding as if Liana had said she planned to jump from the parapets.

"It's a pleasant occupation. You should try it," Liana said, especially since Severn and Zared were now the dirtiest objects in the room.

Zared leaned back in the chair. "I think I'll pass. Did you really tell the Days to go home at night?"

Liana smiled. "Yes, I did. Good night, Severn, Zared." She started up the stairs, then paused when she heard their voices.

"The woman has courage," she heard Zared say.

"Or else she's an utter fool," Severn answered.

Liana continued up the stairs, and an hour later she was in her bedroom, soaking in a wooden tub full of scented hot water and watching the play of flames on the logs.

To her right the door was thrown open with a crash, and Rogan entered like a sudden storm on a peaceful day. "You have gone too far, woman," he bellowed at her. "You have not my permission to dismiss my women."

Liana turned her head to look at him. He wore only his big white shirt, which hung to the top of his thighs, a wide leather belt about his waist, and his braies. His sleeves were rolled up to his elbows, exposing thickly muscled, scarred forearms.

Liana could feel perspiration breaking out on her forehead. He was still yelling at her, but she didn't know what he was saying. She stood in the tub, her slim, firm, full-breasted body rosy and warm from the hot water. "Would you please hand me that drying cloth?" she asked softly in the silence, for Rogan had ceased speaking.

Rogan could only gape at her. For all the many women he'd had, he'd never had the leisure to look, really *look,* at a woman, and now he didn't think he'd ever seen anything as beautiful as this rosy-skinned beauty with the curtain of blonde hair hanging almost to her knees.

I won't let her use her body to make me forget what she has done today, he thought, but his feet took a step toward her and one hand reached out to touch the curve of her breast.

Liana told herself to not lose her head. She wanted this man, oh yes, she so much wanted him, but she wanted more than a few minutes of rutting. She put her hand out and untied the strings of his shirt at his throat, then touched his skin with her fingertips. "The water is still hot," she said softly. "Perhaps you'd allow me to wash you."

A bath was a great waste of time to Rogan's mind, but the idea of being washed by a nude woman . . .

He was out of his clothes in seconds, and when he stood nude before her—*all* of him standing upright—he made a grab for her. But Liana, laughing, side-stepped him.

"Your bath, sir," she said, and Rogan found himself stepping into the tub.

The hot water felt good to his dirty skin and the herbs floating on the water smelled good, but best of all was the woman, his wife, this beautiful . . . "Leah?" he asked, looking at her as she knelt over the foot of the tub, her breasts, pink-tipped and luscious, just grazing the wooden rim.

"Liana," she answered, and smiled at him.

She began to wash him, running soapy hands over his arms, his chest, his back, his face. He leaned against the tub and closed his eyes. "Liana," he said softly. Vaguely, he seemed to remember that this woman had done something unpleasant today, but he couldn't at the moment remember what it was. She was so small and angelic, so pink and white, that he couldn't imagine her doing anything he disapproved of.

He lifted his legs so she could wash them, then obeyed her when she told him to stand and her small, warm soapy hands washed between his legs. The pleasure he felt at her action was so overpowering that he spilled his seed on those small hands. His eyes flew open in alarm and, to hide his embarrassment, he roughly shoved her shoulder and sent her flying hard against the wall.

"You have hurt me," she cried out.

Rogan had killed many people and never felt a thing, but this girl's cry struck some chord in him. He had not meant to hurt her; he had only been unmanned in front of her. To his consternation, he found himself stepping from the tub and kneeling down to her. "Let me see," he said, and bent her forward. Where she had hit the stones, her skin was bruised but not cut.

"It's nothing," he said. "Your skin is too fragile, is all." He ran his big, scarred, callused hand down her small, slim back. "It's skin like the underbelly of a newborn colt," he said.

Liana rolled her eyes at him and almost giggled, but she didn't. Instead, she turned in his arms and put her head on his shoulder. "You enjoyed your bath, didn't you?"

Rogan could feel the blood rushing to his face in embarrassed memory, then as he looked at her, her eyes twinkling, he realized she was *teasing* him. He had seen his brothers laugh with women, but Rogan had found very little that was humorous about women. But this woman made him feel different. "I enjoyed the bath too much," he heard himself say, and was astonished.

Liana giggled against his shoulder. "Can it be enjoyed again?" she asked slyly. "Or is that your last 'enjoyment'?"

For a moment Rogan considered beating her for her

127

insolence, but then his hand slid down her bare rump. "I believe I can manage a bit more." He then did something he'd never done before: He lifted her in his arms and carried her to the bed and gently laid her on it.

As he stood over her and looked down at her, he didn't want to jump on her, thrust inside her, then go to sleep as he usually did. Perhaps it was because of his earlier "enjoyment," as she called it, or perhaps he wanted to touch her as she had touched him, but he lay on the bed beside her, propped on one elbow, and reached out his hand to feel the skin of her belly.

Liana had no idea how new all this was to Rogan, but this was what she had imagined being in bed with a man to be like. He explored her body with his hand as if he'd never seen a woman before. Liana closed her eyes as his hand caressed her legs, running between her thighs, his fingers curling over the smooth, firm roundness of them, then his fingertips entwined in her short woman's hair. His hand moved up to her belly, his thumb running along the side of her navel, then slowly, ever so very, very slowly, his hand moved up to the underside of her breast. He cupped first one then the other, his thumb just grazing the sensitive, hard little point.

She opened her eyes to look at him and saw the softness in his eyes and suddenly she knew why she had agreed to marry him. She had sensed that under his toughness, under his hard outer shell, was a softness he had never let anyone see. A shudder passed through her body as she thought of the pain this man must have experienced in his life to make him into the cold, unfeeling man he showed to the world. But somehow she sensed that the Rogan the world saw was not the inner man.

I love him, she thought. I love him with all my soul

and all my being, and so help me God, I am going to make him love me too.

She put her hand to his jaw, felt the whiskers there, soft now from days without shaving as he seemed to shave only once a week. I'm going to make you need me, she said to herself. And I'm going to make you feel safe enough that I can see the softness in your eyes even when I have clothes on.

The last made her smile and she rolled her body toward his. He held her to him and she could feel his rising passion as his hands stroked her back, then his mouth took hers and he kissed her deeply. His lips ran down her throat and at last to her breast. Liana arched backward and let out a little cry of pleasure.

Rogan was aware of her reactions, and because of the episode in the tub, he was able to control his own need for her. The women he'd had had either been frightened virgins or very willing, experienced women, and always they had wanted to please him. Of course none of them had offered to bathe him, nor had any of them left paper and pens in his room. Perhaps it was merely a wish to repay a debt, but he was enjoying feeling this woman squirm beneath his searching hands. Her pleasure was giving him pleasure.

His lips followed his hands down her body and he found the smell of her and the taste of her sweet and fresh, so unlike the Days, who sometimes smelled so bad he kicked them out of bed. This girl smelled like wood smoke and herbs.

When his head came back up to her lips, he was amazed at how much he wanted her. Her hands clutched at his shoulders and when he entered her, she rose to meet him with a force and power to match his.

Never had he spent such a time in bed with a woman! She was lusty beyond all belief, at one point pushing him to his back and climbing on top of him, her hair wrapping around the two of them like a soft yet strong prison.

Rogan had never considered the woman's pleasure before, but this woman, with her moans and groans, her movements here, her movements there, sent his own pleasure into a fevered pitch until he thought he might die. When he finished at long last, it was an earth-shattering experience to him, affecting him from his toes to the top of his head.

He collapsed on the girl and instead of pushing her away, as he usually did to the women he bedded, he clutched her to him as if he were drowning and she were a buoyant log.

Liana snuggled against him. He seemed to pour over her body as if he were sauce over a pudding. She had never felt so good in her life. "That was wonderful," she whispered. "That was the best thing that has ever happened to me. I knew marriage to you would be like this."

Rogan released his hold on her and moved to the far side of the bed, but Liana moved with him, her head on his shoulder, her arm across his chest, her thigh across his. She was happier than she'd ever been, happier than she'd thought possible.

She had no idea of the turmoil that was coursing through Rogan. He wanted to get away from her, yet he couldn't move.

"What did your brother William look like? Did he have red hair like yours?" she asked.

"I don't have red hair," Rogan said indignantly.

"In the sunlight your head looks as if it's on fire," Liana retorted. "Was William like you?"

"Our father had red hair, but I inherited my mother's black hair."

"So both of you had red hair, then."

"I don't—" Rogan said, then stopped and he almost smiled. "On fire, eh?" Every other woman he'd had had told him he had black hair without a trace of his father's red. That was what he'd wanted them to say and therefore they had.

"What about your other brothers? Were they redheads too?"

He thought of his now-dead brothers, remembering the youth of them, the strength of them. How well they could fight! He never thought he'd someday be the oldest Peregrine and have the responsibility of it all. "Rowland, Basil, and James had a dark mother, so they all had black hair."

"And what of Severn and Zared?"

"Severn's mother was a blonde like . . ." He trailed off. She had taken his hand in hers and now lay there looking at his fingers, entwining hers with his. It was such an odd thing to do, he thought. He should push her out of bed and get some sleep rather than talk to her about painful memories. But remembering his brothers as alive was not painful.

"Like me," Liana said, smiling. "And she was Zared's mother also? But Zared is such a dark young man."

Liana did not see Rogan smile in the dim light. "Yes, indeed. Zared is dark because of a dark mother. Severn's mother died giving birth to him."

"So your father had four wives and seven sons?"

Rogan hesitated before answering. "Yes."

"It must have been good to have brothers. I often wished for another child to be born to my mother. Did you often play together, or were you fostered out to other people?" She felt him stiffen beneath her and wondered what she'd said wrong.

"There was no play in our lives, nor did we foster." His voice was cold. "We trained for war from the time we could stand. The Howards killed William when he was eighteen, James and Basil at twenty and twenty-one, and they killed Rowland two years ago, before he was thirty. Now I must protect Severn and Zared." He took her shoulders and lifted her to look into her eyes. *"I* killed James and Basil. I killed them over a woman, and I'll die before I let it happen again. Get away from me, and stay away from me."

He shoved her back into the feather mattress, then got out of bed and began tugging on his clothes.

"Rogan, I didn't mean—" Liana began, but he was already gone. "Damn, damn, damn," she said, slamming her fist into the pillow, then she turned onto her back and stared at the white-painted ceiling. What had he meant that *he* killed his brothers? And over a woman? *"What* woman?" she said aloud. "I'll have her for breakfast."

The thought comforted her and the thought of there being tomorrow night also calmed her. But most of all, she thought of winning her wager. If the peasants turned over the thieves to her, Rogan would be her slave for an entire day. What would she do with him? Have him make love to her all day? Perhaps just to have him stay with her for a day would be enough. Stay with her and answer her questions, maybe. She drifted off to sleep.

The next morning Liana rose early, meaning to find her husband, but the sight belowstairs made her temporarily forget Rogan. No one was in the Lord's Chamber, so she went down the stairs and outside and took the stairs leading to the retainers' hall. She had not been in this area before, but she was not surprised to find it as filthy as the other part of the castle had been. In the enormous hall, twice as big as the Lord's Chamber, sat about two hundred men at greasy tables on slimy benches eating sand-filled bread and drinking sour wine. No one paid any attention to her when she entered, but they continued scratching, shouting, swilling, belching, and breaking wind.

Liana's good mood and sense of accomplishment left her. Quietly, she left the hall and went outside into the sunlight.

Severn was standing near the south wall stroking the breast of a big peregrine falcon.

"Where is my husband?" she asked.

"Rode out for Bevan this morning," Severn answered, not looking up.

"Bevan? Where your family was starved?"

Severn gave her a quick glance and put the bird on its perch. "That's the one."

"When will he return?"

Severn shrugged and walked away.

Liana followed him, lifting her skirts so she could hurry. "He just rode out? No word to anyone? He didn't tell anyone when he planned to return? I want you to give the men permission to drain the moat."

Severn stopped, turned, and looked down at her. "Drain the moat? Are you crazy, woman? The Howards could—"

"Walk across the thing as it is now," Liana said, glaring up at him. "When will my husband return?"

The stern expression left Severn's face and his eyes began to twinkle. "My brother rode out of here before dawn, saying only that he was going to Bevan Castle. If you asked him to order the moat drained, I imagine that had something to do with his leaving."

Liana didn't say a word.

"Scared to, eh?" Severn said, beginning to smile.

Liana couldn't stop the blood from creeping into her face, as he had guessed correctly.

"I'm not about to give permission and have Rogan come back and see the moat empty," Severn said, and turned away again.

Liana stood staring after him. It upset her that Rogan was gone, but she thought she could perhaps more easily put the castle and the village in order if he weren't there. Severn was a much softer man than Rogan was, she could see that, and she thought perhaps there was a way to persuade Severn, a way she had used to persuade her father to do anything she wanted: food.

Liana sent Joice to fetch her precious recipe book, then Liana straightened her headdress and went up the stairs to the kitchen rooms.

It was late that night when Liana climbed alone into her bed. She was exhausted but happy too, for she now had permission to have a ditch dug to drain the filthy moat.

It had taken all day, but she'd managed to get the kitchens and the retainers' hall somewhat clean and she'd laid before Severn and the Peregrine knights a banquet fit for a king. She'd served roasted beef, pink and juicy, capon in orange sauce, rabbit cooked with onions and raisins, spinach and cheese tarts, eggs in mustard sauce, spiced pears, mince pies, and apple mousse.

By the time Severn and his men stopped gorging themselves, Liana knew she could have anything she wanted from them. Patting his swollen belly, Severn not only agreed to her request, he offered to help dig. She'd smiled and said that wouldn't be necessary, then handed him a plate heaped high with sweet jellied milk cubes.

If only my husband were so easy to win, Liana thought as she sank wearily onto the feather mattress.

She tried not to wonder what her husband was doing at Bevan Castle. Was he in the arms of another woman?

Rogan sat before the fireplace in Bevan Castle, as unaware of the filth and disrepair around him as he was at Moray Castle. He had eyes only for the pretty young peasant girl before him.

When he'd left Moray early that morning, he wasn't sure why he was leaving. He knew only that he'd awakened from sleep and his first thought was of that blonde-haired she-devil he'd married. He'd scratched at the fleas that had so willingly left the old mattress he'd slept on and jumped on his skin, and knew he wanted to put some distance and time between him and the girl.

He'd ordered some men to ready themselves and had ridden out, stopping in the village to pick up Thursday to take her with him. But Thursday had cringed and cried and begged him not to force her to go with him as the Fire Lady would kill her. Rogan had left the girl in disgust. He heard the same from Sunday and Tuesday, so he'd ridden with no woman to Bevan.

Bevan Castle was isolated atop a tall, steep hill, and before he began the climb, he stopped in the village below and took the first pretty, healthy-looking girl he saw and pulled her across his saddle. Now, the girl stood trembling before him.

"Stop shaking," he commanded her, scowling. She was younger than he'd first imagined. He saw her shaking increase and his scowl deepened. "Come here and give me a kiss," he ordered.

Tears began to run down the girl's face, but she stepped toward him and gave him a quick kiss on the cheek. Rogan grabbed her greasy hair and pulled her mouth down to his and kissed her angrily. He felt the girl whimper under him. He released her, pushing her so she fell to the floor.

"Do not hurt me, please, my lord," the girl begged, "I will do as you say, but please do not hurt me."

Rogan's desire left him. He remembered too well a woman who was eager for him, a woman who didn't smell of grease and pig manure. "Get out of here," he said under his breath. "Go before I change my mind!" he yelled when the girl was too frightened to move. He turned away as she scurried from the room.

Rogan went to one of the barrels along the wall and tapped a stream of dark, bitter beer into a dirty wooden mug. One of his knights lay sleeping nearby. Rogan kicked him in the ribs. "Get up," he commanded. "And get some dice. I will need something to help me sleep tonight."

CHAPTER
NINE

Liana put her hand to her aching back. Two long
weeks Rogan had been gone, and in those two weeks
she'd wrought miracles in the castle and the village. At
first the peasants had been afraid to obey her, afraid of
Lord Rogan's wrath, but when a few obeyed Liana and
were not punished, the others began to believe in her.

Village houses were repaired, new clothes purchased, and animals slaughtered to feed the hungry
people. By the end of the first two weeks, the peasants
were looking at Liana as if she were an angel.

The cleaning of the village and castle gave Liana
great satisfaction, except for one aspect: the number
of red-haired children running about. At first she'd
thought it was a coincidence that Rogan should have
the same distinctive dark red hair as some of the
villagers. It was when a little boy, about eight years
old, looked up at her with the same hard eyes of her
husband that Liana demanded to know who was the
father of the boy.

The peasants around her stopped their tasks and stared at the ground in silence. Liana repeated her question, then waited. At last a young woman stepped forward. Liana recognized her as one of the Days, one of the women who used to sleep with Rogan.

"Lord Rogan is the father," the woman said defiantly.

Liana felt the peasants around her cringe as if in anticipation of a blow. "How many of my husband's children are there?"

"A dozen or so." The girl's chin came up a little higher. "And the one I'm carrying."

Liana stood for a moment, unable to move or speak. She didn't know if she was angrier at her husband for having so many bastards or for leaving his own children to exist in poverty. She knew the peasants were watching her, waiting to see what she would do. She took a deep breath. "Gather the children and send them to me at the castle. I will see to their needs."

"With their mothers?" the Day said, her voice and attitude showing she felt herself to be triumphant.

Liana glared at the girl. "You may choose to put your weaned child in my care or you may keep the responsibility of raising it. But no, I do not take on the mothers of the children."

"Yes, my lady," the girl said dutifully, bowing her head.

Near her, Liana heard a few women snicker in approval.

It was late when she left the village, and she wished she could crawl into bed beside Rogan. As usual, she began to daydream about what she would ask of him when he was her slave for a day. Perhaps she'd plan a meal served beside a stream, for just the two of them. Perhaps she'd make him *talk* to her. Just to have him spend a day with her, an *hour* with her, when they both had their clothes on would be an accomplishment. He seemed to put her in the same category as the Days—that she was to sleep with and nothing else.

The loudness of her horse's hooves on the wooden bridge over the now-empty moat brought her back to reality. Behind her rode the ever-present, silent Peregrine knights.

The castle grounds were almost clean now and Liana was able to walk up the stairs to the Lord's Chamber without tripping on refuse.

Once upstairs, she avoided Joice, who had a list of questions and complaints, and climbed upward to the bedchambers above. Several times in the last weeks Liana had sought out the Lady, the woman she'd met that first week, the woman who'd reminded her that men never fought battles over quiet, meek women, but each time the door to her room had been locked.

The upstairs rooms were clean now and a few of them were occupied by her maids, but for the most part they remained empty, waiting for the appearance of guests. At the end of the corridor was the locked door, only this time the door was standing open. Liana paused for a moment to watch the woman, the sunlight on her braided hair as she bent over on a tapestry frame.

"Good evening, my dear," the woman said, turning and smiling pleasantly. "Please come in and shut the door. It makes a draft."

Liana did as she was bid. "I have come to see you before, but you weren't here. Rogan has gone to Bevan Castle." Once again, there was the feeling of having known this woman forever.

The woman separated strands of scarlet silk. "Yes, and you have a wager with him. He's to be your slave for a day?"

Liana smiled and walked toward the woman, looking over her shoulder at the fabric stretched on the frame. It was a tapestry-worked, almost-complete picture of a slim blonde lady with her hand on the head of a unicorn.

"She could be you," the Lady replied, smiling. "What do you have planned for your day with Rogan?"

Liana smiled dreamily. "A long walk in the woods, perhaps. A day spent alone. No brothers, no castle duties, no knights, just the two of us. I want him to . . . to give me his full attention." When the Lady didn't reply, Liana looked at her and saw the smile was gone. "You don't approve."

"It's not for me to say," she said softly. "But then I believe he and Jeanne used to take walks together."

"Jeanne?"

"Jeanne Howard."

"Howard!" Liana said, gasping. "The same Howards who are the sworn enemies of the Peregrines? I have heard little else since I was married—about how the Howards stole the Peregrine lands, killed the Peregrines, starved the Peregrines. Are you saying that Rogan once *courted* a Howard?"

"Rogan was once married to Jeanne before she was a Howard."

Liana sat down on a window seat, the sun warm on her back. "Tell me all," she whispered.

"Rogan was married to Jeanne Randel when he was only sixteen and she was fifteen. His parents and his brother William had been starved at Bevan the year before and the three oldest Peregrine sons were busy waging war on the Howards and so were too busy to marry themselves. They decided Rogan should marry, get a girl's dowry, and give them a few sons to grow to help them fight. Rogan fought against the marriage, but his brothers persuaded him."

The Lady turned to look at Liana. "Rogan has known only hardship and pain in his life. Not all the scars on his body are from battles. His brothers and father put their share on him, too."

"So they 'persuaded' Rogan to marry?" Liana said softly.

"Yes, but he wasn't reluctant after he saw her. She was a pretty little thing, so quiet and soft-spoken. Her mother had died when she was quite young and as a ward of the king she was raised by nuns in a convent. Perhaps going from a convent to marrying a Peregrine was not the easiest thing a child ever did."

The Lady looked at Liana, but Liana did not respond. This morning she'd discovered a dozen illegitimate children of her husband's and this evening she'd discovered he'd had another wife.

The Lady continued. "I think Rogan began to fall in love with her. He'd never had any softness in his life and I think Jeanne's gentleness fascinated him. I remember once they came back from a walk and they both had flowers in their hair."

Liana looked away, not wanting the hurt on her face to be seen. He gave his first wife flowers and he couldn't remember the name of his second wife.

"They were married for about four months when the Howards took Jeanne. She and Rogan were alone in the woods. Rowland had told Rogan not to go out alone, but Rogan thought he was immortal, that when he was with Jeanne, nothing could harm him. I believe they'd been swimming and . . ."—the Lady looked at Liana's stricken face—". . . and napping when Oliver Howard's men set upon them and took her. Rogan couldn't get to his sword, but he managed to pull two

Howards off their horses. He strangled one of them before the others could pull him away. I'm afraid that one of the Peregrines had just killed Oliver's younger brother and Oliver was in a vile mood. He had his men hold Rogan while he shot three arrows into him, not to kill him but to show Oliver's power. Then Oliver and his men rode away with Jeanne."

Liana stared at the woman, imagining the awful scene. "And what did Rogan do?" she whispered.

"Walked back to the castle," the Lady said. "Four miles, with three dripping wounds, he walked back to his brothers. He went with them the next day when they attacked the Howards. He rode with them and fought with them, until, on the third day, he fell off his horse, burning with fever. When he was sensible again, it was nearly two weeks later and his brothers Basil and James were dead."

"He said he killed his brothers," Liana said softly.

"Rogan has always taken his responsibilities very seriously. He and Rowland and young Severn fought the Howards for over a year. The Peregrines did not have the strength or the money to properly attack the Howard castle and it is a vast, strong place, so they fought however they could, stealing Howard supplies, burning the peasants' houses, poisoning what water they could reach. It was a bloody year. And then . . ." the Lady trailed off.

"And then what?" Liana encouraged.

"And then Jeanne returned to Rogan."

Liana waited, but the Lady said no more. Her needle flew lightning-fast in and out of the tapestry silk. "What happened when Jeanne returned?"

"She was six months' pregnant with Oliver Howard's child and very much in love with him. She came to Rogan to beg him to give her an annulment so she could marry Oliver."

"That poor boy," Liana said at last. "How could she do that to him? Or did Oliver Howard force her to come to him?"

"No one had forced Jeanne. She loved Oliver, and he, her. In fact, Oliver had forbidden her to go to Rogan. Oliver planned to kill the husband of the woman he loved. I think Jeanne must have felt something for Rogan because I think her visit saved his life. Rogan came home after he saw Jeanne, and while Rogan petitioned for the annulment, the Peregrines and the Howards did not war with each other."

Liana stood and walked to the far side of the room. She was silent for quite some time. At last she turned back to look at the Lady. "So Rogan and Jeanne used to walk in the woods together, did they? Then I shall plan a celebration. We will dance. I will have singers and acrobats and—"

"As you did at your wedding?"

Liana stopped talking and remembered her wedding day, when Rogan had ignored her. "I want him to spend time with me," she said. "He doesn't notice me except in bed. I want to be more to him than . . . than a day of the week. I want him . . ."

"You want what from him?"

"I want what that slut Jeanne Howard had and threw away!" Liana said violently. "I want Rogan to love me."

"And you are going to accomplish this with walks in the woods?" The Lady seemed amused.

Liana suddenly felt very tired. Her dream of a husband who walked with her and held her hand was not the man who, after being shot with three arrows, continued to fight for days. She remembered Zared's saying Rogan was in his brooding room. Well, no wonder he brooded; no wonder he never smiled; no wonder he wanted nothing to do with another wife.

"What do I do?" she whispered aloud. "How do I show him I'm no Jeanne Howard? How do I make a man like Rogan love me?" She looked to the Lady and waited.

But the Lady shook her head. "I have no answer for you. Perhaps it is an impossible task. Most women would be content with a husband who did not beat them and who used other women's bodies for their needs. Rogan will give you children, and children can be a great comfort to a woman."

Liana's mouth tightened. "Children who can grow up to fight and die for the Howards? Am I to stand by and watch while my husband points to the horses' skulls and teaches my children to hate? Rogan drains all income from me, from the peasants, from wherever he can get it, in order to make war machines. His hatred is more to him than any life on earth. He breeds sons on the peasant girls, then leaves the boys to starve. If for one day he could forget the Howards, forget that now he is the oldest Peregrine. If he could just *see* how his hatred is causing the slow death of his people, then he might—" She stopped, her eyes wide.

"He might what?"

Liana's voice was low. "Weeks ago the peasants asked my permission to celebrate St. Eustace's day. Of course I gave permission. If Rogan could see these people, talk to them . . . If perhaps he could see his own children . . ."

The Lady was smiling now. "He has rarely been away from his family, and I doubt if he will agree to spending the day alone with you. Once, when he was alone, his wife was taken and that eventually led to the death of his two brothers. No, he will not readily agree to whatever you request of him."

The Lady looked at the door and listened. "I believe

I hear your maid searching for you. You must go now."

"Yes," Liana said, distracted, her thoughts on what they'd talked about. She moved to the door then turned and looked back. "May I see you again? Your door is often locked."

The Lady smiled. "Whenever you need me, I will be here."

Liana smiled in return and left the room. She heard the lock turn in the door as soon as it closed. She wanted to knock on the door. There were questions she'd meant to ask the Lady, but she never seemed to remember them when she was in that room.

She changed her mind and didn't knock but went down the hall, then down the stairs. Joice was indeed looking for her. Lord Rogan had returned, and close behind had come nearly the entire village of peasants, a handcart in their midst. On the cart lay two dead men, a father and son.

"They're your thieves," Joice said, eyes wide. "Just like you said. The peasants hanged them. Some of the knights said it was so Lord Rogan wouldn't torture the men. They say the thieves were Robin Hoods, who shared all they stole, and the peasants loved them. But they hanged them for you, my lady."

Liana grimaced at this dubious honor, then smoothed her skirts and went down the stairs to meet her husband. Her heart was pounding in her throat.

Rogan was still on his horse, the fading rays of sunlight flashing on his hair, the big roan stallion between his powerful legs prancing dangerously as it felt its master's anger. Rogan was looking at the castle grounds, frowning at the cleanliness of the place, frowning at the clean peasants who'd lost their lean, gaunt look.

Liana sensed there was to be trouble. She could see it in Rogan's handsome face. "I have won the wager," she said as loudly as she could, trying to draw his attention to her and away from the peasants. Since she was in an advantageous position at the top of the stone stairs, her voice carried to the people below.

She watched, breath held, as Rogan reined his horse around to look at her. He remembers me, she thought with pleasure. And more, he desires me. Her heart began to hammer harder.

But then her breath stilled as she looked into his eyes. He seemed to be angry with her—not just angry, but enraged. No doubt this was how he looked at the Howards. I am not your first wife, she thought as she kept her chin upright and tried to still the trembling in her body. She wanted to run up the stairs to her bedroom and hide under the covers. She wanted to get away from this man's fierce gaze.

"I have won," she forced herself to say. "Come and be my slave." She turned away, no longer able to stand Rogan's glare, and went upstairs to the solar. Perhaps a few minutes alone in the chapel would calm her.

Rogan watched the woman go upstairs, then dismounted, handing the reins to a red-haired stableboy. He watched the boy walk away and he was somehow familiar.

"A woman's slave for a day?" Severn said from beside his brother, laughter in his voice.

Rogan turned his glare on Severn. "Did you give permission to drain the moat? And this?" He waved his arm to include the very different courtyard and the dead men in the cart. "Is all this your idea? When my back is turned—"

"Your wife deserves the credit, not me," Severn said, not losing his good humor. "She has done more in these few weeks than you and I—" He stopped as Rogan pushed past him and went up the stairs.

"Will the killings stop now?" one of the peasants dared to ask.

Severn had his own temper and he strode up the stairs two at a time. Zared was the only person in the Lord's Chamber. "Where is he?" Severn snapped.

"There." Zared pointed to the room they called the brooding room. It traditionally belonged to the head of the Peregrine family—their father, then Rowland, now Rogan. Its privacy was sacred. When a man was inside it, he was to be disturbed for nothing less than imminent attack.

Severn strode up the few steps to the door, then shoved it open without hesitation.

"Get the hell out of here," Rogan bellowed, his voice showing his shock.

"And listen to the men call my brother a coward? To hear them say he won't honor a wager?"

"A *woman's* wager," Rogan sneered.

"But a wager made in public, made in front of me, your men, even the peasants." Severn calmed himself. "Why not give the woman what she wants? She'll probably have you sing a duet with her or carry flowers for her. How bad can it be to be a woman's slave for a day? Especially this woman. All she seems to care about is a clean house and . . . and you. The Lord only knows why. She asked Zared and me hundreds of questions about you."

"And you no doubt told her everything. You seem to like talking to women. You and that married duchess of yours—"

"Don't say anything you'll regret," Severn said in warning. "Yes, I talk to Iolanthe. She has a head on her shoulders, and this wife of yours seems to have one, too. She was right when she said she'd get the peasants to present the thieves. For two years we've flogged people and beat them and they still steal us blind. Yet all she did was feed them and make them take a bath and they're groveling at her feet."

"They'll get so used to eating our cows they'll stop working and expect us to provide them with everything. What will they want next? Silk gowns? Furs to keep out the winter's chill? Peacocks' tongues for dinner?"

"I don't know," Severn answered honestly, "but the woman did win her wager with you."

"She's like the peasants. If I give her what she wants today, what will she demand tomorrow? Will she want to run the whole estate? Shall I let her judge the courts as well? Perhaps I should let her train the men."

Severn looked at his brother for a long moment. "Why are you afraid of her?"

"*Afraid* of her!" Rogan yelled. "I could break her in half with my bare hands. I could order her locked away. I could send her and her uppity maids to Bevan and never see her again. I could . . ." He stopped and sat down heavily in a chair.

Severn looked at his brother in amazement. Here was his big, strong, invincible brother, the man who never flinched before a battle, looking like a frightened child. He did not like to see it. Rogan was always sure of himself, always knew what to do. He never hesitated when a decision was to be made and never wavered once he'd decided what to do. No, Severn amended, Rogan didn't make decisions, he *knew* what to do.

Severn stepped toward the door. "I will make some excuse to the men. Of course no Peregrine will be a slave to a woman. The very idea is absurd."

"No, wait," Rogan said. He didn't look up. "I was a fool to have agreed to her wager. I had no idea she would produce the thieves. Go to her and ask her what she wants of me. Perhaps she wants a new gown or two. I don't want to spare the money, but I will."

When Severn didn't answer, Rogan looked up. "Well? You have something else to do? Go to her."

Severn felt warmth rising at his neck. "She might want something . . . ah, personal from you. If Io won me as a slave for a day, she'd probably tie me to a bed or—" He broke off at the look of interest in Rogan's eyes. "Who knows what your wife wants from you? Maybe she wants you to wear a donkey's tail and scrub the floors. Who knows? This woman listens more than she talks. I guess she knows more about us than we do about her."

"Like a good spy," Rogan said heavily.

Severn threw up his hands. "Spy or not, I like the smell of this place better. Go see what the woman wants. She seems simple enough." He left the room, closing the door behind him.

Moments later, Rogan left his brooding room and mounted the stairs to the solar. He had been in here in the last few years only to fetch a hawk. But the hawks were gone now and the walls looked almost damp with fresh whitewash. Three big tapestries hung on the walls, and his first thought was that he could sell them for gold. There were chairs, tables, stools, and women's sewing frames scattered about the room.

The women in the room stopped their chattering when they saw him and stared at him as if he were a demon from hell. Across the room, sitting on a window seat, was his wife. He remembered that calm stare of hers, but most of all he remembered the feel of her body.

"Out," was all he said, then stood there and waited while the scared women scurried past him.

When the two of them were alone, he didn't move any closer to her. The thirty or so feet separating him from his wife was fine, in his opinion. "What do you want of me?" he asked, his dark brows drawn together in a scowl. "I will not make a fool of myself before my men. I'll scrub no floors or wear any donkey's tail."

Liana blinked at him in astonishment, then smiled. "I have never received any pleasure from making another look like a fool." Very slowly, she reached up and removed her headdress, letting her long blonde hair cascade about her shoulders and down her back. She gave her head a little shake. "You must be tired after your journey. Come and sit by me. I have wine and sweetmeats here."

He stood where he was, glaring at her. "Do you try to entice me?"

Liana gave him a look of exasperation. "Yes, I do. And what is so wrong with that? You're my husband and I haven't seen you in weeks. Come, tell me what you did while you were away and I will tell you of what was found in the moat." She took a silver goblet from a table and poured it full of wine, then carried it to him. "Try it, it's from Spain."

Rogan took the wine and drank, his eyes never leaving hers, then he looked into the cup in surprise. The wine was delicious.

Liana laughed. "I brought some recipes with me and I persuaded your cooks to try them." She put her hand on his arm and gently began pulling him toward the window seat. "Oh, Rogan, I could have used your help. Your people are so stubborn, it was like talking to rocks. Here, try this. It's a pickled peach, and you might like this bread, there's no sand in it."

Before Rogan knew what he was doing, he was half sprawled on the softness of a window-seat cushion, eating one delicious food after another and wasting the day listening to a lot of frivolous nonsense about cleaning. He should, of course, be out training with his men, but he didn't move. "How many gold coins?" he found himself asking.

"We found six gold coins, twelve silver, and over a hundred copper pennies in the moat. There were also eight bodies, which we buried." She crossed herself. "Here, you look uncomfortable. Stretch out and put your head on my lap."

Rogan knew he should leave and he hadn't asked her yet about the wager, but he was tired and the wine was relaxing him. He stretched his legs on the long seat and put his head in her soft lap. The silk of her skirt felt good against his cheek and she caressed his temples and his hair with soft, smooth fingertips. When she began to hum, he closed his eyes.

Liana looked down at the beautiful man sleeping in her lap and she never wanted this moment to end. He looked so much younger when he was asleep, no scowl marring his handsomeness, the weight of responsibility not as heavy on his broad shoulders.

He slept peacefully for nearly an hour until Severn came clanging into the room wearing fifty pounds of armor.

War-trained Rogan sat up with a jolt. "What has happened?" he demanded, all softness leaving him.

Severn looked from his brother to his sister-in-law. He had never seen Rogan even look at a woman before sundown, much less put his head in her lap. It was startling to see such softness in his hard older brother. He found himself frowning.

Severn had been on his sister-in-law's side, but then

Rogan's hardheadedness often made Severn take an opposite side when arguing with his older brother. But he did not like this. He didn't like this woman making Rogan forget where he was supposed to be. Just hours ago Rogan had been dreading seeing his wife again after weeks away from her. Severn had been a bit amused at his brother's temerity, but perhaps Rogan had cause to fear the power of this woman. Could she make him forget his duties? His honor? She was peace-loving with the peasants, but did her nonviolent ways extend to making Rogan forget the Peregrines' war with the Howards?

Severn did not want to see his older brother change. He did not want Rogan's edges softened. It was one thing to play childish games with a woman and quite another to neglect duties to lay about with her in the afternoon.

"I had no idea today was a holy day and meant to be spent in pleasure," Severn said sarcastically. "I beg your pardon. I will leave the men to train alone, without me, and I will go to judge the peasants' disputes since you are too . . . busy."

"Go and train the men," Rogan snapped. "I will judge the courts, and if you do not want to find yourself eating that tongue of yours, keep it still."

Severn turned away in time to hide a smile. This was his brother, the man who scowled and growled, the man who treated him as if he were still a boy. It was all right for the woman to change the castle, but Severn didn't like her trying to change Rogan. As if she could! he thought with a grin. Nothing and no one could change Rogan.

Liana felt like throwing something at Severn. She saw what he was doing, saw the disbelief in his eyes when he'd seen Rogan asleep on a woman's lap. It seemed that everyone conspired to keep all softness from Rogan's life. She reached up to put her hand on his shoulder. "Perhaps I could help in the judgments. I often helped my father," she said. Actually, since her mother's death she had had sole responsibility for judging the peasants' disputes because her father couldn't be bothered.

Rogan was on his feet at once, scowling down at her. "You go too far, woman. *I* will make the judgments. *I* will give justice to my own peasants."

She was on her feet also. "And you have done a fine job of it until now, haven't you?" she said angrily. "Is starving them your idea of justice? Is letting the roofs of their houses fall on their heads what you think they need? If two men come to you with a dispute, what do you do, hang both of them? Justice! You have no idea what the word means. You only know how to punish."

As Liana looked at the rage on his face, she was sure he was going to add her to the long list of people he'd killed. In the heat of that rage, she almost backed away from him, but some great force of willpower made her stay where she was.

Suddenly, his eyes changed. "And what would you do to a man who stole another man's cow? Have them bathe together? Perhaps have them clean their finger-nails twice a day as their punishment?"

"Why, no, I'd—" Liana began, then realized he was *teasing* her. Her eyes twinkled. "I'd have them live with your foul temper for a day. That and the stench of you after weeks without washing should be enough."

"Oh?" he said softly, and stepped toward her. "You do not seem to mind my stench."

He pulled her to him with one arm, and Liana

melted against him. No, she did not seem to mind his stench or his temper or his glares or his disappearances. He kissed her gently at first, then deeper and deeper, until he had to fully support her weight against his strong body.

He pulled his mouth from hers, still holding her. "And what do you want of me as your slave? Shall we spend all day in bed? Shall you stand over me wearing just my helmet and make demands of me?"

Liana opened her eyes. What an interesting idea, she thought, and almost said yes to his suggestion. But she controlled her lust. "I want you to wear peasants' clothes and attend a fair with me."

Rogan blinked a few times, then released her so abruptly she fell back against the window seat. "Not in my lifetime," he said, anger in his face again. "You ask me to go to my death. You *are* a spy. The Howards—"

"*Damn* the Howards!" Liana yelled. "I care nothing for them. I merely want you to spend a day with me. Alone. With no guard watching us, with no brother taunting you for daring to spend an hour with your wife. I want a whole day with you—*with* my clothes on. It cannot happen here, they would not leave you alone. So I ask you to stop, for one whole day, being Lord Rogan and share with me an ordinary day at a peasants' festival." She slowed down, put her hands on his forearms. "Please," she said. "They are such simple people, and their pleasures are so simple. It will be a day of dancing, of drinking, of eating. I believe they plan to put on a play. Can you not spare one day for me?"

Rogan's face did not betray how much her words appealed to him. A day spent in merriment . . . "I cannot go unarmed among the peasants," he said. "They—"

"Wouldn't recognize you. Half the men of the village are the offspring of your father—or you." She said the last with some disgust.

Rogan was shocked at the insolence of her words. He should have locked her away moments after he married her. "And you think they will not recognize you, either?"

"I will wear a patch over one eye. I do not know how I will disguise myself. The peasants will never believe their lord and mistress to be among them. One day, Rogan, please?" She leaned toward him and he could smell lavender from her clothes.

He heard himself say, "Yes," and didn't believe his own voice.

Liana flung her arms about his neck and kissed all the skin she could reach. She couldn't see the look of shock on Rogan's face that slowly softened. For just a moment, a quick, brief moment, he hugged her in return, not a sexual caressing, but just a little squeeze of pleasure.

He released her immediately. "I must go," he murmured, stepping away from her. "And you stay here and don't interfere in my court judgments."

She tried to look hurt, but she was too happy to succeed. "Of course I wouldn't. I'm a good and dutiful wife and I obey my husband in all things. I am merely trying to make your life more pleasant."

Rogan wasn't sure if she was making sport of him or not. He really did need to stop her insolence. "I must go," he repeated, then when she held her hand out to him and he found himself hesitating, he almost ran from the room. He'd go with her to the fair, he thought as he ran down the stairs, and afterward he'd send her to Bevan to stay. And he'd have his Days returned. Yes, he'd do that. This wife was getting entirely out of hand and interfering in his life.

But even as he was thinking of sending her away, he was also thinking of taking his helmet to their bed-chamber that night.

CHAPTER TEN

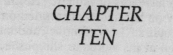

*L*iana looked at her husband's sleeping profile in the early morning light and smiled. She shouldn't be smiling at him, but she was. Last night she'd waited in bed for him for hours, but he hadn't come to her. At last, with her jaw set, a torch in her hand, she went downstairs to look for him.

She didn't have to go far. He was in the Lord's Chamber just below, alone with Severn, the two of them drunk almost to the point of oblivion.

Severn lifted his head from the table and looked at Liana. "We used to get drunk," he said, his words thick and slurred. "My brother and I used to be together all the time, but now he has a wife."

"And you *still* get drunk together," she said pointedly. "Here," she said to her husband. "Put your arm about my shoulders and let's go upstairs."

"Wives change things," Severn mumbled from behind her.

Liana had all she could do to help Rogan up the

157

stairs. "Your brother needs a wife," she said to Rogan. "Perhaps he'll leave us alone if he has his own wife."

"She has to have lots of money," Rogan said as he leaned heavily on her and concentrated on the steep, narrow spiral stairs. "Lots of money and lots of hair."

Liana smiled at his words as she pushed open the bedroom door. Rogan staggered to the bed and was asleep instantly. So much for a night of lovemaking, Liana thought, then snuggled against his dirty body. He was right. She didn't seem to mind his stench at all.

Now in the early morning, smiling down at him, she felt exhilarated and happy because today was the day he was to spend with her. For one whole day he was hers.

"My lady?" Joice's voice came through the door.

"Yes," Liana called, and Joice entered, careful the door didn't squeak.

Joice took one look at the sleeping Rogan and frowned. "You aren't ready? The others will be up soon and they will see you." Her voice was full of disapproval of her mistress's plan.

"Rogan," Liana said, leaning over her husband, whispering softly in his ear. "Rogan, my love, you must wake up. Today is the fair."

He put his hand up and touched her cheek. "Ah, Thursday," he murmured. "You get on top today."

"Thursday!" Liana gasped, then punched him in the ribs. "Wake up, you drunken dung heap! I'm your *wife*, not one of your women."

Rogan put his hand over his ear, then turned, blinking, to look at her. "What are you yelling about? Is something wrong?"

"You just called me by another woman's name." When he looked blank, having no idea why that should bother her, she sighed. "You have to get up. Today's the fair."

"What fair?"

"Men!" Liana said through her teeth. "The fair you promised to take me to. The wager, remember? I have peasants' clothes for us and we're to leave the castle the moment the gates are open. My maid is going to lock herself in this room all day, and I have put it about that what I want from you is a day in bed. No one will know we're gone."

Rogan sat up. "You have taken a lot on yourself," he said, frowning. "My men should know where I am at all times."

"If they do, they will hover about you and all the peasants will know who you are. Are you going back on your word?"

Rogan thought that women who talked of honor and keeping one's vows should be put in the same category with flying pigs. They shouldn't exist, and if they did, they were a damned nuisance since they wouldn't stay in their pens.

Liana leaned toward him, her beautiful hair spilling over his arms. "A day in pleasure," she said softly, "nothing but eating, drinking, dancing. No men to worry over. Nothing at all to worry about." She smiled as she had an inspiration. "And you might be able to hear whether the peasants know anything about the Howards' doings."

Rogan considered that. "Where are the clothes?"

Once he'd made up his mind, Liana was able to get him to move quickly. When they were dressed, she was sure no one would recognize them—as long as Rogan remembered to drop his shoulders and keep his head slightly bowed. Peasants didn't walk the way the lord of the manor did.

They left the bedroom and got to the gate just as Rogan's men were lifting the portcullis. No one looked at them. Once across the drawbridge, over the empty moat, Rogan stopped. "Where are the horses?"

"Peasants don't ride horses. They walk."

Rogan balked. Just stood there unmoving.

Her first thought was to remind him that he used to walk with Jeanne Howard, but she restrained herself. "Come on," she coaxed. "We'll miss the play if we don't hurry. Or maybe I can purchase that old donkey over there. For a few coins I imagine he'll—"

"There's no need to spend money. I can walk as well as the next man."

They walked the four miles to the village together, and around them swarmed many people, strangers arriving to sell goods, travelers, relatives from other villages. As they neared the village, Liana could feel Rogan begin to relax. His eyes were still wary, for he was a soldier and he watched the people suspiciously, but when they all seemed to be laughing and looking forward to the day, some of his suspicion left him.

"Look there," Liana called, pointing at the pennants flying from the tops of the tents set up by the visiting merchants. "What shall we have for breakfast?"

"We should have eaten before we left," Rogan said solemnly.

Liana grimaced and hoped he wasn't going to starve them all day in order to save a few pennies. The fair had been set up on a barren field outside the walls of the village.

"This field will never grow grain again," Rogan grumbled. "Not after all these feet have trampled it."

Liana gritted her teeth and wondered if taking Rogan to the fair had been such a good idea after all. If he spent all day looking at what the peasants did wrong, he'd have a lot to punish them for later.

"The play!" Liana said, pointing toward a big wooden stage that had been set up at one end of the field. "Some of the players have come from London, and the whole village has been working on it for the last week. Come on or we won't get a seat." She took Rogan's hand and began pulling him forward, leading him to a place on one of the benches in the middle of the audience. Near her was a woman with a basket of rotten vegetables that she could sling at the performers if she didn't like what they did.

Liana nudged Rogan to look at the vegetables. "We should have brought some too."

"A waste of food," Rogan growled, and Liana wondered again if this had been such a good idea.

There was a patched and dirty curtain across the stage and now a man dressed in harlequin clothes, one leg red, one black, opposite arm red, the other black, with a black and red tunic, came out to announce that the name of the play was *The Taming of Lord Buzzard*.

For some reason, this announcement made the people around them howl with laughter.

"I guess it's a comedy," Liana said, then added, looking at Rogan's dour face, "I *hope* it's a comedy."

The curtain was pulled aside to reveal a bleak scene: Bare trees in pots stood at the back, and in the foreground was an ugly old man squatting down over a heap of straw that was dyed red to look like a fire. He held a stick out that had three rats on it.

"Come on, daughter, dinner is almost ready," the man called.

From behind the curtain to the right came a woman —or what looked to be a woman. She turned toward the audience and she was actually a very ugly man.

The audience howled. In her arms was a fat straw doll, and when she bent to put the "baby" down then stood, the audience saw that she had an enormous bosom, so enormous its weight tipped her forward. She looked at the rats. "They look delicious, Father," she said in a high voice as she squatted down across from him.

Liana smiled up at Rogan and saw that he was barely watching the play. He was looking at the people around them as if he were trying to find enemies.

From the left side of the stage came another actor, a tall man, his shoulders thrown back, his head held high. On his head was a red wool wig and on his nose was a paper beak like a hawk's.

"What is going on here?" the tall actor demanded. "I am Lord Buzzard and you are eating my livestock."

"But, my lord," the father whined, "they are only rats."

"But they are *my* rats," Lord Buzzard said arrogantly.

Liana began to feel a little nervous. This play couldn't possibly be a parody of Rogan, could it?

On the stage, Lord Buzzard grabbed the old man by the scruff of the neck and pushed him face down into the straw fire.

"No, my lord," cried the ugly daughter as she stood up, her tattered cloak falling away from her vast bosom.

"Ah-ha!" Lord Buzzard said, leering. "Come here, my beauty."

The reference to the woman-dressed man as a beauty made the audience laugh.

The daughter took a step backward as Lord Buzzard came toward her. He kicked the straw baby with his foot, sending it flying across the stage.

It was then that Lord Buzzard opened his long cloak. Affixed around his waist, strapped to his legs, was an enormous set of genitals. It was padded straw, eighteen inches long, eight inches around, and below it hung two big round gourds.

Liana's heart dropped to her feet. "Let's go," she said to Rogan, said really loudly, because the audience was screaming with laughter.

Rogan's eyes were now fixed on the stage. He clamped a hand down on Liana's shoulder and held her in place. She had no choice but to watch.

Onstage, Lord Buzzard, with his coat held open, went across the stage after the ugly woman until they were out of sight. Instantly, one of Rogan's red-haired sons came onto the stage and took a bow. He was obviously the product of Lord Buzzard's union with the woman.

From stage left came an old woman carrying a dark bundle, which she put in the middle of the stage, not far from where the father still lay in the straw fire.

"Now, daughter, we will at last be warm," she said, and from the right came another very ugly man dressed as a woman. Only this man stuck out behind instead of in front. He had padded buttocks that could have been used as a shelf and an absolutely flat chest.

While the audience was watching this, another of Rogan's red-haired sons ran across the stage, sending the audience into new gales.

Liana didn't dare look at Rogan. Tomorrow he'd probably order the whole village drawn and quartered.

Onstage, as the mother and her jut-butted daughter were warming their hands over the pile of black, Lord Buzzard strutted onstage, his paper hawk beak looking even larger.

"You are stealing my fuel," Lord Buzzard shouted.

"But it is only cow dung," the old woman wailed. "We were freezing to death."

"You want fire, I will give you fire," Lord Buzzard said. "Take her and burn her."

From the left came two men, big, fierce-looking brutes with scars painted on their faces so that they looked like monsters more than men. They took the old woman's arms, as she wailed and screamed, and pulled her to the back of the stage, where they tied her to one of the barren trees and placed red-dyed straw bundles about her feet.

Meanwhile, Lord Buzzard looked at the daughter. "Ah, come to me, my beauty," he said.

The ugly man playing the daughter turned to the audience and made a face so ugly—he pushed his lower lip up over the tip of his nose—that even Liana gave a bit of a laugh. Once again Lord Buzzard pulled his cloak back to reveal the grotesque genitals and chased the "girl" off the stage, while behind them the mother screamed. Two red-haired boys came running from opposite sides of the stage and crashed into each other.

"There's more where we came from," one boy announced gleefully to the audience.

Liana was about to insist to Rogan that they leave when she got an even greater shock. From the left came a young girl, very pretty, wearing a long white gown and a blonde wool wig that reached all the way to her feet. Liana knew this actress was supposed to be her. And how would these cruel people portray her?

From the right came Lord Buzzard and a man dressed as a priest; the priest began to read a marriage ceremony. Lord Buzzard, obviously bored, didn't look at the pretty girl in white. Instead, he played to the audience, making kissing faces at the girls, winking, flipping his cloak open now and then to show what he had. The girl in white kept her head down, her hands clasped.

When the priest pronounced them married, Lord Buzzard grabbed the girl's shoulders then picked her up and began shaking her. Coins fell out of her clothes, and Lord Buzzard's men ran onto the stage and scurried to pick them up. When there was no more money falling from the lady in white, he set her down, turned his back on her, and strutted offstage, still flirting with the audience and flipping his cloak. The lady walked to the back of the stage, her head bowed.

Immediately, onstage came a man leading a cow. Lord Buzzard met him center stage.

"What is this?" Lord Buzzard demanded.

"My lord," the man said, "this cow ate your vegetables."

Lord Buzzard patted the cow's head. "Cows need to eat." He started to walk away, but then turned back to glare at the man. "Did *you* eat any of my vegetables?"

"I had one bite of turnip that fell from the cow's mouth," the man said.

"Hang him!" Lord Buzzard ordered, and his scarred knights hurried onstage.

The man fell to his knees. "But, my lord, I have six children to feed. Please have mercy."

Lord Buzzard looked at his men. "Hang the whole family. There'll be fewer to feed."

The knights dragged the man to the back of the stage and put a rope around his neck. He stood beside the man in the fire, the old woman at the stake, and the lady in white.

The lady looked at these people and shook her head sadly.

Onstage sauntered two pretty, plump young women

who Liana recognized as two of the Days. The audience, especially the men, cheered and whistled and the Days stretched and bent over and did what they could to show off their voluptuous bodies. Liana stole a look at Rogan. He was sitting as immobile as a statue, his eyes and attention totally on the stage.

On instinct, she reached across him and took his hand in hers, and to her surprise, he clung to her hand.

She looked back at the stage. Lord Buzzard came back onstage, halted at the sight of the Days, then leaped at them, his cloak flying open. The three of them went tumbling to the floorboards.

It was at this sight that the lady in white came alive. She hadn't minded when her husband had ignored her at their wedding or shaken coins from her or when he'd hanged a man for eating a bit of turnip a cow had spit out—but she minded about the other women.

She ripped off her white dress to reveal a red one underneath. From behind a pot containing a bare tree, she took a red headdress with tall paper flames attached to it and jammed it on her head over the blonde wig.

"The Fire Lady!" the audience yelled in delight.

The red-dressed Fire Lady took bundles of red-painted straw from the feet of the old woman tied to the tree and began throwing them at the three people tumbling about in the center of the stage. The Days jumped up, screaming and acting as if they were putting out fires from their clothes and hair, and ran offstage.

The Fire Lady looked down at Lord Buzzard and from her pocket she withdrew a big collar such as used to tie up a mean dog. She fastened it onto Lord Buzzard's neck, took a leash, and led him offstage.

The audience yelled and cheered and jumped on the benches and danced, while onstage all the dead people came to life again. Six of Rogan's sons came out and threw flower-covered nets over the dead trees so that it looked as if even the trees were coming back to life. The people onstage began to sing and all the actors came onstage, the Fire Lady leading Lord Buzzard on all fours. He tried to flip his cloak aside to show the audience, but the Fire Lady smacked him across the head and he was quiet again.

At long last, the curtain was pulled closed, and when the audience stopped cheering and laughing, they began to file out of the benches.

Rogan and Liana sat still, neither of them moving, hands clasped in Rogan's lap.

"I don't guess the peasants are so simple, after all," Liana managed to say at last.

Rogan turned to look at her, his eyes telling her what an understatement her words were.

CHAPTER
ELEVEN

*T*he audience filed out of the benches, laughing, slapping one another's backs, and recalling one scene of the play after another. "Did you see—?" "I liked the part where—"

Liana and Rogan sat where they were, hands clasped, until the last person had left the audience.

Gradually, as her shock left her, Liana felt her body filling with anger. In the last weeks she had dared her husband's rage for these people. She had exhausted herself seeing that they were fed and clothed, and they repaid her with this . . . this ridiculing farce.

She clutched Rogan's hand. "We'll go back and get your men," she said, anger pounding in her temples. "We shall see if these people will be so ungrateful after your men get through with them. They think they have seen the Peregrine wrath, but they have seen nothing."

Rogan didn't say anything, but when she looked at him, he didn't appear to be angry as much as thoughtful.

"Well?" she said. "You didn't want to come, and you were right. We'll return and—"

"Who played Lord Buzzard?" Rogan asked, interrupting her.

"He looked like one of your father's by-blows," Liana snapped. "Shall I return alone?" She stood and started to move past him, but he still held her hand and wouldn't let her pass.

"I'm hungry," he said. "Do you think they sell food here?"

Liana gaped at him. A moment ago he'd refused to part with the few pennies needed to buy them food. "The play didn't make you angry?"

He shrugged as if he didn't care, but there was something deeper in his eyes—something that Liana meant to discover. "I never killed anybody for eating my rats," he said somewhat defiantly. "They can have all the rats they want."

"What about using your cow dung for fuel?" she asked softly. She was standing between his big legs and he was still holding her hand. Somehow, this hand-holding was more intimate than their few couplings. He said the play didn't bother him, but the way he was holding on to her told another story.

"I have never *killed* anyone for that," he said, looking off into the distance, "but the dung does fertilize the fields."

"I see," Liana said. "Flogging?"

Rogan didn't answer, but his dark skin seemed to flush. She felt very motherly toward him at that moment. He wasn't a vicious man, a man who enjoyed killing or got pleasure from seeing others suffer. He had been trying to protect his family and provide for them the best way he could.

"I am starving," she said, smiling at him, "and I

saw a stall heaped with cream cakes. Perhaps a few cakes and some buttermilk will cheer both of us."

He allowed her to lead him away, and she wanted very much to know what he was thinking. When he reached inside his coarse woolen peasant garb and withdrew a little leather bag and gave the cream-cakes vendor some pennies, she felt elated. She couldn't be sure, of course, but she doubted if he'd ever spent money on a woman before.

He bought them a mug of buttermilk and they shared the mug while the vendor waited for the return of the wooden cup.

With food in her belly, Liana began to be able to think of the play with less anger. In fact, looking back on it, it was almost humorous. She would never have guessed that the peasants could be so daring—or so honest.

She looked into the mug and tried to keep from smiling. "They may have been wrong about the rats, but they were right about certain physical attributes of the lord," she said.

Rogan heard her, but at first he didn't understand her meaning. Then, remembering the outrageously exaggerated straw genitals of Lord Buzzard, he began to feel the blood creep to his face. "You have a sharp tongue on you," he said, meaning to chastise the wench.

"If I remember correctly, you liked my tongue."

"Women shouldn't talk of such things," he said sternly, but his eyes betrayed him.

Liana knew by the way he was looking at her that she had sparked his interest. "Did you *really* bed ugly women? Ugly but sticking out in front or back?"

He looked as if he were about to reprimand her again, but instead his eyes softened. "Your father should have beat some manners into you. Here," he said, taking the empty mug away from her. "If you are through eating me into poverty, let's go see the games over there."

Her teasing had pleased him and pleasing him made her feel joyous. As they walked, she slipped her hand into his and he did not push her away.

"Will it change back?" he asked, looking ahead as they walked.

She had no idea what he was talking about.

"Your hair," he said.

Liana squeezed his hand and laughed in delight. Joice had dyed her blonde hair and eyebrows black so that the peasants wouldn't recognize Liana's distinctive hair. There wasn't much of it visible beneath the coarse linen covering pinned over her braided hair. "It will wash out," she said, then looked up at him. "Perhaps you'll help me wash it."

He looked down at her, desire in his eyes. "Perhaps."

They walked on together, saying nothing, holding hands, and Liana felt jubilant.

Rogan paused on the outskirts of a crowd of people. He could see over their heads, but Liana couldn't. She stood on tiptoe, then squatted down, but she couldn't see through the people. She tugged on Rogan's sleeve. "I can't see," she said when he looked at her. She had a romantic vision of his lifting her to his shoulders and holding her, but instead, acting as if he owned the place—which he did—he pushed his way through the crowd to the front. "Don't call attention to us," she hissed, but he paid no attention to her. She gave weak smiles of apology to the people around them as she was pulled along by Rogan.

The people were looking with curiosity at Rogan, especially at his hair curling along his neck beneath his woolen hood. Liana began to stiffen in fear. If

these people, hating the Peregrines as they did, should
find out the master was alone and unprotected among
them, they would no doubt murder him.

"Another of the old lord's bastards," she heard a
man near them whisper. "Never seen this one before."

She began to relax and for once thanked God for the
fertility of the Peregrines. Still clutching Rogan's
hand, she looked at what he did. On a flat grassy place,
in the middle of a large circle, were two men, both
naked from the waist up, fighting each other with long
wooden poles held in both hands. One man, short,
muscular, with short arms, looked to be a forester or a
woodcutter. He was very ordinary-looking.

Liana's eyes went to the other man—as did the eyes
of every other woman in the crowd outside the circle.
This was the man who'd played Lord Buzzard. He'd
looked good onstage, but now, half-nude, skin glisten-
ing with sweat, he was magnificent.

Not as magnificent as Rogan, Liana reminded herself and stepped closer to her husband.

Rogan was intent on the fight, interested in the way
this half-brother of his handled himself. He was crude
and untrained, of course, but there was speed in his
movements. The little woodcutter was no match for
him.

Rogan's attention was taken from the fight when his
wife stepped closer to him. He glanced down at her.
She was watching his half-brother with wide-eyed
interest, and Rogan began to frown. It was almost as if
she found this half-Peregrine desirable.

Rogan had never felt jealousy before. He'd shared
the Days or any of his women with his brothers, with
his men. As long as he wasn't inconvenienced, he
didn't care what the women did. But right now he
didn't like the way his wife was looking at his scrawny,
weak, bumbling, incompetent, red-haired—

"Think you could beat 'im?" said a toothless old man standing next to Rogan.

Rogan looked down his nose at the old man.

The man cackled, his bad breath filling the air. "Just like them Peregrines," he said loudly. "The old master bred arrogance in his sons."

The Peregrine half-brother in the ring glanced at the old man, then at Rogan, and in his surprise, he looked away from his opponent. The woodcutter clipped the young man on the side of the head. The man stepped back, put his hand to his temple, and looked at the blood on his fingertips. Then, with a look of disgust on his face, he sent the woodcutter sprawling in three hard blows.

Immediately, he went to stand before Rogan on the sidelines.

Liana saw that the two men were about the same age, but Rogan was heavier and, to her eyes, much, much more handsome. Beside her, a young woman gave a sigh of lust. Liana clutched Rogan's hand hard with her own and plastered herself to the side of him.

"So, I have another brother," the young man said.

His eyes were as piercing as Rogan's, Liana thought, and something in them made her sure that he knew who Rogan was. "Don't—" Liana began.

"Shall we give the people a fight or not?" the man challenged. "Or are you ruled by a woman?" He lowered his voice. "As Lord Rogan is?"

Liana felt her heart sink, for she knew Rogan would never resist the challenge. The two of them had politely ignored the last scene of the play, when the Fire Lady had collared Lord Buzzard, but she knew Rogan was aware of it. He wouldn't allow himself to be insulted twice in one day.

Rogan released her hand and stepped into the

circle. Liana knew she could do or say nothing without putting both their lives in jeopardy. Her breath held, she watched the two men walk together into the ring, facing each other. They were so much alike: same hair, same eyes, same square, determined jaw.

Rogan looked down at the pole on the ground, then to Liana's horror, he removed his concealing hood, then pulled his shirt off over his head. There was a moment's pleasure as he tossed his garments to her and she caught them, but then Liana's fear returned. Surely someone would recognize him now. She didn't like to think *who* would recognize him, since it could be one or all of the women he'd bedded. "Half the village," she muttered to herself.

She scanned the crowd and saw two of the Days standing on the opposite side of the circle. Now their faces showed puzzlement, but Liana had no doubt that soon the women would realize who Rogan was.

Swiftly, she began to make her way toward the women.

"You say one word and you will regret it," she said when she reached the women. One of the Days cowered, her face showing her fear, but the other woman was bolder and smarter. She saw the danger Liana and Rogan were in.

"I want my son to be raised as a knight," the woman said.

Liana opened her mouth to refuse this outrageous and bold request, but she closed it. "You will see that no one else knows," she countered.

The woman looked Liana in the eyes. "I will tell people he comes from a village to the south and that I have met him before. My son?"

Liana couldn't help admiring this woman who risked so much for her child. "Your sons will be educated and trained. Send them to me tomorrow."

She moved away from the women and made her way back to where she had been.

Rogan and his half-brother were circling each other, long poles held horizontally in their hands. They were imposing men, both young and strong, broad-shouldered, slim-hipped, muscles well defined.

But it didn't take half a brain to see who was the better fighter. Rogan was obviously testing his half-brother, toying with him to see what he could do, while the half-brother, anger in his eyes, was fighting with all his might. The brother attacked and Rogan easily sidestepped, then quickly brought his pole to the back of his brother's knees.

"Are you used to fighting only women?" Rogan taunted.

Anger was getting the best of his brother, causing him to make stupid mistakes.

"No one has ever beaten Baudoin before," the toothless old man next to Liana said. "He'll not like being bested."

"Baudoin," Liana said aloud, frowning. She didn't think it was a good idea for Rogan to make an enemy of this brother as he was doing. Rogan had spent most of his life training with sticks and swords, while this young man no doubt spent most of his time behind a plow.

After a while, it was obvious to everyone watching that Rogan was growing tired of this game that gave no challenge. He stood in front of his brother, put his pole in one hand, standing it on end and . . . stretched.

It was an insulting move, and Liana's sympathies went to Baudoin at being so humiliated.

Baudoin's eyes turned dark with rage, and he lunged at Rogan, murder in his face. The crowd gasped.

Barely looking at his brother, Rogan sidestepped and brought his stick crashing down on the back of Baudoin's head. The young man went sprawling, face down, unconscious, in the mud and grass.

Without a look of concern for his brother, Rogan stepped over his inert body and walked toward Liana, took his clothes from her, and slipped them over his head. He pushed his way through the crowd, his shoulders and head back, not looking at Liana but obviously expecting her to follow him. He ignored the peasants about him, who clapped him on the shoulder in congratulations and asked him to have a drink with them.

Rogan was feeling very proud of himself. He'd bested the man who'd made his wife look at him with desire. He'd shown her who was the best man. And he was proud of how he'd done it. There would be no doubt in her mind as to who was the better man. He could have beat that overconfident half-brother with one hand tied behind his back.

Very aware that Liana was following him, he led her toward the woods. When she showed how pleased she was with him, he wanted to be alone with her. Once, after he'd won a tournament, two young ladies had come to his tent to congratulate him. That had been a night to remember!

But now all he wanted was his wife's praise. Perhaps she'd kiss him the way she had when he'd said he'd go to the fair with her. He didn't stop walking until he was deep in the woods, then he turned and looked at her.

She didn't throw her arms about his neck, nor did she give him one of her smiles that he'd come to know: a smile that was beginning to make him think of pleasure and softness and laughter.

"I won," he said, his eyes alive.

"Yes, you won," she said flatly.

He didn't understand her tone. It was almost as if she were angry with him. "I beat the man rather easily."

"Oh yes, it was very easy for you. Easy to humiliate him, to make the people laugh at him."

Rogan didn't understand her and he didn't try. She had gone too far this time. He drew back his hand to strike her.

"Will you beat me now? Will you beat someone else who is weaker than you? Will you beat *all* your relatives? Me, your wife, your brothers. Why not get your children and tie them to the trees and flog them?"

Rogan knew the woman was crazy; she made no sense. He lowered his hand and turned away from her to walk back to the village.

Liana planted herself in front of him. "What were you thinking of to beat the boy so badly? You made him look like a fool."

Rogan's own temper came to the surface. He grabbed her shoulders and yelled into her face. "Did you hate seeing him made a fool of? Would you rather it was *me* on the ground? Would you have comforted *him* with his head in your lap?" He dropped his hands from her shoulders. He had revealed too much of himself. He walked past her.

Liana stood alone for a moment, staring at the ground as she thought about his words. His meaning came slowly to her and she had to run to catch him. She stood before him. "You were jealous," she said, wonder in her voice as she looked up at him.

He didn't answer but walked around her.

She stepped in front of him again and put her hands on his chest. "Did you really beat that boy so badly just to impress me?"

Rogan looked into the distance over her head. "I wanted to test his strength and quickness, and when I'd done that, I was finished with him." He glanced at her, then away. "He is not a boy. He is my age or perhaps older."

Liana began to smile. She didn't like what he'd done to his half-brother, but oh how good it felt to think her husband was jealous of the way she'd looked at another man. "He may be as old as you, but he's not as strong as you or as skilled nor as handsome." She took his arm and tried to lead him into the forest, but he stood where he was.

"I have been too long away from my men. We should return to the castle." His body was rigid.

"But the wager was for you to be my slave for a whole day," Liana said, unable to keep from whining slightly. "Come, we'll sit here in the woods. We won't have to return to the fair."

Rogan found himself following the woman. Somehow she was able to make him forget duty and responsibility. He had neglected his work more since he'd married her than he had ever done before.

"Come, sit here beside me," she said, indicating a grassy, flower-strewn patch beside a little stream.

She could see by his face that he was still angry and she started to smile at him when a movement in the trees behind him caught her eye. "Look out!" she managed to shout.

Rogan instinctively sidestepped and so missed the knife that came at his back.

Liana stood where she was and watched, horror on her face, as Baudoin attacked Rogan with a knife. She saw blood on Rogan's arm, but in the frenzy of activity, she couldn't tell how bad the wound was.

This time Rogan did not have such an easy time of

subduing his half-brother. Baudoin was enraged, and he meant to kill.

Liana could do little more than watch as the men wrestled with each other, tumbling, rolling over and over on the grass, the knife flashing between them now and then. Rage added strength to Baudoin, and Liana could see that Rogan was fighting for his life.

Glancing about her, she saw a short, stout tree branch. She picked it up, weighing it in her hands, then moved closer to the two powerful men. She had to jump back as they rolled near her, then step forward when they rolled away. The two heads, their faces buried in each other's bodies, were so alike she was afraid she'd hit the wrong man.

Then there was a chance. Baudoin wrenched his right arm free and held the knife above Rogan's throat.

The next moment he collapsed helplessly as Liana brought the club down on his head.

For a moment Rogan didn't move. He lay there, his limp half-brother sprawled on top of him. He didn't like to admit to himself that he might have been killed if it hadn't been for a . . . a woman.

He pushed Baudoin off him and stood, unable to look at his wife. "We'll go back and send the men for him," he murmured.

"And what will your men do to him?" Liana asked as she examined the wound on Rogan's arm. The skin was barely broken.

"Execute him."

"Your own *brother?*" Liana asked.

Rogan frowned. "It will be quick. No burning or torturing."

Liana was thoughtful for a moment. "You go and get the men. I will join you in a while."

Rogan looked at her and his pulse pounded in his temple. "You mean to stay here with him?"

Her eyes met his. "I mean to help him escape your injustice."

"My—?" Rogan said, aghast. "He just tried to *kill* me. If that means nothing to you, it means a great deal to me."

She went to him and put her hands on his arms. "You have lost so many brothers, and most of them were half-brothers. How can you bear to lose another? Take this man and train him. Train him to be one of your knights."

He stepped away from her, gaping at her. "Do you tell me how to run my men? Do you ask me to live with a man who tried to kill me? Do you hope to rid yourself of me so you can have this man?"

Liana threw her hands in the air in a gesture of helplessness. "What a fool you are! I chose *you.* Do you have any idea how many suitors I had? They desperately wanted my father's money, and they courted me in every possible way. They wrote poetry to me, sang songs to my loveliness. But *you!* You shoved me in a bog and told me to wash your clothes and, fool that I am, I agreed to marry you. And what have I received in return for my stupidity? Other women in your bed while you ignore me. The stench of you. And now you dare to accuse me of liking other men. I have cleaned that cesspit you call a home. I have given you better food, I have been an enthusiastic bed partner, and you dare to accuse me of adultery? Go on, kill the man. What do I care? I will return to my father and you can have all the gold and no troublesome wife."

Her anger was leaving her and she felt tired and deflated, and near to tears. She had failed with him. Just as Helen had warned, she had failed.

"What bog?" was all Rogan said after a moment.

Liana was swallowing her tears. "By the pond," she said tiredly. "You made me wash your clothes. Shall we go now? He will waken soon."

Rogan stepped toward her, put his fingertips under her chin, and lifted her head to look at him. "I had forgotten that. So you're the hellion who beat the holes in my clothes?"

She jerked away from him. "I replaced your clothes. Shall we go now? Or perhaps I should leave and you can stay behind and kill your brother. Perhaps he has sisters and you can abduct them and get yourself a new set of Days."

Rogan caught her arm and turned her to face him. Yes, she was that girl at the pool. He remembered lying there, aware that he was being watched and pleased to find it was a pretty woman. She'd shown fire then and even more fire the night she'd put a torch to his bed.

He gave her something he hadn't given a woman in years: He smiled at her.

Liana felt her knees grow weak at his smile. His handsome face was transformed into boyish good looks. Was this the man his first wife had seen? If so, how could she have ever left him?

"So," he said, "you agreed to marry me because I tossed you in a bog?"

No matter how good he looked, she wasn't going to answer him—not when he used that tone of voice. He made her sound like a brainless, lustful peasant girl, no more than one of his Days. She turned away, her back straight, head held high, and started back toward the village.

He caught her and, to her disbelief, lifted her in his arms like a baby, then tossed her high. "What do you have planned for me now? Another bed burning? Or maybe you'll set the whole castle on fire this time?" He tossed her up again. "For someone so little you have a mighty way of getting what you want."

Her arms went about his neck to keep from falling.

"That's better," he said, and kissed her neck.

Liana's anger melted and Rogan knew it because she could feel his silent laughter against her neck. "You!" she said, and smacked his shoulder. "Put me down. Are you going to kill your brother?"

He looked at her and shook his head. "You don't let go of something, do you?"

She put her hand up and caressed his cheek. "No," she said softly. "When I decide I want something, I never let it go."

His eyes turned serious as he looked at her as if he were puzzled about something, and he started to reply to her, but a groan from Baudoin on the ground behind them caught his attention. Rogan put Liana down so quickly she stumbled against a tree.

When she recovered her balance, she saw Rogan standing over his half-brother, the knife in his hands.

Liana began to pray. She prayed fervently, with all her heart, for her husband to show mercy to this young man.

"And how will you kill me?"

She opened her eyes to see Baudoin standing straight and proud before Rogan, showing no fear.

"Fire?" Baudoin asked. "Or will your torturers work on me? Are your men hidden in the woods and spying on us? Will they burn the village because of what was in the play?"

Liana looked at the two men, Rogan with his back to her, and held her breath. She knew her husband could kill Baudoin easily if he wanted, but she prayed he would not. Rogan tossed the knife from one hand to the other and remained silent.

"What do you do to earn your keep?" Rogan asked at last.

The question seemed to startle Baudoin. "I buy and sell wool."

"Are you an honest man?"

Baudoin's face showed his anger. "More honest than the man who fathered us. More honest than my illustrious brothers. *I* do not leave my children to starve."

Liana could not see Rogan's face, but she feared Baudoin's taunts were signing his own death warrant.

When Rogan spoke, it was softly and somewhat hesitantly. "I have lost several brothers in the past few years. I cannot lose more. If I were to bring you into my household, would you swear an oath of fidelity to me? Would you honor it?"

Baudoin was stunned—so stunned he could not speak. He had hated his half-brothers in their castle on the hill all his life. He had lived in poverty while they had had everything.

Liana could see Baudoin's hesitation and she could guess its meaning. She could also guess that Rogan's generosity would soon turn to anger if it weren't readily accepted. Quickly, she stepped between the two men.

"You have children?" she said to Baudoin. "How many? What are their ages? When you come to live with us, I'll see that they're educated. They can go to school with Rogan's sons."

"What sons?" Rogan said, glowering down at her. This wool merchant was refusing to pay homage to him! He should have killed him an hour ago, but he hadn't because of his interfering wife. He stepped toward her.

Liana took Baudoin's arm in such a way that she was protecting him and herself. "All your little red-haired sons, of course," she said brightly. "Can your wife sew?" she asked Baudoin. "I need some women who can sew. Or spin. Or weave. When you're out training with Rogan, she can stay with me. Rogan, why don't you tell your *brother*"—she emphasized the word—"how hard you'll work him. Perhaps he'd rather continue buying and selling wool."

"I am to try to *persuade* him?" Rogan said in disbelief. "Shall I tell him of the comfort of the bed? Or tantalize him with offers of meat every day?"

Baudoin was recovering from his shock. He had inherited their father's intelligence and no one had ever accused him of being a fool. "Forgive my hesitancy, my lord," he said loudly, taking Rogan's attention from his wife. "I am most grateful for your offer and I . . ." He paused and his eyes hardened. "I will defend the Peregrine name with my life."

Rogan looked at the man for a long moment, and Liana could see that he was wrestling with something inside himself. Please, she prayed to herself, please believe him.

"Come to me tomorrow," Rogan said at last. "Now, go."

When Baudoin was gone, tears of relief came to Liana's eyes. She went to Rogan and put her arms about his neck and kissed him. "Thank you," she said. "Thank you so much."

"Will you be so thankful when I am returned with that man's sword in my heart?"

"I do not think . . ." she began, but she didn't *know* that Rogan wasn't correct. "Perhaps I have made an error. Perhaps you should make him a clerk or send him to your other castle or—"

"Are you turning coward on me?"

"When it comes to your safety, I will risk nothing."

"Women have said such to me before," he said, "and it turned out they were not to be trusted."

She put her lips next to his. "Who said this to you? Jeanne Howard?"

One moment she was in his arms and the next she was on the ground, looking up into the face that had made grown men tremble.

CHAPTER
TWELVE

*H*e turned on his heel and started walking quickly through the forest, away from her and away from the village.

Liana began to run after him. She was glad for the short peasant skirt as she leaped over logs and around trees. But she couldn't catch Rogan. He was out of sight within minutes.

"Damn him and his temper," she said aloud, stamping her foot in anger.

She hadn't realized she was so close to the edge of the stream or that the land fell away so sharply. The bank gave way under her and she went sliding downward, on her back, for about twenty feet, screaming as she went.

When she hit bottom, Rogan was there, a short sword drawn from someplace under his tunic, standing over her.

"Who did this?" he demanded.

Liana had no time to bless her good luck at having

brought him back. "I fell," she explained. "I was chasing you and I fell."

"Oh," he said, uninterested, as he put his sword back under his rough garment.

He stood there looking as if he had no idea of what to do next. "Carry me to the water, slave," Liana commanded, holding out her hand in an arrogant way. When he didn't move, she said, "Please."

Bending, he picked her up in his arms and walked her to the stream. She put her arms around his neck and nuzzled against him. "Was Jeanne pretty?" she asked.

He dropped her into the ice-cold water.

Sputtering, Liana came up for air. Rogan was already walking away again. "You're the worst slave there ever was!" she called after him. "You're going to forfeit the wager."

As she stood up in the water, he came back to her and by the look on his face Liana almost wished he hadn't.

"I'll forfeit no wager to you, woman," he said in a low growl. "There are some things in my life that are no one else's business and . . . and . . ."

"Jeanne Howard," she said. Her teeth were beginning to chatter.

"Yes, that woman has caused the deaths of—"

"Basil and James," she supplied.

He stopped and glared at her. "Do you make light of me?" he whispered.

Her eyes were pleading with him. "Rogan, I've never meant to make light of something as awful as death. I was merely asking my husband about his first wife. Every woman is curious about the other women in her husband's life. I've just heard so much about Jeanne and—"

"Who told you?"

"The Lady." When Rogan obviously didn't know who she meant, she said, "I believe she's Severn's lady, although she's somewhat older than he is."

Rogan's face lost its hard look. "I wouldn't dare remind Iolanthe that she's older than Severn if I were you." He paused. "Io told you about . . ."

He didn't seem able to say his first wife's name, and this bothered Liana. Was he still so much in love with her? "I've never met Iolanthe, but the Lady mentioned her. Rogan, I'm freezing. Couldn't we talk over there? In the sun?"

Twice he'd walked away from her when she'd mentioned that woman's name and both times he'd returned, and now he was considering remaining with her to "talk." He grabbed Liana's hand and pulled her from the stream.

When they were in the sun, he folded his arms across his chest and set his jaw. He was never, ever again in his life going to agree to spend a day with a woman—especially not this one. She had a talent for picking at his sorest spots. "What is it you want to know?" he asked.

"Was she pretty? Were you very much in love with her? Is she the reason the castle was so dirty? Did you vow to never love another woman because she hurt you so? Why would she want Oliver Howard instead of you? What's he like? Did she make you laugh? Is it because of Jeanne that you never smile? Do you think I can ever replace her in your heart?"

When the questions at last stopped, Rogan just stood there looking at Liana. His arms were at his sides and his mouth was open a bit in astonishment.

"Well?" Liana said, encouraging him. "Is she? Was she? Tell me!"

Rogan wasn't sure what he'd expected from her

when he'd asked her what she wanted to know, but these frivolous, unimportant, lovesick questions were not it. His eyes began to twinkle. "Beautiful?" he said. "The moon was afraid to come up over Moray Castle because it couldn't compete with the beauty of . . . of . . ."

"Jeanne," Liana said thoughtfully. "Then, she was much prettier than me?"

He couldn't believe she was taking this seriously. Truthfully, he didn't remember what his former wife looked like. It had been so many years since he'd seen her. "Much," he said in mock seriousness. "She was so beautiful that . . ." He searched for a comparison. ". . . that charging war horses would halt before her and eat from her hand."

"Oh," Liana said, and sat down on a rock, her wet clothes making squishing noises. "Oh."

Rogan gave the top of her bowed head a look of disgust. "She could never wear pretty clothes because if she did, she hurt men's eyes. She had to wear peasants' clothes all the time just to keep from blinding people. If she rode into the village, she had to wear a mask or otherwise men would throw themselves under her horse's hooves. Diamonds looked dull next to—"

Liana's head came up. "You're teasing me." There was hope in her voice. "What did she *really* look like?"

"I don't remember. She was young. Brown hair, I think."

Liana realized that this last was the truth, that he didn't remember much about Jeanne's looks. "How can you forget someone you loved so much?"

He sat down on the grass, his back to her, and looked at the stream. "I was just a boy, and my brothers ordered me to marry her. She . . . she betrayed me, all of us. James and Basil died trying to get her back."

She went to him and sat beside him, her cold wet side next to the warm dryness of him. "She's what has made you sad?"

"Sad?" he said. "The death of my brothers has made me sad. Seeing them die one by one, knowing that the Howards have taken everything I ever wanted in life."

"Even your wife," she whispered.

He turned and looked at her. He hadn't thought of his first wife in a personal way in years. He couldn't remember her face, her body, anything at all about her. But as he looked at Liana he thought that if she left, he would remember a great deal about her—and it wouldn't just be her body either, he thought with astonishment. He'd remember some of the things she'd *said*.

He put his hand out and touched her damp cheek. "Are you as simple as you seem?" he asked softly. "Is whether someone loves you or thinks you're beautiful the most important thing in your life?"

Liana didn't like to sound so frivolous. "I can watch the accounts of the estates. I can produce thieves. I can judge court cases. I can—"

"Judge?" Rogan asked, leaning away to look at her. "How can a woman make a decent judgment? The judgments are not about love and who has the cleanest floor—they're about issues of importance."

"Give me an example," Liana said evenly.

Rogan thought it better not to burden a woman's mind with too many serious matters, but he also wanted to teach her a lesson. "Yesterday a man and three witnesses came to me with a document signed with a seal. The document said the man was the owner of a farm, but the farm's previous owner would not leave. That man had put his seal to the paper as collateral for a debt. Now the debt went unpaid, but the first owner remained on the farm. How would you have settled the matter?" he asked smugly.

"I would make no judgment until I'd heard the first owner's testimony. The king's courts have ruled that a seal is too easy to forge. If the man was educated enough to have a seal, perhaps he could also write his own name. He would have put his seal *and* his mark on the paper. I would also question whether the witnesses were friends of the first man or not. All in all, the case does not sound straightforward to me."

Rogan gaped at her. The document had indeed proved to be a false one, made by a man who was angry at having seen his young wife talking to the owner's son.

"Well?" Liana said. "I hope you did not send men to throw the poor farmer off his land."

"I did not," he snapped. "Nor did I burn anyone for eating rats."

"Or impregnate a daughter?" she said teasingly.

"No, but the farmer's wife was a beauty. Big—" He held his hands in front of him.

"You!" Liana said, and lunged at him.

He caught her, pretended that her weight had knocked him down, then held her closely to him. He kissed her.

"I did well in the judgment, didn't I? The document was false, wasn't it?" She was lying on top of him, feeling his strong, hard body under hers.

"Your clothes are wet," he said. "Maybe you should take them off and let them dry."

"You're not going to distract me. Was the document false or not?"

He lifted his head to kiss her again, but she turned her face away.

"Was it?" she asked.

"Yes, it was false," he said, exasperated.

Liana laughed and began kissing his neck.

Rogan closed his eyes. He'd had so few women in his life who weren't afraid of him. The high-born women of the courts usually turned up their noses at him, so Rogan told himself he preferred the servant girls. They were usually fearful of his scowls and frowns. But this woman laughed at him, yelled at him—and refused to obey him.

". . . and I can help," she was saying.

"Help in what?" he murmured.

"The judgments." She was running her tongue along his collarbone.

"Over my dead body," he said cheerfully.

She wiggled on top of him. "I'm over your body, but it doesn't feel very dead to me."

"You're an impudent wench," he said, kissing her.

"How shall you punish me?"

He put his hand behind her head and rolled her over, throwing his big leg over hers. "I will wear you out."

"Impossible!" she said before his mouth came down on hers.

From the trees came a sound of people walking, which, at first, the lovers did not hear.

"Gaby, I tell you this is a bad idea," came a man's voice.

"Nothing ventured, nothing gained, I always say," answered a woman.

Liana felt Rogan's body stiffen, then quickly he took his short sword from under his tunic and knelt over her in a gesture of complete protection.

Through the trees came Baudoin and a small, plump woman, a little girl in her arms, a basket on her arm, and a boy between them.

Liana and Rogan just stared, not understanding the meaning of this intrusion.

"There you are," the plump woman said, coming forward. "Baudoin has told me everything. You must forgive his temper. I'm his wife, Gabriel, but everyone calls me Gaby, and these are our children, Sarah and Joseph. I told Baudoin that if we're going to live with you, we ought to get to know you. My father was a knight, nothing as high as an earl, mind you, but a man of respect. I knew Baudoin was the son of a lord, so I pleaded with my father to let me marry him." She gave the tall, handsome young man a look of adoration. "And I've never regretted a minute of it. Aren't you cold, my lady, in those wet clothes? The dye's coming out of your hair and it's all over your face. Here, let me help you get clean."

Rogan and Liana, in their astonishment, hadn't moved. He still knelt over her, knife drawn, protecting Liana beneath him. When the woman Gaby held out her hand, Liana didn't move.

Baudoin broke the silence. "Go on," he said. "Everyone does what she says." The words were mean, but there was a tone of love in his voice. The couple didn't look as if they belonged together. Baudoin was tall, lean, exceedingly handsome, and angry-looking. Gaby was short, plump, pretty, but far from beautiful, and she looked as if she'd been born with a smile on her face.

Liana took the woman's offered hand and followed her to the stream. Liana was used to women of Gaby's class being fearful of her, but ever since she'd come to the Peregrine land, nothing has been as she'd once known it.

"Now, sit there and behave yourself," Gaby said as she set her daughter on the ground. She looked back at Liana. "I heard what happened this morning. Broth-

ers shouldn't fight. I always told Baudoin that someday his brothers in the castle would see the light, and I
was right. He's a good man, is my Baudoin, and he'll
do whatever is needed. Look at them. Two peas in a
pod."

Liana looked at the two men standing near one
another, not looking at each other, not speaking, the
little boy between them just as silent.

"Lean over here and let me wash your hair," Gaby
directed.

Liana did as she was bid.

"Does yours talk as little as mine?" Gaby asked.

Liana was unsure of what to do—whether to be
friends with this woman or not. It was odd how
clothes affected one's mind. If she were wearing her
best blue silk she would have expected this woman to
bow before her but, somehow, while wearing peasant's
wool, she felt almost as if she were . . . well, equal to
this woman. "If I chain him in one place he will talk,
but not much," Liana finally said.

"Don't give up the fight. He'll pull into himself
completely if you allow it. And make him laugh.
Tickle him."

"Tickle him?" Black-dyed water was streaming past
Liana's face.

"Mmm," Gaby said. "Ribs. They're good men,
though. They're not fickle in their affections. If he
loves you today, he'll love you forever. He won't be
like some men and love you today, somebody else
tomorrow, and somebody else the next day. There,
that should do it. Your hair is blonde again."

Liana sat up, slinging her wet hair back. "And now
we can't return to the fair. Someone might recognize
me."

"No," Gaby said seriously. "You don't want to go

back there. There was talk this morning of who the mysterious man was who beat Baudoin. You shouldn't return." Her face brightened. "But I have brought food and we can stay here in this pretty spot."

Gabriel didn't tell Liana that she'd spent a year's savings on the feast she'd brought with her. Under Gaby's happy exterior was a very ambitious woman —but she was not ambitious for herself. She was ambitious for the man she loved more than life itself.

She had been twelve when she'd first seen the handsome, cold-eyed Baudoin and she had decided then that she'd have him no matter what it took to get him. Her father had wanted her to make a good marriage, not to marry some bastard son with no prospects. But Gaby had wheedled and whined and pleaded and nagged until her father at last made an offer to Baudoin's stepfather.

Baudoin had married her for her dowry, and the first years together had been hard. He'd had many other women, but Gaby's love was stronger than his lust. Gradually he began to notice her, to come to her for love and comfort, and when the children were born, he found he enjoyed them, too.

In the six years of their marriage, Baudoin had gone from being a hellion who jumped from one bed to another to being a successful merchant who most of all enjoyed his wife and children.

This morning, when he'd seen Lord Rogan in the crowd, he'd recognized his half-brother immediately. For the first time in years his old rage had come to the surface. Hours later he'd found Gaby and, after much word-pulling from her, had told her what had happened in the forest. He was ashamed of having attacked a man from behind and he told Gaby about the offer he'd accepted, but said that they must leave the area and start over again elsewhere, that he could not bear to face Lord Rogan again.

Gaby gave a quick prayer of thanks to God for at last giving them this opportunity, and then she proceeded to work on Baudoin. She used every technique she could think of to break Baudoin's reserve. Once this was accomplished she knew she had to work on the lord and his kind, forgiving wife. And she knew that today, while the lord and his lady were dressed in peasants' garb, was her opportunity. Tomorrow, when they were in silk and she was in wool, the gulf between them would be too great.

So she'd taken the money from its hiding place, purchased beef, pork, chicken, bread, oranges, cheese, dates, figs, and beer, and put them into a basket and gone in search of Baudoin's illustrious relatives. She didn't let herself think of Rogan's reputation, which had been so well portrayed in the play (and she refused to think about Lord Rogan's having seen Baudoin playing him), but concentrated on being amusing and *equal*.

Liana didn't have to say much when she was near Gaby, but then no one did, for Gaby talked enough for an army. At first Liana was reserved with the woman. She didn't like her presumption, didn't like the way the woman had forced herself into what was to have been her time alone with Rogan.

But after a while, Liana began to thaw. It was so good to hear *talk*. With Rogan she had to force every word from him and there were no guests at Moray Castle, no one to talk with except her maids and the Lady—who too often stayed behind a locked door.

And, too, Liana liked the way Gaby adored Baudoin. Her eyes roamed over him in a possessive way that was part wife, part mother, part she-monster who meant to suck the life from him. I wonder if I look at Rogan like that, she thought.

The men looked at one another warily, not knowing what to say or how to react to each other, until Gaby suggested Rogan teach Baudoin how to fight with long poles.

The women sat on the ground eating cheese and bread and watched the men train. Rogan was a good teacher, if a harsh one. He knocked Baudoin into the cold stream three times. But Baudoin wasn't his father's son for nothing. The fourth time Rogan meant to send his half-brother into the water, Baudoin pivoted and Rogan went splashing face down into the icy water.

Liana was on her feet instantly and running to her husband. He looked so startled as he sat there in the water that Liana began to laugh, as did Gaby. Even Baudoin smiled. It took Rogan a moment, but he smiled also.

Liana put her hand out to help him up but, still smiling, he pulled her down into the water with him. "Not fair," she cried. "I was nearly dry."

He stood, then lifted her out of the water and carried her to the grassy place in the sun and sat down beside her. He removed his shirt, and when Liana shivered, he pulled her into his arms so that she leaned back against him. Liana knew she'd never been so happy in her life.

"What's to eat?" Rogan asked. "I'm starved."

Gaby pulled luscious food from the basket, and the four adults and two children began to eat. For the most part it was Gaby who talked, telling amusing little stories of village life. She was remarkably tactful when it came to avoiding all reference to the Peregrine family's terrorizing of the village.

Liana could feel Rogan beginning to relax. He asked Baudoin some questions about being a wool merchant, even asked him if he had any ideas how to improve the Peregrine wool production.

The little girl, Sarah, only a toddler, just able to walk, picked up a date and on her chubby legs made her way, with her father's help, to Rogan. She stood and stared at him for a while until Rogan turned to look at her. He'd never paid much attention to children, but he noted that she was a pretty child with intense dark eyes that studied him.

The child handed him the date, and when Rogan took it, she seemed to think this was an invitation. She turned and plopped into his lap, snuggling her back against his chest.

Rogan looked down at the soft curly hair in horror.

"Never met a stranger," Gaby said. "That's my Sarah."

"Take her," Rogan said under his breath to Liana. "Get her off me."

Liana suddenly became deaf. "Here, Sarah, give these figs to your Uncle Rogan."

Solemnly, the child took a fig and held it to Rogan's mouth. When he tried to take it from her, she gave a squeal of protest. Looking as if it were the most unpleasant thing he'd ever done, he opened his mouth and allowed her to put the fig inside.

Liana kept up a running stream of conversation with Gaby and pretended she was taking no notice of Rogan and the child, but she kept the little girl supplied with dates and figs. When the child tired of feeding her uncle, she settled back against Rogan and went to sleep.

All too soon, the sun dropped low in the sky and Liana knew it was time to go home. She didn't want this pleasant time to end, didn't want to return to gloomy Moray Castle and, perhaps, a husband who ignored her. She slipped her hand in Rogan's and put her head on his shoulder. For a long while they sat there, entwined, the sleeping baby on his lap.

"This has been the best day of my life," Liana whispered. "I wish it would never end."

Rogan tightened his arm around her. It had been such a wasteful day and he planned never again to be so frivolous, but he agreed that it had been . . . well, pleasant.

It was Sarah's waking and crying that made them realize they had to return to their respective homes.

"You'll come tomorrow?" Liana asked Gaby, and saw tears of gratitude in the woman's eyes. Already, Liana had plans of making Gaby her mistress of the household. Gaby would make sure the maids kept the place clean, and Liana would have more time to spend with her husband.

A few minutes later, in the growing darkness, Rogan and Liana began to slowly walk back to Moray Castle. Hands clasped, they were quiet for a while.

"I wish we didn't have to go back," Liana said. "I wish we could be like Gaby and Baudoin and live in a simple hut somewhere and—"

Rogan snorted. "They were ready enough to give up their simple hut. That meal must have cost them a year's wages."

"Half a year," Liana said in the tone of someone who spends a great deal of time with account books. "But they're in *love*," she said dreamily. "I could see it in Gaby's eyes." She looked up at Rogan. "It must be how I look at you."

Rogan was looking ahead at the walls of Moray Castle. It had been too easy for them to leave this morning. What if the Howards were to dress as vegetable sellers and beg entry? He'd have to tighten vigilance.

"Did you hear what I said?" Liana asked.

Perhaps he should require a badge to be worn by the peasants who were allowed to enter. Of course a badge could be stolen, but—

"Rogan!" Liana had stopped walking and, clutching his hand, she made him halt too.

"What is it?"

"Were you listening to me?" she asked.

"Heard every word you said," he answered. Perhaps something besides a badge. Maybe a—

"What did I say?"

Rogan looked at her blankly. "Say about what?"

She tightened her lips. "I was telling you that I love you."

Perhaps a password, changed daily. Or maybe the safest thing would be just to designate certain peasants to enter, with no new faces allowed in, ever.

To Rogan's consternation, his wife dropped his hand and marched ahead of him, and from the way she walked, she looked to be angry. "Now what?" he muttered. He'd done everything she wanted of him today and yet she still wasn't pleased.

He caught up with her. "Something wrong?"

"Oh, so you noticed me," she said haughtily. "I hope I wasn't disturbing you by telling you that I love you."

"No," he said honestly. "I was just thinking about something else."

"Don't let my declarations of love interrupt," she said nastily. "I'm sure a hundred women have sworn they love you. All of the Days. But then you even had Months once. And of course Jeanne Howard probably told you every day."

Rogan was beginning to see through her cloud of illogic. This was another one of those woman things and not serious at all. "She wasn't a Howard when she was married to me."

"I see. But you don't deny that she told you repeatedly that she loved you. You've probably heard it so many times it means nothing coming from *me*."

Rogan thought for a moment. "I don't remember any woman telling me she loved me."

"Oh," Liana said, and slipped her hand back into his. They walked in silence for a few minutes. "Do you love me?" she asked softly.

He squeezed her hand. "I have a few times. And tonight I'll—"

"Not *that* kind of love. I mean, inside of you. Like how you loved your mother."

"My mother died when I was born."

She frowned. "Severn's mother, then."

"She died when Severn was born, when I was two. I don't remember her."

"Zared's mother?" Liana asked softly.

"I don't think I felt much of anything for her. She was scared of us all. Used to cry a lot."

"Didn't anyone try to comfort her?"

"Rowland told her to stop crying so we could get some sleep."

Liana thought about that poor woman, alone with a dirty castle full of men whose chief concern was that her crying disturbed their sleep. And she was the wife who was starved to death at Bevan Castle. If Rogan had not loved the women in his life, he must have loved his brothers. "When your oldest brother died—"

"Rowland did not die, he was killed by the Howards."

"All right then," she said impatiently. "Killed.

Murdered. Slaughtered unfairly without provocation. Did you miss him after his death?"

Rogan took a while to answer as images of his strong, powerful brother floated through his head. "I miss him every day," he answered at last.

Liana's voice lowered. "Would you miss me if I died? Say, if the plague took me?"

He looked down at her. If she died, his life would return to the way it had been. His clothes would be crawling with lice. The bread would be filled with sand. The Days would return. She wouldn't be around to curse him, ridicule him, publicly embarrass him, or make him waste his time. He frowned. Yes, he'd miss her.

And he bloody well didn't like the idea of missing her.

"I wouldn't have to go to any more fairs," he said, and walked away from her.

Liana stood rooted where she was. She didn't like to think how much his words hurt. They had been together such a short time and he meant so much to her, yet she was less than nothing to him.

She vowed to herself that she'd never let him see how he'd hurt her, that she'd keep her pain to herself. She thought her face was impassive, with no expression showing to give herself away, but when Rogan turned back, he saw his pretty little wife with her lower lip extended and her eyes big with unshed tears. He searched his mind to figure out what was wrong with her. Did she dread returning to the castle?

He went to her and put his fingers under her chin, but she jerked away.

"You care nothing for me," she said. "If I were to die, you could get another rich wife and keep her dowry."

Rogan gave a bit of a shudder. "Marriages are too

much trouble," he said. "My father had the stamina of a thousand men. He went through four marriages."

In spite of her intentions, tears began to roll down Liana's face. "If I died, you'd no doubt toss my body in the moat. Good riddance!"

Rogan's confusion showed. "If you died I'd . . ."

"Yes?" she asked, looking up at him through lashes heavy with tears.

"I would . . . know that you were gone."

Liana knew this was the best she was going to get from him. She flung her arms about his neck and began to kiss him. "I knew you cared," she said.

To the consternation of both of them, people around them began to applaud. They had been so involved in their own dispute that they hadn't been aware of the people around them who had been gleefully watching and listening.

Rogan was more embarrassed than Liana. He grabbed her hand and started running. They stopped not far from the castle walls and suddenly he, too, was reluctant for the day to end.

There was a vendor nearby with a wooden tray fastened to a belt around his shoulders. In the tray were painted wooden toys of men that danced at the end of a stick. The vendor, seeing Rogan's glance, hurried forward and demonstrated the funny little doll. When Liana laughed at the doll's antics, Rogan found himself parting with two precious pennies for the thing.

Liana clutched the doll eagerly. If Rogan had given her emeralds, she wouldn't like them as much as the doll. She looked up at Rogan with love.

Rogan turned away from her look. Such a frivolous day, such a waste of time and money spent on a bit of a girl who asked stupid questions. And yet . . .

He put his arm about her shoulders and watched as

she fooled with the toy. He felt good as he watched her. He felt at peace, something he thought he'd never felt before. He leaned down and kissed the top of her head. Never before had he kissed a woman for any reason other than lust.

Liana snuggled her body closer to his and Rogan knew he'd pleased her. It was absurd, of course, but somehow, pleasing her pleased him.

With a sigh of regret, he led them to the castle.

CHAPTER
THIRTEEN

Severn sat at the now-clean table in the lord's chamber, eating cheese that had no mold and perfectly cooked beef, and chuckled.

Zared looked up. "Care to share your humor?"

"A whole day in bed with a woman," he said. "Not even I believed Rogan could do it, but once again I underestimated my brother." His eyes showed his pride. "The woman won't be able to walk. She'll probably spend today in bed, too—resting."

"Maybe Rogan will be the one wanting to rest."

"Ha!" Severn snorted. "You know nothing about men. Especially not about men like our brother. He'll put that woman in her place. You'll see. No more trying to run this place after yesterday. Rogan won't neglect the training field to lay about in her lap." There was bitterness in his voice. "She'll stay in her room from now on and not try to interfere in our lives. No more of this constant cleaning and—"

"Cooking," Zared interjected. "I rather like the place better. I sure like the food better."

Severn pointed his eating knife at Zared. "Luxury

can be the downfall of a man, and no one knows that better than our brother. Rogan—"

"Lost the bet."

Severn squinted his eyes. "Yes, he may have lost the bet, but he got what *he* wanted for payment."

"Perhaps," Zared said, slathering sweet, freshly churned butter onto a thick slice of bread. "But then it was her decision about what she wanted to do, wasn't it? And she did win the wager, didn't she? She produced the thieves when you and Rogan couldn't. And she—"

"Luck," Severn said, jaw set. "Blind, stupid luck. No doubt the peasants were ready to turn the thieves over and she happened to arrive at the right time."

"Uh-huh," Zared said. "Sure."

"I don't like your tone," Severn snapped.

"And I don't like your stupidity. The woman has done a lot of work in a short time and she deserves credit. And what's more, I think Rogan's falling in love with her."

"Love!" Severn gasped. "Love! Rogan would never be so weak. He's had a hundred women, a thousand, and he's never fallen in love. He wouldn't. He's too sensible."

"He wasn't so sensible about Jeanne Howard."

Severn's face began to turn an unbecoming shade of purple. "What do you know of that woman? You were a kid when she was here. Her treachery *killed* Basil and James." He calmed himself a bit. "Anyway, Rogan knows what women are like, especially what *wives* are like." He looked at Zared and grinned. "And besides, Rogan never has any use for a woman once he's bedded her. After yesterday, he'll be so sick of this woman he'll probably send her to Bevan to stay and then things will return to normal around here."

"Normal meaning rats on the stairs and dead

bodies lost in the moat? You know what's wrong with you, Severn? You're jealous. You don't want your brother giving his attention to anyone except you. You don't—"

"Jealous! I'll tell you what's wrong with me: I fear Rogan's attention turning from the treachery of the Howards. If this woman softens him, he'll forget to watch his back and an arrow will pierce it. A man can't be a Peregrine and wear skirts as well. *You* should know that."

"I do," Zared said softly. "But what if Rogan does . . . care for her?"

"He won't. Trust me. I know my brother better than he knows himself. He can't even remember the woman's name, so there's no danger of his loving her."

Zared started to speak, but a noise on the stairs made them both turn.

Rogan and Liana entered the room, both of them resplendent in silk brocade, Rogan's hair damp, as if he'd just washed it. Liana had her arm entwined with his and he had his hand over hers.

More unusual than the clothes and the posture was the look on Rogan's face. If he wasn't quite smiling, he was close to it and his eyes were alive as he looked down into the adoring face of his wife.

"Perhaps," Rogan was saying.

"Are you afraid I will contradict you before the peasants?" Liana asked.

"You contradict *me?*" he asked. "Such a thing might make the peasants believe you'd . . ."—he hesitated—" . . . tamed me."

Liana laughed, touching her forehead to his arm. As they walked to the table, they didn't seem to notice the open-mouthed astonishment on the faces of Severn and Zared.

"Good morning," Liana said cheerfully, then seated herself at Rogan's right hand. "Tell me if any food isn't to your liking and I'll speak to the cook—after the court session."

"I see," Rogan said in mock seriousness. "And if you do not participate in the courts, what will we have for dinner?"

Liana smiled sweetly at him. "What you have always eaten: sandy bread and maggoty meat, with moat water to drink."

Rogan turned twinkling eyes to Severn. "This woman blackmails me. If I do not allow her to help judge the court cases, she will starve me."

Severn had been too stunned by this new behavior of his brother's to be able to speak, and now he did not trust himself. He came out of his chair so quickly it fell to the floor. He turned on his heel and stomped from the room.

Rogan, having lived with brothers who were moody and angry most of the time, paid no attention to Severn.

Not so Liana. She turned to Zared. "What is wrong with him?"

Zared shrugged. "He doesn't like being wrong. He'll get over it. Rogan, you look like you enjoyed yourself yesterday."

Rogan started to say something about the fair, but he thought it best that only a few people know where he'd been yesterday. "Yes," he said softly. "I did."

Zared saw Rogan look at Liana with wonder on his face. Rogan would remember the woman's name now, Zared thought, and again wondered if he was falling in love. What would a Rogan in love be like? Would he turn his brooding room into a chamber for writing poetry?

Zared sat quietly at the table and watched the two

of them and saw a brother who didn't act like a Peregrine. Perhaps Severn was right. *This* brother would never be able to lead an attack on the Howards.

When Rogan finished eating, he gave Liana a lusty look and said, "Come with me, my beauty," at which Liana convulsed with laughter.

Zared, at that point, began to agree with Severn. This was not the brother Zared had always known, the Rogan who scowled and frowned and hated.

Quietly, thoughtfully, Zared left the table, but Rogan and Liana didn't notice.

Severn's anger stayed with him throughout the day. In the afternoon he was on the training field with the men, but Rogan wasn't. "Probably back in bed with the woman," he muttered.

"My lord?" asked the knight Severn was training with.

Severn took his anger out on the knight, attacking him in the mock battle with a ferocity he usually used only on the battlefield.

"Enough!" Rogan bellowed from behind Severn. "Are you trying to kill the man?"

Severn halted, sword in hand, and turned to his brother. Beside Rogan was a man who looked very much like him. "What's one of our father's bastards doing here?" Severn snarled.

"He is to train with us. I put him in your charge." Rogan started to turn away, but Severn caught Rogan's shoulder and pulled him around.

"Like hell I'll train the bastard. If you want him here, you train him. Or should we let your wife train him, since she seems to run the Peregrines now? Was he her idea?"

Severn had hit too close to the truth, and Rogan grabbed an iron pike from the hands of a knight standing nearby. "You will eat those words," Rogan said, and went for his brother.

Severn took a pike too. The men fought long and hard while their knights watched in silence, for they sensed that this was not like the usual petty fights of the brothers but something deeper and more serious.

Rogan was not fueled by rage as his brother was. In fact, he felt less angry than he had in years, so he merely defended himself against his brother's attacks.

Both men were surprised when Rogan's foot caught behind him and he fell. Rogan started to get up, but Severn held the pointed end of the iron pike to his brother's throat.

"This is what that woman is doing to you," Severn said. "She might as well castrate you; she already has a chain about your neck."

It was too close to what the peasants had implied in the play. Rogan's rage came to the surface. He pushed the pike aside and leaped up, going for Severn with his bare hands.

Six knights jumped on Rogan and four on to Severn to hold the men apart.

"You always were a fool about women," Severn shouted. "The last wife of yours cost the lives of two brothers, but I guess we mean nothing to you when you have a wife."

Rogan went dead still. "Release me," he said to his men, and the men stepped back. They should not have interfered. Rogan was the lord and he had every right to do what needed to be done to his brother.

Rogan stepped close to his brother. Severn's blue eyes were still hot with anger; he was held back by the knights. "I have given you another brother to train," he said quietly. "I expect you to do it." He turned and walked back to the castle.

* * *

It was hours later that a sweat-dripping Severn mounted the stone stairs over the kitchen and entered Iolanthe's apartments. Here the richness of this large, sunny room was stunning. Gold glowed, silk embroideries shone, jewels on the ladies' gowns sparkled. But by far the most beautiful thing in the room was Iolanthe. Her beauty, her figure, her voice, her movements, were all without flaw, of such exquisite loveliness that often people could not speak when they saw her.

When Io saw the anger on Severn's face, she lifted her hand and dismissed her three women to their own chambers. She poured delicious wine into a golden goblet, handed it to Severn, and when he downed it in one gulp, she refilled it.

"Tell me," she said softly.

"It's that damned woman," Severn said.

Io knew who he meant because Severn had been complaining about Rogan's new wife for some time now.

"She is a Delilah," he said. "She is taking his very soul from him. She rules him, the men, the servants, the peasants, and even me. She ordered *my* room to be whitewashed! There is no place sacred from her touch. She invades Rogan's brooding room and he doesn't so much as reprimand her."

Io was watching him thoughtfully. "And what has she done today?"

"Somehow she persuaded Rogan to bring one of our father's bastards into the castle, and *I* am to train him. He's a *wool merchant.*" Severn said the last with horror.

"How did you get the lump on your forehead?"

Severn looked away. "So the man had a bit of luck with the poles. He'll never be a knight, no matter how much that woman wants it. And today I heard that she

211

sat beside Rogan at court. What next? Will he ask her permission to piss?"

Iolanthe watched Severn, saw his jealousy, and she wondered what this wife of Rogan's was like. Io had stayed in her pretty apartments, leaving only for walks on the battlements, and watched what was happening below. At first she would have wagered that no woman could effect a change on that hardheaded, insensitive, hate-obsessed Rogan, but the weeks had proved her wrong. She and her ladies had watched with amazement as the castle had been cleaned (Iolanthe and her ladies refused even to walk down the stairs through the filth) and she'd listened for hours to the kitchen maids tell stories of what the Fire Lady was doing. Io especially liked the story of Lady Liana's setting Rogan and one of his whores on fire. "Should have been done a long time ago," she'd said.

Io looked back at Severn. "He cares for her, then?"

"I don't know. It's as if she's put a spell on him. She's draining him of his strength. Today in training *I* knocked *him* down."

"It could have nothing to do with your being angry while he was not?"

"Before she came, Rogan was *always* angry. Now he . . . he *smiles!*"

Io could not hide a smile of her own. She did her best to stay out of the Peregrine-Howard feud. The only thing she cared about was Severn. Of course she did not tell him of her love. She had long ago guessed that at the mention of the word *love,* he would flee. And now she knew she was right. He was raging because his brother cared for his wife.

Io wondered how this Liana had made Rogan notice her. It wasn't beauty, because she'd seen divine-looking women make fools of themselves over

Rogan yet he'd not glanced at them, and she'd heard this little wife of his was pretty but certainly no beauty. No, it wasn't beauty that attracted the Peregrine men or Severn would be in love with Iolanthe.

As Io looked at Severn, his handsome face colored by his anger, she thought she'd sell her soul to the devil if he'd love her. He made love to her, true, he spent time with her, even asked her advice on problems, but she never deluded herself that he loved her. So she took what he gave her and never let him know she wanted more.

"What is this woman like?" Io asked.

"Meddlesome," Severn snapped. "Into everyone's business. She wants to run everyone—the knights, the peasants, Rogan, everyone. And she is simpleminded. She believes if she cleans something, it will cure the problem. No doubt she believes that if we bathed with the Howards, we could forgive each other."

"What does she look like?"

"Ordinary. Plain. I cannot see what Rogan sees in her."

Neither could Io, but she wanted to find out. "I am coming to supper in the Lord's Chamber tomorrow night," she announced.

For a moment Severn looked astonished. He knew Io didn't like Rogan, and the castle outside her apartment disgusted her. "Good," he said at last. "Perhaps you can teach the woman to behave like a woman should. Invite her to spend time with you. Keep her out of the courts and away from the peasants —and away from my brother. Maybe if you can get the woman to mind her own business, things can return to the way they should be."

Or perhaps she can teach me how a woman should behave, Io thought, but said nothing to Severn.

* * *

Liana looked out the window for the thousandth time. Yesterday Rogan had returned from the training field and his good mood was broken. Since they returned from the fair, he'd been so sweet, so much like the man she sensed he could be, but in the evening he'd been sullen and angry. He locked himself in his brooding room, as Zared called it, and wouldn't let her in.

It was late that night when he came to bed beside her, and sleepily she rolled next to him. For a moment she thought he was going to push her away, but then he clutched her to him and without a word made violent love to her. Liana almost complained about his fierceness but some instinct told her to be quiet, that he needed her.

Afterward, he'd held her tightly.

"Tell me what happened," she whispered.

For a moment she thought he might talk to her but he rolled away, his back to her, and went to sleep. In the morning he got out of bed and left without a word.

So now she was waiting for him to return from the training field for supper. At dinner he'd eaten with his men, leaving Liana alone with her ladies and Zared. It had been a lonely meal.

Liana dressed carefully to go downstairs. It never hurt to look your best when you were with a man.

When she entered the Lord's Chamber, the air was heavy with silence. Zared, Severn, and Rogan were already seated and eating, none of them speaking. Liana had already guessed that Rogan's anger had something to do with his brother, but she had no idea what had caused it. She could have asked Zared, but she wanted Rogan to tell her what had happened.

She seated herself to Rogan's left and began to eat after she was served. She searched for some topic of conversation. "Did Baudoin arrive today?" she asked.

It didn't seem possible, but the silence increased. When the two older men said nothing, she looked at Zared.

"Not a bad fighter," Zared said. "But then our father always bred good men."

"He's not our brother," Severn snapped.

Zared's eyes flashed. "He's as much my brother as you are."

"I'll teach you who's a Peregrine and who isn't," Severn said.

All three of them were on their feet at once, Severn going for Zared's throat, Rogan going for Severn.

This scene was halted in mid-action by the arrival of a woman. Liana looked under the arch that was formed by Severn's hands around Zared's throat, and her eyes opened wide in astonishment. Standing in the doorway was the most beautiful woman she'd ever seen. No, not just beautiful: perfect, flawless, a standard of beauty for all time. She was swathed in cloth of gold so that she was radiant, like a pillar of sunshine on a dark night.

"I see that nothing has changed," said the woman. Her voice was cool and arresting and at once made everyone feel calmer. She walked forward, as gracefully as an angel, floating, yards of fur-trimmed cloth trailing behind her. "Severn," she said, and looked at him as a mother might look at a disobedient child.

Severn immediately dropped his hands and looked a bit sheepish. Then, obediently, he pulled out a chair for her. When she was seated, she looked up at the three Peregrines who were still standing. "You may sit," she said, as a queen might give an order.

Liana couldn't take her eyes off the woman. She was what every woman hoped to look like. She was so lovely, so elegant, so graceful—and best of all, she had men jumping to do her bidding.

"Io, you have honored us," Rogan said. "Why?"

There was no mistaking the hostility in Rogan's voice, and when Liana looked at him, she saw what was almost a sneer on his lips. That sneer pleased her very much.

"I came to meet your wife," the woman said.

Liana almost asked, Me? but she caught herself. Then she drew her breath in sharply. If Rogan forgot her name again in front of this beautiful woman, she just might fall dead on the spot.

"Liane, Iolanthe," Rogan said, and went back to eating.

Close enough, Liana thought and wondered if the blacksmith could make a brand of her name and sear it on Rogan's forearm, where he could see it when he forgot.

"Hello," Liana said. What was she to say to this woman? "Did you buy your dress fabric in London?"

"France. My husband is French."

"Oh." She gave the woman a weak smile.

The meal went downhill after that. Rogan didn't speak; Severn didn't speak. Zared seemed as intimidated by the woman as Liana felt. Only Iolanthe seemed comfortable. Three of her own women stood behind her and served her food on gold plates. She didn't say anything but watched the others with curiosity—especially Liana, who grew so nervous she couldn't eat her soup.

At long last, Iolanthe rose to leave and Liana felt her shoulders relax in relief. "She is very beautiful," she said to Severn.

Severn, nose in his soup bowl, merely grunted.

"Isn't her husband a little concerned about her living here with you?"

216

Severn turned eyes of hatred on her. "You may interfere in other people's business, but not in mine. Io is *my* business, not yours."

Liana was stunned by his animosity. She looked at Rogan, half expecting him to leap at his brother. But Rogan didn't seem to have heard.

"I meant no insult to you," Liana said, "nor do I mean to interfere. I just thought—"

"Didn't mean to interfere!" Severn mocked. "That's all you've done since you arrived. You've changed everything: the castle, the grounds, the men, the peasants, my brother. Let me tell you, woman, you keep your nose out of my business and you leave Iolanthe alone. I don't want her corrupted."

Liana leaned back in her chair, astounded at this attack. Again she looked at Rogan. Why wasn't he defending her? He was looking at her with interest and she suddenly realized that she was being tested by him. She may be only a Peregrine by marriage, but she had to prove herself to be a Peregrine.

"All right," she said calmly to Severn. "You may have everything you had before I came." She stood and went to the fireplace, where there were cold ashes from that morning, picked up the big scoop nearby, and filled it with ashes. She walked across the room to Severn, with all eyes on her, then dumped the ashes on his food and clothes. "There," she said. "Now you are filthy and so is your food. From now on I will see that you have what you've always had."

Severn, soot on his chin and clothes, stood up, enraged. His hands made claws as he went for her throat.

Liana paled and stepped backward.

Severn never reached her because Rogan, while never looking up from gnawing on a beef joint, stuck his foot out and tripped his brother, sending Severn sprawling.

When Severn caught his breath, he bellowed, "You better do something about that woman."

Rogan ran his sleeve across his mouth. "She looks like she can take care of herself."

Liana had never felt so proud of herself in her life. She'd passed!

"But I wouldn't like it if you laid a hand on her," Rogan continued.

Severn stood, slapping soot from his clothes, which had been clean a few minutes before (Liana had directed the maids to wash his garments). He glared at Liana again. "Stay away from Io," he muttered, then left the room.

Liana felt jubilant. These Peregrines had their own rules of conduct, but she was beginning to understand them. Best of all, Rogan *had* defended her. Not from hateful words, but when his brother might have physically harmed her, he had stepped in.

Smiling—not only visibly, but also deep inside herself—she sat back down at the table. "More peas, Zared?" she asked.

"Clean peas?" Zared asked in mock fright. "The way *I* like my peas? Clean, the way I like my clothes and room and the peasants and the men *and* my brother?"

Liana laughed and looked at her husband, and the dear lovely man *winked* at her.

Later that night, Rogan held her in his arms and kissed her and made sweet love to her. Whatever had been bothering him seemed to have solved itself.

Afterward, he didn't turn away but held her close to him and Liana heard his soft, slow breathing as he fell asleep.

"Iolanthe isn't the Lady," she said sleepily.

"What lady?" he murmured.

"The Lady who lives above the solar, who told me about Jeanne Howard. She's not Iolanthe, so who is she?"

"No one lives above the solar, not until you came."

"But—" Liana said.

"Stop talking and go to sleep or I'll let Severn have you."

"Oh?" she replied, faking interest. "He's awfully good-looking. Maybe—"

"I'll tell Iolanthe you said that."

"I'm asleep," Liana answered quickly. She'd rather face Severn than the frightening Iolanthe.

As she drifted into sleep, she wondered again who the Lady was.

CHAPTER
FOURTEEN

The next morning, Gaby and her children arrived at the castle and at last Liana had someone to talk to. And best of all, Gaby told Liana of the disagreement Rogan and Severn had had over Baudoin.

"But my husband defended me?" Liana said softly.

"Oh yes, my lady. He told Lord Severn to keep his mouth shut, and Lord Severn has done everything he can to make my Baudoin quit and return to the village. But my Baudoin will *never* quit."

"No," Liana said with resignation. "Peregrines don't ever seem to quit or back down or even relent."

"That's not so, my lady," Gaby said. "Lord Rogan has changed since you arrived. Yesterday you walked across the bridge and Lord Rogan stopped yelling at one of his knights and watched you."

"Did he?" Those were sweet words to Liana. "And he does defend me to his brother?"

"Oh yes, my lady."

Liana couldn't seem to get enough from Gaby. At

times it seemed she'd had no influence on Rogan, that he was the same man who couldn't remember her name. But he remembered it now. Just this morning he had held her in his arms and kissed her and whispered her name in her ear.

Three weeks after Baudoin and Gaby's arrival, Rogan and Severn were still at such odds that they were barely speaking. Liana tried to get Rogan to talk to her about his anger, but he would not. Yet in bed he clung to her. Sometimes she felt as if he wanted her to make up for all the softness he'd lacked as a child.

In the evenings after supper, sometimes he came to the solar with her and sat sprawled on a cushioned chair and listened to one of her ladies play a lute and sing. She'd started to teach him to play chess, and when he realized it was a game of strategy, rather like war, he quickly became quite good. Zared began to join them, and Liana was pleased to see the young man sitting cross-legged on the floor holding a skein of yarn for one of the women to wind. One evening Rogan had been lounging on the window seat, Zared seated on the floor nearby, and Liana had seen Rogan reach out his hand and caress Zared's head. The boy had smiled up at Rogan with a look of such love and trust and adoration that Liana felt her knees weaken.

With each day Liana felt her love for her husband grow deeper and stronger. She had sensed from the beginning that there was more to him than what people saw, that there was a softer side.

Not that the softer side was easy to see. They'd had a couple of arguments that nearly brought the roof down on their heads. Rogan refused to believe Liana was good for anything but bed pleasure and providing him with food and drink. And no matter how many times she showed him otherwise, he never even remembered, much less learned anything from what she'd done.

Even though she'd passed his test and he even joked with her about it, in the end she had to fight him to allow her to help judge the local disputes. She pointed out how she had delivered the thieves to him, but it made no difference. He had decided she couldn't judge the cases, and no amount of reason or logic was going to dissuade him.

She finally broke down in tears. Rogan was not a man who fell apart at the sight of a woman's tears, but what he hated was her lack of smiles. He seemed to think it was her duty to always be happy and cheerful. After a day and a half of Liana's misery, he relented and said she could sit beside him in the court cases. She had thrown her arms about his neck and kissed him—and then she'd tickled his ribs.

Severn had walked into the Lord's Chamber and seen the two of them rolling about on the floor, Liana's headdress knocked off, her hair cascading about her as she tickled his big brother into helpless laughter. Severn's rage had sobered them immediately.

Severn, Liana thought. She was still amazed that her brother-in-law could cause her so much unhappiness. When she'd first arrived, he'd seemed to be on her side, but as Rogan had changed, so had Severn. Now, it was almost as if he hated her, and he did everything he could to turn Rogan against her. Not that Rogan even mentioned what was going on to Liana. No, she had to rely on Gaby for that information. On the training field Severn taunted his brother, ridiculed him for being led by a woman.

The more Liana heard about what Severn was doing, the more comfort she tried to provide Rogan.

In the evenings she sometimes saw how torn he was, as if he warred inside himself whether he should give in to the pleasures of her solar or stay alone in his brooding chamber.

His brooding chamber caused their second big fight. After he'd spent two nights alone in there, Liana went inside. She didn't knock or ask permission for entry, she just walked in, her heart pounding in her ears. He'd yelled at her. He'd blustered and fumed, but there was something in his eyes that told her he didn't actually mind her invasion.

"What are those?" she'd asked, pointing to the stack of papers on the table.

He'd argued some more, but at last he'd shown her his sketches. Liana didn't know much about war machines, but she knew something about farm machinery and this wasn't all that different. She'd made a few suggestions and they had been good ones.

It had been a lovely evening, just the two of them together in that little room, bent over the papers. Several times Rogan had said, "Like this?" or, "Is this better?" or, "Yes, I think that might work."

As he often did, Severn had ruined the evening. He'd pushed open the half-open door, then stood gaping at the two of them. "I heard she was in here," he'd said softly, "but I didn't believe it. This room was sacred to our brother Rowland and to our father. But now *you* let a woman in here. And for what?" He nodded toward the sketches on the table. "To tell you how to build war machines? Is there nothing of the man left in you?"

Liana was pleased to see that when Severn stomped away, he was scratching his arm furiously. She knew that once again lice were infesting his clothes and she hoped they ate him alive. She turned to her husband. "Rogan . . ." she began.

But he was already on his feet. He left her alone in the room and as far as she knew, he had not visited the room since.

Her heart went out to Rogan as she saw him fight within himself. Part of him wanted the softness and tenderness she offered, but part of him wanted to please his angry brother. He trained and worked many hours during the day, trying to be the leader of the Peregrines, to prove to his men and especially to his brother that he was still worthy of his position as their master. And in the evening he never fully relaxed during the pleasures Liana offered.

She tried her best to keep her rage at Severn under control, but it was difficult. She wrote a letter to her stepmother, asking Helen if she knew of any young heiresses Severn might marry. If she could find a wife for Severn, perhaps he'd leave Rogan to her.

It was the third fight that turned the tables and made Rogan side with Severn against her.

Liana was boiling with rage when she stormed down the stairs into the Lord's Chamber. Severn and Rogan were sitting at the table, calmly eating breakfast but not speaking to each other.

Liana was so angry she could hardly speak. "Your . . . your brother was in bed with three women this morning," she spat at Rogan.

Rogan looked at Severn in wonder. "Three? The most I've ever had was four. I was worn out the next day."

"When was that?" Severn asked, as if Liana weren't there.

"A year ago at the tournament at—"

"Not *him!*" Liana shouted. "Zared! Your little brother, that *child,* spent the night with *three* women."

The two men just stared at her stupidly. She

doubted if they had any idea what was wrong with Zared's being in bed with three women. "I won't have it," she said. "Rogan, you have to stop this."

To further increase her fury, Rogan's eyes began to twinkle. "Yes, I will have to do something."

She advanced on him. "Don't patronize me. That boy looks up to you. He idolizes you. He thinks the sun rises and sets on you and I'm sure he's merely imitating you."

Severn grinned and slapped Rogan's shoulder. "Just imitating his big brother," he said, laughing.

Liana turned on Severn, her anger at him coming to the surface. "At least Rogan is making an effort. But you! You, with a married mistress living in the same house as that innocent child."

Severn was on his feet and glowering down at her. "My life is none of your business," he shouted at her. "And Zared is—"

Rogan stood, cutting his brother off. "We will take care of Zared."

"As you take care of everything else—including your wife?" Severn sneered, then slammed from the room.

Rogan watched his brother go, then sat down heavily in his chair. Severn's words had upset him.

"That man needs a wife," Liana said.

"A wife?" Rogan said. "Iolanthe would tear the woman's eyes out."

He looked so dejected sitting there that she wanted to say something to amuse him. "We'll have to find a woman strong enough to handle Severn and Iolanthe."

"There is no such woman."

She caressed his forehead. "No? I have handled you, and you are stronger than twenty Severns and

Iolanthes." She meant her words as a jest, but Rogan
didn't seem to take them as such. He looked up at her
with eyes glittering with anger.

"No woman controls me," he said under his breath.

"I didn't mean—" she began, but he stood, his
expression still angry.

"No woman controls me or my family. Go back to
your sewing, woman, where you belong." He left her
alone in the room.

He left her alone all that day, that evening, and that
night. She was frantic with worry and she was sure
he'd gone to another woman. "I will kill her so slowly
she will pray for death," Liana seethed as she paced
their chamber.

At midnight she went to Gaby, woke her from
Baudoin's arms, and had Gaby find out where Rogan
was. It didn't take Gaby long to return and tell Liana
that Rogan was getting drunk in the Great Hall with
half a dozen of his men.

Somehow the news made Liana feel very good. He
was as upset about their argument as she was. No
more was he the man who ignored her, who couldn't
pick her out from a group of women.

When at last she went to bed, if she didn't sleep
soundly, she did sleep.

She was awakened before dawn by the unmistakable
sound of steel on steel. "Rogan," she said, her heart
tight with fear. She threw a robe over her nakedness
and began to run.

The Howards had tried to sneak into the Peregrine
castle before dawn. They tossed great hooks over the
parapets and started climbing up the ropes.

It had been so many months since the Howards had
attacked, and the Peregrines had been so involved in
their own internal squabbles, that there had been a

feeling of safety. Watchfulness had lulled; senses were no longer as alert.

Twelve of the twenty Howard attackers were over the wall before the sleepy guards on the parapets heard them. Two Peregrine knights died without ever waking up.

Rogan, in the Great Hall, lying on the floor in a drunken stupor, had difficulty rousing himself. Severn was there before he was fully aware of what was happening.

"You sicken me," Severn said, then tossed his brother a sword and ran out of the room.

Rogan made up for lost time. If his head did not clear instantly, his body remembered its long training. He kicked his men awake and within seconds he was in the courtyard fighting beside Severn and Baudoin.

It didn't take long to kill the Howard attackers, and as Severn meant to slay the last one, Rogan stopped him.

"Why?" he demanded of the man. "What does Oliver Howard want?"

"The woman," the Howard man said. "We were to take her and hold her." The man knew he was going to die. He gave Rogan an insolent look. "He said his younger brother needs a wife and the Peregrine brides make excellent Howard wives."

Rogan killed the man. He thrust his knife into the man's heart and twisted and kept twisting until Severn pulled him away.

"He's dead," Severn said. "They're all dead. As well as four of our men."

Fear was coursing through Rogan's body. If Severn had not been here . . . if he'd been a little drunker . . . if his men hadn't heard . . . They could have had Liana by now. "I want this place searched," he said. "I want every granary, every garderobe, every chest searched. I want to make sure no Howards are here. Go!" he shouted at the men standing near him.

"At last you care about the Howards," Severn said. "But only because of *her*. You have placed all our lives in danger—me, Zared, yourself. You risk what little property we have left because of her. Is it nothing to you that tonight four of your men were killed and a dozen others wounded while you were in a drunken stupor? And why? Because of a quarrel with that woman? You have killed two brothers over a wife. Will it take the deaths of the rest of the Peregrines to satisfy you?"

At that moment Liana came flying down the stairs, long blonde hair streaming behind her, her robe opening to show slim bare legs. She threw herself at Rogan, her arms about his neck. "You're safe," she cried, tears wetting his shoulder. "I was terrified for you."

For a moment Rogan forgot the bloodstained men around him, as well as his scowling brother, and hugged her trembling body to his. It was only luck that she was still here and not taken by Howard's men. He stroked her hair and soothed her. "I'm unhurt," he whispered.

He looked up to see the face of one of his men, one of his father's men, a man who'd followed Rowland into battle, and he saw disgust on the man's face. Disgust that a Peregrine would be standing here in the early dawn, two dead men at his feet, and cooing to a woman.

Over the past few weeks, Rogan knew that his men had sided with him over Severn because Rogan had never slacked in his training. And they hadn't seen the way Rogan sat in the solar with his wife in the evening and listened to women singing. Nor had they seen

Rogan allowing his wife to help him design machines of war.

But now, as Rogan looked into the eyes of his men, he knew their loyalty had just changed. How could they follow a man who, because of a quarrel with his wife, was too drunk to hear an attack? How could he control them? In the village play, the peasants had portrayed him as being "tamed," as a man whose wife had put a collar on him and led him away. At the time, the idea had seemed too absurd to consider, but now he saw some truth in the play.

He had to establish his control before his men or lose their respect forever.

He abruptly pulled Liana from him, then shoved her away. "Get back to the house, woman, where you belong."

Liana had some idea of Rogan's embarrassment. She straightened her shoulders. "I will help. How many wounded are there?" She turned to the man who'd been watching Rogan with so little respect. "Take these men to the kitchen, it'll be warmer there. And fetch—"

Rogan had to stop her. "Obey me!" he bellowed.

"But there are wounded men here."

His men, wounded and well, were watching him intently and Rogan knew that it was now or never. "I married you for your money," he said evenly and loudly enough for all his men to hear, "and not for your advice or your beauty."

Liana felt as if she'd been kicked in the stomach. She wanted to reply, but her throat closed and she couldn't speak. Around her she could feel the men's smirks. Here was a woman who had been put in her place. Slowly, she turned and started back into the castle.

For just a moment Rogan almost went after her, but he didn't. "Get these men up," he said. He'd make it up to her tonight. Maybe a gift. She had liked that little doll from the fair so much, maybe—

"Take them where?" Severn asked.

Rogan saw respect once again in his brother's eyes. "The Great Hall," he said. "And get a leech to sew them up. Then bring me the men who were on guard duty."

"Yes, brother," Severn said, and for a moment put his hand on Rogan's shoulder.

To Rogan, the hand felt heavy with responsibility.

"He did it," Severn said proudly to Iolanthe. "I knew that when we needed him, he'd be there. You should have seen him yesterday morning. 'I married you for your money, not for your advice or your beauty.' That's what he told her. Now maybe she'll stop interfering in Peregrine business."

Io looked at him over her tapestry frame. She'd heard all about what had happened yesterday. "Where did your wise brother sleep last night?"

"I don't know." Severn hesitated. "With his men, maybe. He should have broken the bedroom door down. That woman needs to be taught a lesson."

Io watched Severn scratching. It had been so good when, for a while, he was clean. "You have nearly got the castle back to the way it was. Your brother is sleeping with his men, and I imagine he is as unhappy as he ever was. I don't guess he's smiling now, is he?"

Severn stood and walked toward the window. Zared had said Severn was jealous, and part of him was beginning to wonder if that was correct. Yesterday Severn had won. He'd forced Rogan into publicly denying his wife, into making her retreat from him. And what had he won? The last twenty-four hours had been miserable. He hadn't realized how much Rogan had changed since he'd married that woman.

The old Rogan had returned in full force. On the training field he was a vicious taskmaster. He had broken the arm of one knight who wasn't quick enough. He had gashed the cheek of another. And when Severn had protested, one blow from Rogan had sent him sprawling.

Severn turned back to Io. "Rogan is as angry as he ever was."

Iolanthe could read his thoughts. There wasn't a malicious bone in Severn's body—which is one reason why she loved him. But he was like most men in that he didn't like change. He had loved, worshiped, his older brothers and one by one he'd seen them die until only Rogan was left. And now he was afraid of losing him, too.

"So what are you going to do to get them back together?" Io asked as she couched gold thread onto the needlepoint background.

"Together?" Severn gasped. "Have Rogan lounging about in the solar all afternoon? The place will fall apart. The Howards will kill us in our sleep. They'll—"

"Rogan is going to kill you with work if you do not rectify your interference."

He opened his mouth to contradict her but shut it and sat back down in the chair.

"I guess she's not so bad," he said after a moment. "And maybe the place did need a bit of cleaning." He looked at Io. "All right, a lot of cleaning, but she didn't have to—" He stopped, not knowing what else to say. "She didn't have to take him away so completely," he said at last.

"She loves him," Io said. "That's a fatal thing to happen to a woman." She looked at Severn with love, but he didn't notice. Iolanthe admired this pale, plain Liana, who'd been able to do what Io could not. "Send Liana an invitation to supper, make it from Rogan, then send Rogan an invitation from Liana."

Severn scratched furiously at his shoulder. "Do you think she'll have my clothes washed?"

"If you give her back Rogan, I'm sure she will."

"I will think about it," Severn said softly. "If Rogan gets worse, I'll consider it."

"Does he think he can win me back so easily?" Liana asked Gaby. They were alone in the solar, Liana having sent her other women away. "Does he think that a single invitation from him will make me come crawling back to him? After the way he humiliated me?"

"But, my lady," Gaby said pleadingly, "sometimes men say things they don't mean, and it's been a whole week now. Baudoin said Lord Rogan is worse than he ever was, that he never sleeps or lets the men rest. He doubled the guards on the parapets, and any guard who so much as blinks is flogged."

"Of what concern is that of mine? He has my money; he has what he wants." The deep, deep hurt she'd felt at his words had not abated in the past week. She had been lying to herself in thinking that he cared anything about her. He had married her for her money and money was all he wanted from her. Well he had that now and he no longer had to put up with her. She wouldn't try to come between him and the peasants. She wouldn't nag him to allow her to judge the court cases. In fact, perhaps she'd just take her ladies and go to that other castle he owned, or maybe she'd retire to one of the estates of her dowry—if he could spare the revenue.

"You mean to refuse his invitation?" Gaby asked.

"I will pack a bag full of gold plates and put them on the chair in my place. That should satisfy him. Then he wouldn't have to look at my ugliness."

"But, my lady, I'm sure he didn't—"

Gaby kept talking, but Liana didn't listen. The thought of the gold and her lack of beauty had given her an idea. "Fetch the blacksmith to me."

"My lady?"

"Send the blacksmith to me. I have a job for him to do."

"If you will tell me what it is, I'll—"

"No, this is my secret."

Gaby stood where she was. "Do you mean to accept the invitation?"

"Oh yes," Liana said. "I will accept my husband's invitation and he will get my gold and he will not have to look upon my plain face."

Gaby still didn't move. "Sometimes it is better to forgive and forget than to keep on with the fight. Marriage is—"

"*My* marriage is based on gold and nothing else. Now, go!"

"Yes, my lady," Gaby said meekly, and left the solar.

Three hours later, Liana was dressing to attend the supper her husband had invited her to. Joice was helping her, as Liana didn't want Gaby's disapproval —and disapproval she knew it would be.

Nor did she want the Lady's disapproval. As Liana mounted the solar stairs, she'd seen that the Lady's door was unlocked and standing ajar. "I will always be here when you need me," the Lady had said, and it was true. Whenever she'd come to a crisis with Rogan, the door had been open.

But tonight Liana did not want to talk to the Lady, because Liana did not want to be dissuaded from what she was about to do. Her hurt was too deep and too raw to do anything else. Was she to say she forgave him? If she did, what would he do to her next time? He could humiliate her daily and expect her to forgive him anything.

So Liana ignored the invitation that the Lady's open door signaled and instead dressed with Joice's aid.

"Get out of here!" Rogan bellowed to Severn. They were in one of the rooms over the kitchen, a room that had once been occupied by a Day. It was already dirty, since no cleaning had been done in a week, and a big rat gnawed on a bone in a dark corner.

"I thought you might like to wear something that stank a little less, that's all. And maybe shave."

"Why?" Rogan asked belligerently. "To eat with a woman? You were right. It was better before she interfered. I think I'll send her to Bevan."

"And how many men must leave here to protect her? The Howards will—"

"The Howards can have her, for all I care." Even as Rogan said it, he winced. Damn the bitch to hell, anyway! He'd tried to see her after what he'd said, but she'd locked the door against him. His first impulse had been to beat the door down and show her who was master in his home, but then he'd felt like a fool for caring. Let her stay behind the locked door if she wanted, it didn't matter to him. He'd told the truth when he'd said he'd married her for her money.

But during the past week he'd . . . well, he'd remembered things. He'd remembered her laughing, remembered the way she threw her arms about his neck when he'd pleased her, remembered her opinions and suggestions, remembered her warm, willing body at night. He remembered the things she caused to happen: music, good food, a courtyard that he could walk across without stepping in a pile of horse manure, the day at the fair. He remembered holding her hand. He remembered watching Gaby wash her hair.

He glared at Severn. "Since when have you cared whether I dressed for my wife or not?"

"Since there was sand in my bread two days ago and since Io started being less than warm to me."

"Send her back to her husband, and I'll send . . ."—he could hardly say her name—". . . I'll send Liana," he said softly, "away."

"Probably be better for both of us," Severn said. "A lot quieter, certainly. And we could get some work done. And we wouldn't have to worry about the Howards attacking us to get at our women. But on the other hand, the men have been complaining about the bread. Perhaps . . ." He trailed off.

Rogan looked at the dark green velvet tunic Severn still held. Perhaps, since she had sent him an invitation, it meant she was ready to apologize for locking him out of their room and for allowing sand in the bread and rats in the rooms. And if she was ready to apologize, perhaps he was ready to forgive her.

Liana waited until all of Rogan's men were seated in the Great Hall and Rogan and Severn and Zared sat at the high table. Joice lowered the veil over her mistress's face.

"You are sure, my lady?" Joice asked grimly, her disapproval showing in her tight mouth.

"More than sure," Liana said, and put her shoulders back.

Every man and the few women in the Hall were quiet as Liana entered, Joice holding her long, fur-trimmed train. Liana's face was covered by a veil that reached to her waist.

Solemnly, slowly, she walked toward the high table and stood there waiting until Severn nudged Rogan, and Rogan stood and pulled her chair out for her. As Liana sat down, still the room was silent, every eye on the master and mistress.

Rogan seemed to have no idea what to do to break the silence. "Would you like some wine?" he asked at last, his voice ringing in the high-ceilinged stone room.

Very slowly, Liana put her arms under her veil and raised it. There was an audible gasp through the room as they saw her. About Liana's face, suspended from strings attached to her headdress, were coins: gold coins, silver coins, copper coins. In each one a hole had been punched, a string attached, and then fastened to her headdress.

As the astonished crowd watched, Liana took a pair of scissors and cut a silver coin from in front of her face. "Will this be enough to pay for the wine, my lord?" She cut off a gold coin. "Will this cover the cost of the beef?"

Rogan gaped at her, looking at the coins she cut away.

"Do not look so fearful, my lord," she said loudly. "I will not eat so much that you will be exposed to my ugliness. I am sure the sight of the money pleases you more than my plain face."

Rogan's face turned cold. He did not say a word to her, but rose and left the Hall.

Zared turned to Severn, who looked as if he might be ill. "Eat up, Severn. Tomorrow we'll probably get rocks in our bread and Rogan is going to work all of you into the grave on the training field," Zared said cheerfully. "You were smart to try to keep Liana from interfering."

Liana, with all the grace and dignity she could muster, left the Hall.

CHAPTER
FIFTEEN

N o!" Liana snapped at Gaby and Joice. "Don't put
that there. Nor over there. And certainly not there!"

Joice backed out of the room as soon as possible,
but Gaby stayed in the solar, looked at the back of
Liana's head, and bit her tongue. Not that she'd kept
her mouth shut in the two weeks since that awful
supper when Lady Liana had appeared wearing the
coins, but she'd learned it did no good. "He has what
he wanted," was all Lady Liana would say to Gaby's
pleadings that she and Rogan talk to each other.

And Lord Rogan was worse than his wife. Gaby had
wheedled Baudoin into broaching the subject to the
lord, but Rogan had nearly put a pike through
Baudoin's belly.

So, because of the anger between the master and
mistress, the whole castle, as well as the village, was
suffering. The bakers refused to deliver fresh bread
because Rogan refused to pay them, and Liana refused
to have anything to do with the household. So there
was, once again, sand in the bread. The courtyard was

full of manure because no one ordered the men to clean it. The peasants were hungry. The moat, with only a foot of water in it, already contained half a dozen rotting cow carcasses. Whereas this had been the normal way of life before, now everyone complained. The men complained about the lice and the fleas in their clothes and the manure under their feet. They complained about Rogan's temper. They complained about Lady Liana not doing her job properly. (No one seemed to remember the way they'd fought her when she first arrived.)

All in all, after two weeks there wasn't a person within a ten-mile radius who wasn't affected by this argument between the lord and his lady.

"My lady——" Gaby began.

"I have nothing to say to you," Liana snapped. Two weeks had done nothing to calm her temper. She had made every effort to please her husband, to be a wife to him, and he had ignored her and humiliated her in public. He, a man of great beauty, might think that the plainer people of the world had no feelings about their lack of looks, but he was wrong. If he thought she was so ugly, then she'd spare him having to look at her.

"It's not me," Gaby said. "The lady Iolanthe asks to see you."

Liana's head came up. "Severn has had his way. He has won and he has his brother the way he was. I see no reason to see Severn's mistress."

Gaby gave a bit of a smile. "The gossip is that Lord Severn and his . . . the Lady Iolanthe are quarreling also. Perhaps she'd like to commiserate with you."

Liana wanted to talk to someone. Gaby constantly preached forgiving Rogan for everything. She thought Liana should go to him and apologize, but Liana was sure he'd reject her. How could a woman as plain-faced as she was have any influence on a man like

Rogan? And how could someone as dazzling as Iolanthe understand Liana's problem? "Tell her I cannot accept," Liana said.

"But, my lady, she has invited you to her apartments. It's said that she's never invited anyone inside there before."

"Oh?" Liana said. *"I* am to go to her? I, the lady of the manor, am to visit my brother-in-law's married mistress? Tell her no."

Gaby left the room, and Liana looked back at her tapestry frame. She was seething over the presumption of the woman, but part of her was also curious. What did the beautiful Iolanthe have to say to her?

The invitation was reissued daily for three days, and each time Liana refused it. But on the fourth day she looked out the window and into the courtyard and saw one of the Days, her generous bosom pushing against the coarse wool of her greasy dress.

Liana turned to Joice. "Fetch my red brocade gown, the one with the cloth-of-gold underskirt. I am going visiting."

An hour later Liana was dressed so that she knew she looked her best. She had to go outside and cross the courtyard to reach the stairs to Iolanthe's apartments, and she could feel every eye on her. But she looked straight ahead and ignored all of them.

When she at last reached the apartment and a maid opened the door, it took Liana a moment to recover her composure—and close her gaping mouth. Never had she seen a room of such wealth. There were gold and silver-gilt dishes everywhere. There were *rugs* on the floor, deep-piled, intricately patterned carpets. The walls were hung with silk tapestries of delicate scenes and so intricately woven, a flower no bigger than a thumbnail had a dozen colors in it. The beamed ceilings were painted with pastoral scenes.

The windows had leaded panes with colored-glass inserts that shone like jewels.

And in the room were carved chairs with cushioned seats, carved sewing frames, beautiful chests inlaid with ivory. There was nowhere she could look that was not of exquisite beauty.

"Welcome," Iolanthe said, and in her silver gown she was the most beautiful object in the room.

"I . . ." Liana took a breath to recover herself. "You had something to say to me?" Earlier, Liana had thought of telling this woman how immoral she was and how she would spend eternity in hell for being married to one man and living in sin with another, but in Iolanthe's presence, no such words came to Liana.

"Won't you have a seat? I have had something prepared for us to eat."

Liana took the seat offered and sipped watered wine from a ruby-studded gold chalice.

"You'll have to go to him," Iolanthe said. "He's too stubborn to give in to you, and besides that, I doubt if he knows how."

Liana set the chalice down with a thunk and stood. "I'll not listen to this. He has insulted me repeatedly, and this is the final straw." She started for the door.

"Wait!" Iolanthe called. "Please return. That was rude of me."

Liana turned back.

Io smiled at her. "Forgive me. It has been difficult lately. Severn has been in the worst temper. Of course I've told him this is entirely his fault, that if he hadn't been so jealous of his brother, Rogan would never have said he'd married you for your money and you would never have had to resort to the veil of coins."

Liana sat back down. "True," she said, and picked up her wine goblet again. "He said, in front of his men, that he couldn't bear my ugliness."

Iolanthe stared at the blonde woman. So, she thought, it wasn't the money. It was that Rogan had insulted his wife's looks. Rogan and Severn were such divine-looking men that it was easy to see how a woman could feel intimidated by them. Every morning Io studied her own reflection in the mirror and, at her age, she was teaching herself to smile without crinkling her eyes. She lived in terror of the day when Severn no longer believed her to be beautiful. She couldn't imagine how she'd feel if Severn said that he wanted her husband's money and not her person.

"I see," Io said at last.

"Yes," Liana said. "And *I* see, too. I thought I could make him love me. I thought I could make myself indispensable to him, but he never wanted me. Nor did anyone else want me here. It's ironic. My stepmother tried to tell me this, but I wouldn't listen. I thought I knew more than a woman who'd had two husbands. She was right. Even my maid Joice was right. Joice said men didn't want wives. In my case not only my husband didn't want me, but his brother didn't, his mistresses, his men—no one wanted me except the Lady, and now even her door is locked against me."

Iolanthe listened to this speech of self-pity and understood it very well. As long as a woman felt desirable, she could feel confident. She could set his bed, with him and his mistress in it, on fire; she could dare to make a wager that he would lose; she could tempt his wrath by countermanding his orders for the castle staff. But when a woman felt undesirable, much of her strength left her.

Io had no idea what to do. Never in all of time could she hope to get Rogan to go to Liana. Rogan was a stubborn man who had no idea what was good for him. He wouldn't like thinking any woman had ever had any influence on him. "Who is the Lady?" Io asked, stalling for time while she thought about this problem.

At first Io barely listened to Liana's explanation, but something in her words caught her attention. "She lives above the solar?"

"In a single room that is almost always locked. But she seems to sense when I'm troubled, for then the door is open. She has been my greatest friend since I arrived. She told me about Jeanne Howard. She told me that men do not fight battles over timid women— or over ugly women," Liana added.

"Is she an older woman, quite pretty, with soft brown hair?"

"Yes. Who is she? I've meant to ask her, but every time I see her—" She broke off as she watched Iolanthe ring a little silver bell. A maid appeared, Io whispered something to her, and the maid disappeared.

Iolanthe stood. "Would you mind if we went to this room and met your Lady?"

"The room is locked. It has been since I . . . since I went to supper with my husband."

"I have sent my maid to fetch the key. Shall we go?"

Liana's lone appearance earlier had slowed movement in the courtyard, but when Io and Liana appeared together, everyone came to a halt and stood gaping at the two women. Iolanthe was a rare enough sight, but her with another woman was impossible to believe.

Liana ignored the staring people both inside and outside the castle and led Iolanthe to the locked door above the solar. "When she doesn't want to be disturbed, she keeps the door locked. I think we should respect her privacy."

Io didn't say anything, but when her maid reappeared, a big key in hand, she inserted it into the lock.

"I don't think—" Liana began, but broke off. The room, which had been the one clean place in the castle when she arrived, was bare. No, not bare, for she could see, under years of cobwebs and rodent droppings, the Lady's furniture. There was the cushioned bench Liana had sat on. There was the Lady's tapestry frame. The windows that had had sunlight streaming through them were broken, and a dead bird lay on the floor.

"I don't understand," Liana whispered. "Where is she?"

"Dead. Many years ago."

Liana crossed herself even as she denied this. "Are you saying she's a ghost? That's not possible. I talked to her. She's as real as you or I. She told me things, things other people didn't know." Her eyes widened.

"I've heard she does. I've never seen her, nor has Severn, and I don't know if Rogan has or not, but several other people have. She seems to love helping people in need. Years ago a maid who was pregnant was about to throw herself into the moat when she heard the Lady, as you call her, singing and spinning. The Lady talked her out of suicide. Didn't you wonder why no one lived in these rooms? Half the men refused even to go into the solar to fetch the birds, and *no* one would come up here."

Liana was trying to take this in. "No one told me. No one so much as hinted."

"I guess they thought your cleaning would do away with her. She never harms anyone. As ghosts go, she is benign."

Liana walked through the thick dust on the floor to the tapestry frame. On it was an old, unfinished piece of work of a lady and a unicorn—what the Lady had been sewing when Liana had visited. Liana suddenly felt as if she'd lost a very dear friend. "Who is she? And why does she haunt the Peregrines?"

"She is Severn's grandmother, Rogan and Zared's too. She was Jane, the first wife of old Giles Peregrine. Their son was John, Severn's father. After Jane died, Giles married Bess Howard and it was her family who said Jane had never been legally married to Giles and therefore her son and his children were bastards. This castle and Bevan belonged to Jane's family; she grew up here."

"And so she comes back here to haunt."

"Years after her death, she was in this room when her son John arrived home after the king declared him illegitimate. He locked the door on her and never unlocked it again. Only she unlocks it now. Some people say John was a fool, that his mother came to tell him something and he wouldn't listen."

"She probably wanted to tell him to stay away from the village girls," Liana said bitterly.

"No," Io said. "Everyone believed she wanted to tell him where the parish registers were."

"What registers?"

"John could never prove that his parents had been married. All the witnesses to the marriage either died or mysteriously disappeared and no one could find the registers that recorded the marriage. Most people believed the Howards had destroyed them, but some people said old Giles had hidden them from his grasping second wife." Io smiled. "If you see your Lady again, you might ask her where the registers are. If there were proof the marriage did take place, perhaps the king would restore the Peregrine estates to Rogan and Severn and this feud with the Howards would stop."

Liana wondered if Rogan would love her if she

found the registers. No, probably not. She'd still be plain-faced even if she were the richest woman in the world. "We should leave," she said, "and lock the door. She should have her privacy."

They left the room. Io locked the door and handed the key to her maid, who had been quietly waiting outside.

"Will you go to him?" Io asked.

Liana knew who she meant. "I cannot. He does not want me; he wants gold. Now that he has it, he should be content."

"Gold makes a cold bed partner."

A lump formed in Liana's throat. "He has his Days. Now, will you excuse me? I have a bit of embroidery that needs finishing."

They walked down the stairs to the solar, and Iolanthe bid Liana farewell.

That evening Severn came to Iolanthe's apartments. He was limping and there was a blood-dripping gash on the side of his head. Io motioned to her maid and soon Io was bathing his head with a linen cloth.

"I am going to kill my brother," Severn said through his teeth. "That is the only way to stop him. Did you talk any sense into that wife of his?"

"I had as much success talking to her as you have had with your brother."

"Watch that!" Severn said, wincing. "I don't want new wounds. At least I can understand Rogan. He's been very tolerant of that woman, allowing her to sit by him while he judged the courts, letting her do what she could in the village, even giving her a full day in bed."

"He has been *most* generous," Io said sarcastically.

"He has, actually. I never thought he'd be so generous with a wife."

"What did you think? That your sweet-tempered brother would drop her in this filthy castle with servants who ridiculed her, that he'd ignore her, that he wouldn't remember what she looked like until she set him on fire?"

"Women!" Severn muttered. "You are such illogical creatures."

"My logic is fine, it's your brother who—"

Severn pulled her into his lap and kissed her neck. "Let's forget my brother."

She pushed away from him and stood. "How many weeks has it been since you had a bath?"

"You never used to care whether I bathed or not."

"I thought horse manure was your natural scent," she shot back at him.

Severn stood up. "This is all that woman's fault. If she—"

"If *you* hadn't interfered, things would be fine now. What are you going to do to make up for what you've done?"

"We've been through this, remember? I was willing to admit that I'd been . . . well, a little overzealous with Rogan, so at *your* suggestion I sent them invitations to supper. And you saw where that went, didn't you? That stupid bitch showed up wearing coins. Rogan should have accepted her offer of payment. What he should have done was—"

"He *should* have told her she's beautiful," Io interrupted. "She thinks your oversexed brother doesn't desire her. I can't imagine why. He'll bed anything that's even three-quarters female."

Severn smiled proudly. "Great cocksman, isn't he?"

"Let's not go into my opinions of your brother. You

have to get Rogan to tell Liana he thinks she's beautiful and he desires her above all other women."

"Sure. And I'll move a few oceans, too. You want London moved while I'm at it? You've never tried to get Rogan to do something he doesn't want to do."

"Is he back sleeping with his Days now?"

Severn grimaced. "No, and I think that's half his problem. This is the longest he's gone without a female since . . ." He thought a moment. ". . . since the Howards took his first wife. Don't give me that look," he said to Io. "My brother can handle women whether he's married to them or not. Maybe he just doesn't want a woman right now. I can understand that, what with the way his wife has behaved. Wearing those coins was the last straw."

"It's up to you," Io said sweetly. "Why don't you get Rogan to send Liana back to her father, get rid of her completely. Then you could bring in a wagonload of beautiful, nubile young girls so your brother could have a dozen per night."

"And which one will see that we have pies to eat?" Severn muttered. "Damn you, Io! And damn that Liana. Damn *all* women! Why can't you leave a man alone? Rogan only married her to get money. Why did he have to . . . to . . ."

"To what?" Io asked innocently. "Fall in love with her? Begin to need her?"

"That isn't what I meant at all. Damn both of them! Somebody ought to lock them in a room together and throw away the key. Both of them make me sick." His head came up.

"What is it?"

"Nothing. Just a thought."

"Tell me," Io urged.

It was a while before Severn began talking.

* * *

That same evening Severn sent a peace offering to Liana. She sat alone in her solar with her ladies, as she did every evening. Usually, she was undisturbed by anyone from the castle—as if she didn't exist, or as if they wished she didn't exist—so she was very surprised when a scarred old knight brought up a jug of wine and said it was from Lord Severn to his beautiful sister-in-law.

"Do you think it's poisoned?" Liana asked Gaby.

"Perhaps with a love potion," Gaby answered. She'd never give up trying to reason with Liana.

The wine was spicy and warm and Liana drank more than she meant to. "I suddenly feel very tired," she said. She was so tired that her head felt too heavy to hold up.

It was at that moment that Severn entered the solar. All of Liana's women perked up at the sight of the handsome blond giant, but Severn had eyes only for Liana.

Gaby was looking at her mistress in alarm as Liana's eyes closed and her head lolled against the back of her chair. "I'm afraid something's wrong."

"She'll sleep it off," Severn said, elbowed Gaby out of his way, then picked Liana up.

"My lord!" Gaby gasped. "You cannot—"

"I *am,*" Severn answered as he carried the sleeping Liana from the room and started up the spiral stairs. He went up past the bedrooms above the solar, up another flight until he came to a heavy iron-clad oak door. He shifted Liana, tossing her over his shoulder while he took a key hanging at the end of a chain suspended from his belt and opened the door.

It was a small room with a garderobe off to one side and another heavy, barred door leading out to the walk along the top of the parapets. The room was usually used for housing guards, but today the guards were gone. Sometimes the room was used as a prison and that's what Severn wanted it for.

Severn pushed the door open and stood for a moment while his eyes adjusted to the dim light. Lying on the bed, sound asleep, was Rogan and for a moment Severn reconsidered his plan. But then a couple of fleas began scurrying about on his back and he knew that what he was doing was right. He dumped his sister-in-law on the bed beside his brother and gouged at the fleas.

"There," he said as he looked down at the two of them. "You can stay in here until we have some peace."

CHAPTER
SIXTEEN

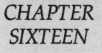

It took Liana a while to wake up in the morning. It was as if she couldn't open her eyes. She stretched her arms, then her legs, as she luxuriated in the soft warmth of the mattress.

"If you want something to eat, you better get up and get it."

Her eyes flew open to see Rogan sitting at a small table devouring chicken, cheese, and bread.

"What are you doing here?" she demanded. "Why have you brought me here? The wine! You drugged it."

"My brother did. My brother, whose days on this earth are limited, drugged the wine."

"And he brought me here?"

"He brought both of us here while we were sleeping."

Liana sat up and looked about the spare little room: a bed, a table and two chairs, and a candle stand. "He has betrayed us to the Howards," she said softly. "Does he mean to turn the castle over to them?"

Rogan looked at her as if she were the village idiot. "My brother may be stupid at times as well as stubborn, but he is not a traitor."

"Then why has he done this?"

Rogan looked back at the food.

Liana got out of bed. "Why has he drugged us and put us in here?"

"Who knows? Now, eat."

Liana felt her temper rising. She went to the doors and pulled on them, then beat her fists against them and shouted to be released, but no one came. She went to each of the two narrow arrow slits and shouted down from them, but no one answered. She turned back to Rogan. "How can you eat? How long are we to be prisoners? How do we get out of here?"

"My father made this room to keep prisoners. We cannot get out."

"Until your stupid, overbearing brother lets us out, that is. Why did I ever marry into a family like this? Do any of you men have any sense?"

Rogan just looked at her with hard eyes, and Liana immediately regretted her words. "I . . ." she began.

He put his hand up. "You may return to your father as soon as we are released from here."

He pushed away from the table and went to stand by the narrow window. She walked beside him. "Rogan, I . . ."

He walked away from her.

The day was spent in silence and anger. Liana looked at Rogan and remembered his telling her that her money meant everything to him. So be it, she thought. She would return to her father or retire to one of her dower estates and live without the Peregrine family, with their horses' skulls hanging over the mantel.

Food was lowered to them in a cloth bundle that would fit through the arrow slit. Rogan took the food and yelled up at Severn about what he planned to do to him when he was released. Rogan took his food to the other side of the room and refused to sit at the table with Liana.

Night came and they still were not speaking. Liana lay down on the bed and wondered where Rogan planned to sleep. She started to protest when he lay down beside her, his back to her, but she didn't. She just made sure she wasn't touching him.

But as the early morning sun touched the arrow slit, Liana woke to find herself held tightly in her husband's arms. She forgot about feuds and arguments and kissed his sleep-softened mouth.

Rogan woke instantly and kissed her with all the hunger he felt. After the kiss, they were both lost and there was a frenzy of clothes being discarded as they frantically sought each other's skin. They came together fast and furiously, with a passion that had built up over the past two weeks.

Afterward, they lay in each other's arms, plastered together by sweaty skin, clinging to one another. Liana's first impulse was to ask if Rogan really thought she was ugly and if he actually meant to send her away, but she refrained.

"I saw the ghost," she said at last.

"In the chamber below us?"

"She's the Lady I thought was Iolanthe. Remember I told you she was older than Severn? She told me about Jeanne Howard."

He didn't answer her, and Liana turned in his arms to look at him. "You've seen her, too, haven't you?" she asked after a moment.

"Of course not. There is no ghost. It's just a—"

"A what? When did you see her? Was she sewing or spinning?"

He took a while to answer. "Sewing. The tapestry with the unicorn."

"Did you ever tell anyone?"

"Not until now."

His words made Liana feel triumphant. "When did you see her? What did she say to you?"

His voice was soft. "It was after Oliver Howard took . . . her."

"Jeanne."

"Yes, that one," Rogan answered. "The woman came to me and told me she wanted Howard, that she carried his brat. She asked me to stop the feud. I should have killed the bitch with my own hands."

"But you couldn't."

"I didn't, anyway. I returned here to get supplies—we'd been fighting the Howards for a year—and early one morning I shot an arrow to test a bow and the wind caught the arrow and carried it into a window over the solar. At least, that's what I thought at the time. I also thought I heard a woman scream. I went to the solar, then to the rooms above. No one had lived in them for years because of the stories of the ghost. My father used to curse her because when he had guests, she always appeared and frightened them."

"Were you frightened when you went to get your arrow?"

"I was too angry then at the Howards to care about a ghost. I'd lost my two brothers, and every arrow was needed."

"Was she there?"

She saw Rogan smile slightly. "I thought a ghost would be . . . foggy, I guess. She was so real-looking. She had my arrow and she gave me a scolding, said I'd nearly hit her. At the time I never thought about the fact that I had been shooting away from the castle walls."

"What did you talk about?"

"It was odd, but I talked to her as I've never talked to anyone else."

"Me, too. She knew so much about me. Did you talk about Jeanne?"

"Yes. She told me my wife was not the one."

She looked at him. "The one for what?"

"I don't know. It made sense when I was with her, but none whatever when I left. I guess it had something to do with the poem."

Liana's eyes widened. "What poem?"

"I haven't thought of it in years. Actually, it seems to be more of a riddle. Let's see . . .

> *"When the red and white make black*
> *When the black and gold become one*
> *When the one and the red unite*
> *Then shall you know."*

Liana lay quietly in Rogan's arms and thought about the riddle. "What does it mean?"

"I have no idea. Sometimes I used to lay in bed and think about it, but I never came up with anything."

"What does Severn think? Or Zared?"

"I never asked either of them."

She pushed away to look at him. "Never asked? But it could have something to do with the parish registers. The Lady is your grandmother, and if anyone knows where the registers are, she does."

He frowned. "The woman is a ghost. She's been dead a long time. Maybe I didn't see her and I dreamed the riddle."

255

"*I* didn't dream the story about you and Jeanne Howard. The Lady told me how beautiful Jeanne was and how much you loved her."

"I hardly knew the Howard bitch, and I don't remember her as being especially good to look at. Certainly nothing like Iolanthe."

Liana pulled the sheet over her bare breasts and sat up. "Oh, so now it's Iolanthe you want. You could get money *and* beauty."

Rogan's confusion showed on his handsome face. "Iolanthe is a bitch. I'm sure she's the one who planned this." He motioned to the locked door.

"Why? In an attempt to get me to forgive you for telling me before your men that I was hideously ugly?"

Rogan sat up, his mouth dropping open. "I never said any such thing."

"You did! You said you married me for my money, not for my advice or my beauty."

Rogan's confusion deepened. "I only spoke the truth. I didn't even see you before the wedding, except when I didn't know who you were, so how could I have married you for anything besides money?"

Liana could feel tears of frustration coming to her eyes. "I married you because I thought you . . . that you desired me. You kissed me when you didn't know I had any money."

Rogan had never made an effort to understand the female mind and now he knew why. "I also kissed you when I knew you were rich." His voice was rising as he got out of bed and leaned over her. "I kissed you after you interfered between me and the peasants. I kissed you after you wheedled me into seeing a play that made me look like a fool. I kissed you—"

"Because I'm your wife and for no other reason," she said. "You told everyone you thought I was ugly.

Maybe I'm not as beautiful as Iolanthe or as pretty as your first wife, but there are some men who've said I was quite pleasing to look at."

Rogan threw up his hands in exasperation. "You're not bad when you're not sniveling."

Liana started to cry in earnest at that. She lay down in bed, her knees drawn up, and cried so hard her shoulders shook.

As Rogan looked down at her, at first he felt nothing but anger. She was accusing him of something, but he wasn't sure what. She was making it seem that he was in the wrong for what he'd said. He had merely told the truth and he had said it to keep her from stepping between him and his men. What in the world did his words have to do with her looks? And *desire?* Hadn't he just proved this morning that he desired her? And damnation, he hadn't touched another woman in two whole weeks. Two long, long weeks!

He knew he had every right to be angry with her. *He* should be the one being comforted, but as he watched her cry, he felt something inside himself soften. When he was a boy he'd cried just as she was doing now and his big brothers had kicked him and laughed at him.

He sat on the bed by her head. "Tell me . . . what's wrong," he said hesitantly, feeling awkward and embarrassed.

She didn't answer but just cried harder.

After a moment he lifted her and pulled her onto his lap and held her close. Her tears wet his shoulder as he stroked her hair away from her face. "What's wrong?" he asked again.

"You think I'm ugly. I'm not beautiful like you or Severn or Zared or Iolanthe, but the jongleurs have written poems to my beauty."

Rogan started to say that for money anyone would do anything, but he wisely caught himself. "Not as beautiful as me, eh? Or Severn? I might agree with you about me, but we own pigs better-looking than Severn."

"Better-looking than me, too, no doubt," she cried anew.

"I think you're prettier now than when I first saw you."

Liana sniffed and lifted her head to look at him. "What does that mean?"

"I don't know." He smoothed her hair back. "When I saw you at the church, I thought you were a pale little rabbit and I couldn't tell you from the other women. But now . . ." He looked in her eyes. "Now I find you quite pleasant to look at. I have . . . thought about you these past weeks."

"I have thought about you every minute of every day." She clutched him to her. "Oh, Rogan, tell me anything about me, tell me I'm stupid, tell me that I'm a great nuisance and a bother, but please don't tell me I'm ugly."

He held her close. "You should never tell your secrets to a person. They'll use them against you."

"But I trust you."

Rogan couldn't help but feel that her trust was a burden and a responsibility. He held her away from him. "I will tell you that you are the most beautiful of women if you will not unman me before my men."

It was Liana's turn to be shocked. "Me? Never would I do such a thing. *Never!*"

"You countermanded my orders for the peasants."

"Yes, but you were flogging innocent people."

"You tried to burn me in my bed."

"But you were in bed with another woman," she said indignantly.

"You seduce me away from my work with sweetmeats and music and pretty smiles."

She smiled at him as his words convinced her of how right she was to have married him.

"And you disobeyed my orders before my men."

"When?"

"The morning the Howards attacked."

"I was merely——"

"Interfering," he said sternly. "It wasn't any of your business. If I hadn't been drunk, you might have——" He stopped. He didn't want to tell her that while he lay in a drunken stupor, the Howards might have taken her prisoner.

"I might have what?"

His face changed, and Liana could see he was hiding something. "What might I have done?"

Rogan moved away from her and got out of bed. "If that damned brother of mine doesn't send us food, I'll hang him after burning him."

"If you hadn't been drunk, I might have what?" She wrapped a sheet around herself and followed his nude form into the garderobe. Even as he began to use the urinal, she didn't hesitate. "Might have what?"

Rogan grimaced. "If I ever capture a Howard spy and want information, I'll send you to him."

"Might have what?" she asked again.

"Been taken," he snapped, turning back to the room.

"The Howards wanted me?" Liana whispered.

Rogan was angrily pulling on his braies. "The Howards seem to always want what the Peregrines have: our land, our castles, our women."

"We could make them a gift of the Days." Rogan did not find humor in her words. She went to him and put her arms about his neck. "You were so angry that morning because the Howards threatened to take me? Rogan, you *do* love me."

"I don't have time for love. Get dressed. Severn may come in."

She let the sheet fall off her body so that her bare breasts were against his chest. "Rogan, I love you."

"Humph! You haven't spoken to me in weeks. You've made everyone's life miserable. Even Zared's room has rats in it. And I'm so light from lack of decent food, my horse doesn't know me. My life was better when no woman said she loved me." What he said did not agree with how tightly he held her.

"Severn has taught me something," she said. "I swear to you that never again will I leave you alone. If you hurt me—and I've no doubt you will do so often—I promise I will tell you why I am angry. Never again will I shut myself away from you."

"It's not me who matters, but the men need decent food and—"

She stood on tiptoe to kiss him. "It is you who matters to me. Rogan, I will never betray you as Jeanne once did. Even if the Howards were to take me, I would still love you."

"The Howards will never take another Peregrine," he said fiercely.

"And I am now a Peregrine?" she asked, smiling.

"An odd one, but a Peregrine more or less," he said reluctantly.

She hugged him and didn't see the way Rogan smiled into her hair, the way he closed his eyes as he held her. He didn't like to think how much he'd missed her in the past few days or how much her frivolous chatter had come to mean to him. He had lived his life without her and done very well, but she had entered his life meekly, then literally set him on fire. Nothing had been the same since. Pleasure, leisure, softness, had never been part of his life. But this snippet of a girl had introduced them all into his life and it was amazing how quickly he'd adapted.

He pulled away from her, her face held in his big hands. "I think my stupid brother locked us in here to get you to clean his room and to talk to the bakers."

"Oh? And who is to persuade me to do what he wants?"

"Perhaps I can," Rogan said suggestively, and swung her into his arms. "You told everyone we once spent a whole day in bed. Now you shall make your lie true."

They made love to each other long and slowly, their first needy passion already spent. They explored each other's bodies with their hands and tongues, and when they at last came together, it was leisurely, slowly, caressingly. Liana had no idea how Rogan watched her, how he wanted to give pleasure to her, how he wanted her to enjoy their lovemaking.

Afterward, they lay in each other's arms and held one another.

"Do we hang your brother or kiss his feet?" Liana whispered.

"Hang him," Rogan said firmly. "If there was an attack—"

Liana rubbed her thigh over his. "If there were an attack, you'd be too weak to fight, so it wouldn't matter."

"You are a disrespectful wench. You ought to be beaten."

"By whom?" she asked insolently. "Surely not the worn-out oldest Peregrine."

"I'll show you who is worn out," he said, rolling over on her, making Liana giggle.

But a thud on the floor near them caught Rogan's attention. Immediately, he covered Liana's body with his as he looked about for the cause of the noise. "At last, my damned-to-hell brother has sent us food." He scurried off Liana, out of bed, and went to the package that Severn had managed to swing through the narrow arrow slit and then release so it dropped on the floor.

"You're more interested in food than in me?" she asked.

"At the moment, yes." He brought the food to the bed and they ate there. When bread crumbs dropped on Liana's bare breasts, Rogan licked them off.

They stayed in bed together all day. Liana got Rogan to tell her about his life, about when he was a boy, about the things he'd dreamed about and thought about as a child. She couldn't be sure, but she didn't think he'd ever really talked to anyone before in his life.

At sundown Liana mentioned using some of her dowry wealth to add on to Moray Castle. Rogan was speechless with horror at the idea. "This is not Peregrine land," he said. "The Howards took—"

"Yes, yes, I know. But you have now lived here two generations. Our children will make the third. What if it takes another five generations to get the Peregrine lands back? Will all of them have to live in a place where the roof leaks? Or live in a place this small? We could add a wing to the south—a proper wing, with paneled walls. We could add a chapel and—"

"No, no, no," Rogan said, standing up and glaring down at her in bed. "I'll not put money in this puny place. I'll wait until I have the lands the Howards stole."

"And until then you'll spend every penny that I brought you for making war?" Liana's eyes blazed. "You married me so you can wage war?"

Rogan started to yell that yes, that's why he'd married her, but his eyes changed. "I married you because of your beauty that surpasses all other women's," he said softly. "Including my first wife."

Liana looked up at him, her mouth open in astonishment, then she leaped from the bed and threw herself at him, her legs about his waist, her arms about his neck. "My beautiful husband, I love you so much," she cried.

Rogan hugged her tightly. "I will spend the money how I see fit."

"Yes, of course, and as an obedient wife I would never contradict you, but just let me tell you of my ideas for enlargement."

Rogan groaned. "First you part me from my women, then you burden me with a bunch of red-haired brats, and now you propose to tell me how to spend the money I have worked so hard for."

"Worked so hard for!" she said. "You didn't even attend the wedding feast I had planned so carefully. And you insulted my stepmother."

"She needed insulting. She needs a hand applied to her backside."

"And you'd like to do it?" Liana asked archly.

"I wouldn't want to touch her," he said softly, looking at Liana in the fading light. "Now, come to the table because my bound-for-hell brother has sent down supper."

They spent the night in each other's arms, and as they fell asleep, Rogan murmured that he'd "think about" enlarging Moray Castle and Liana felt as if she'd won a great battle.

When she awoke in the morning, she looked up to see Rogan staring stonily straight ahead. She propped herself up on one elbow to follow his line of vision and saw the door to their room standing open. Liana didn't know when any sight had depressed her so much.

"We could close it again," Liana whispered.

"No," Rogan said. "I must face the ridicule of my men."

Liana had not thought how his men would look at their master, who, because of a spat with his wife, had been locked away in a tower chamber.

They were allowed no time to speculate because Gaby came bustling into the room, talking as fast as her teeth and tongue could move. It seemed that Severn had spread the rumor that Rogan had ordered his wife to be locked into the room with him in order to chastise her. Rogan's reputation was intact.

"And what of mine?" Liana asked.

"They believe you to be a proper wife," Gaby said primly.

"A proper wife?" Liana gasped.

"Don't call her that," Rogan said, "or we'll never have any peace. I want no more fiery beds."

Gaby kept her mouth shut on her opinions about Liana's behavior as a wife. Gaby had won her husband through years of self-denying love and she expected every other woman to do the same thing.

Reluctantly, Liana left the chamber with her husband. She had learned something while in this room. She had learned that what was important to a woman was not necessarily important to a man. Rogan had not called her ugly, and better yet, he didn't think she was plain.

Somehow, she felt that they had come to a bridge and had crossed it safely. Liana could see no obstacles in their future path.

CHAPTER
SEVENTEEN

*F*or six long, glorious weeks, Liana was the happiest person on earth. She and Rogan had feared his men's ridicule, but what they had not foreseen was that the men were so grateful to once again have good food on their table and the rats out of their rooms that they didn't really care what had brought about the change.

And Moray Castle did indeed change. The men, rather than ignore her or fight her, now tugged their forelocks in respect as Liana walked past. Severn couldn't be nice enough to her, and Iolanthe began to join them for dinner.

But best of all was Rogan. His eyes followed Liana wherever she went. He only went into his brooding chamber to fetch something and instead spent each evening in the solar with Liana and her ladies. Severn, instead of fighting his brother, began to join them, as did Zared and Io.

It was the morning after such a lovely evening that Liana realized she was going to have a baby. She had always assumed she'd be ill as she'd seen other women be in their first months, but she wasn't ill. She hadn't been tired, hadn't felt in any way unusual, except that now she could barely get into her clothes. She put her hands on her hard, expanded belly and dreamed of a little red-haired child.

"My lady?" Gaby said from behind her. "Are you well?"

"Fine. Lovely. I have never felt better. What are you doing?"

Gaby had a basket full of herbs over her arm. "Lord Rogan and Baudoin were wrestling and they rolled into stinging nettles. I shall prepare an infusion of these to help relieve the pain."

Liana winced. Stinging nettles could be very painful. Near her father's house grew an herb that helped stop the pain much more than what Gaby carried. When Liana first arrived at Moray Castle, she remembered seeing the herb along the road. How far away was that? Ten, twelve miles? With a good horse she could be there and back by sundown. And tonight, as she rubbed the herb on her husband's fiery skin, she'd tell him about their child.

She dismissed Gaby. It wouldn't be easy to escape Moray Castle. Rogan had given her strict orders never to leave the grounds without an escort. And since the Howard attack, he'd told her she could not leave the castle even if all the Peregrine knights accompanied her.

Liana looked down at her brocade dress and smiled. Of course if she left the castle as someone else and not as Lady Liana, then she had nothing to fear. She dug into a trunk at the foot of the bed and found the peasants' clothes she'd worn to the fair. All she had to do was cover her hair, keep her face down, and steal a horse.

An hour later she was galloping eastward, away from Moray Castle, away from the village, and toward the herbs that would give her husband relief. The wind on her face and the muscles of the horse between her legs felt wonderful. She laughed aloud to think of the child she was carrying and of the happiness that was hers.

She was so engrossed in her thoughts that she neither saw nor heard the riders come from the trees. They surrounded her before she saw them.

"Look at this," one of the five men said. "A peasant girl on an animal like that."

Liana didn't need to be told who these men were. They were richly dressed, and there was an arrogance about them that could come only from their being retainees to a powerful man. These men were Howards. Her only hope was that they didn't find out who she was.

"I have stolen the horse," she said in a whining voice. "Oh please do not tell my mistress."

"And what will you give us for not telling?" one handsome young man taunted.

"Anything, sir, oh anything," Liana said, tears in her voice.

Another man rode up behind them. He was older, with gray hair at his temples, a thick, muscular body, and what looked to be a permanent frown on what might have once been a handsome face. "Throw the girl off and take the horse," the man commanded. "It's a Peregrine horse, so I'll take it."

In spite of herself, Liana gave the man a sharp look. Could this be Oliver Howard, the man who'd stolen Rogan's first wife? Liana put her head down and started to dismount, but two men had their hands on her, clutching at her body, searching for her breasts and hips. She twisted away from them—and her hood fell off. Her long blonde hair went cascading down her back.

"Look at this," one man exclaimed, touching her hair. "I think I'd like some of this little horse thief."

"Bring her here!" the older man ordered.

With her arms pinned behind her, Liana was taken to stand beside the man's horse. She kept her eyes lowered.

"Look at me," he commanded. "Look at me or I'll make you wish you had."

Defiantly, not wanting him to see her fear, Liana looked up at him. As he studied her, years of anger lines seemed to melt from his face, until at last he threw back his head and gave a roar of mirthless laughter.

"Well, Lady Liana, let me introduce myself. I am Oliver Howard," he said at last. "And you, dear lady, have given me what I have spent my life wanting. You have given me the Peregrines."

"Never," she said. "Rogan will never surrender to you."

"Not even for your return?"

"He didn't surrender for Jeanne and he won't for me," she said, and hoped her voice was as strong as her words. Inside, she was trembling. What would Rogan think when they took her? Would he believe she would betray him as Jeanne had so many years ago?

"Take her," Oliver Howard said to one of his men. "Put her on your horse in front of you. It will be your life if she escapes."

Liana felt too bleak to fight off the man's hands on her body. What was happening was her own fault; she had no one to blame but herself.

The man who held her on his horse whispered into her ear. "The Howards have a charm for Peregrine women. Will you wed one of them? Will you divorce Peregrine and become a Howard as the first one did?"

She didn't bother to answer, which seemed to amuse the man.

"It won't matter what you do," the man said, laughing. "Lord Oliver will make your husband believe you have become a Howard. We will win in the end."

Liana told herself that Rogan would never believe she'd betrayed him, but inside her, she was afraid.

They rode for two days. When they stopped at night, Liana was tied, sitting, to a tree and the men took turns staying awake to guard her.

"Perhaps you should assign two men to me," Liana sneered at Oliver Howard. "I am so strong and mighty that were I to escape the ropes, I might beat them."

Oliver did not smile. "You are a Peregrine and they are treacherous people. You might have the devil help you escape." He turned his back on her and went inside one of the three small tents hidden in the trees.

During the night it began to rain. The men guarding her took turns, no man staying in the rain for longer than an hour. There was no mention of untying Liana and putting her inside the dry warmth of a tent.

In the morning she was cold, wet, and exhausted. The man who held her on his horse didn't grope her as he had before. Instead, he was quiet and Liana felt her weary muscles beginning to relax. She fell asleep against him and didn't wake until sundown, when they reached what Rogan called the Peregrine estates.

They could see the towers from a mile off, and as they approached, Liana's lethargy left her. Never had she seen anything like the buildings looming before her. There were no words to describe the size of the estate: *vast, huge, enormous*—all seemed inadequate. There was a series of six "small" towers guarding the tunnel and outer wall that led to the gate in the inner wall of the castle. Each of these towers was larger than the single tower of Moray Castle.

Behind the inner walls were towers of such magnitude that Liana could only stare at them. She could see another wall inside and slate-roofed buildings.

They came first to a wooden bridge over a moat that was as wide as a river. In time of war, the bridge could easily be chopped away. They rode over a stone bridge, another wooden one, and then they were inside the tunnel. Above her were murder holes that in time of war were used for pouring hot oil on the enemy.

In the fading light again, they crossed another wooden bridge over another moat and at last they reached the inner gate, which was flanked by two tall, massive stone towers. Again, murder holes were above them, as well as the spikes of an iron portcullis.

They entered a grassy area with many half-timbered houses built against the walls. The place was clean and prosperous-looking.

They kept riding to go through another tunnel, this one flanked by two towers that were larger than those of any castle her father owned. Inside, they came to acres of a beautiful courtyard. Here were stone buildings with leaded-glass windows: a chapel, a solar, a Great Hall, storerooms where people bustled in and out with food and barrels of drink.

Liana sat on the horse and stared. She had never, in her wildest thoughts, imagined a place of this size or this wealth. So this is what the Peregrines are fighting for, she thought. This is what has caused the deaths of three generations of Peregrines. This is what makes the Peregrines hate the Howards.

Looking at the wealth around her, she began to understand Rogan better. No wonder he looked on small, decaying Moray Castle with contempt. That castle, including walls, could be placed three times inside the inner ward of this castle.

This is where Rogan belongs, she thought. This is where the size of him, the look of him, the power of him, would fit.

"Take her to the top of the northeast tower," Oliver Howard said, and Liana was pulled from the horse and half-dragged across the long courtyard to the thick, massive tall tower in the northeast corner. The men led her up stone spiral stairs, past rooms she barely glimpsed. But all looked clean and cared for.

There was an iron-barred door at the top of the tower, and one of the men unlocked it and shoved Liana inside, locking it behind her. It was a small room with a mattress on a wooden frame in one corner, a little table and chair in another, and a door to a garderobe to the west. There was one window looking north, and out of it she could see the hundreds of yards of outer wall that surrounded the vast grounds. Men walked on the parapets and kept watch.

"Against the Peregrines' puny force," Liana said bitterly.

She put her hand to her head, feeling dizzy and tired. She'd spent last night tied to a tree in the rain, and that, together with the emotion she'd spent, was exhausting her. She went to the bed, lay down, and pulled the blanket of fulled wool over her and went to sleep.

When she awoke, it was late the next morning. As she struggled from bed to go to the garderobe, she swayed on her feet and when she put her hand to her forehead, her skin felt hot. Someone had been in the room and there was water, bread, and cheese on the little table. She gulped the water, but the food held no appeal for her.

She went to the door and banged on it. "I must speak to Oliver Howard," she shouted, but if anyone heard, he didn't answer. She slid down the door to sit on the cold stone floor. She had to be awake when someone entered her room. She had to talk to Oliver Howard and somehow persuade him to release her. If Rogan and Severn tried to take her from this place, they would be killed.

She fell asleep, and when she awoke, she was in bed, uncovered, and drenched in her own sweat. Again, someone had been in her room, but even opening the door and carrying her to the bed hadn't awakened her. She staggered from the bed and poured a cup of water, her hands so weak she could barely lift the pitcher. She collapsed crosswise on the bed.

When she woke again, it was to someone roughly shaking her. Wearily, she opened her eyes to see Oliver Howard looming over her. The dark room, the candle-light coming from behind him, made him look blurry and indistinct.

"Your husband shows no interest in having you returned," he said fiercely. "He has ignored all ransom requests."

"Why do you want what little he has?" she asked through dry, cracked lips. When he didn't answer, she continued. "Our marriage was arranged. My husband is no doubt glad to be rid of me. If you ask at our village, you will hear of the horrors I have done to him."

"I have heard it all. I have even heard how he went

unarmed into the village to attend a fair. I would have been there, had I heard of it sooner, and I would have taken him. I would have killed this Peregrine as he's killed my brothers."

"As you have killed *his* brothers." Liana's words lost most of their force since she was too weak to lift her head. But even as weak as she was, she wanted to save Rogan. "Release me or kill me, it won't matter to him," she said. "But do it soon. He will want a new heiress for a wife." If it is soon, she thought, then Rogan will not have time to attack.

"I will see how much he doesn't care," Oliver said, and motioned to one of his men.

Liana saw the scissors flash in the candlelight. "No!" she gasped and tried to twist away, but the men's hands were too strong. Hot, feverish tears rolled down her cheeks as the man cut her hair away, leaving it no more than shoulder length. "It was my only beauty," she whispered.

Neither Oliver nor his two men took notice as they slammed from the room. Liana's shorn hair was in Oliver's hand.

Liana cried for a long time, never once touching her shortened hair. "He will never love me now," she kept repeating. Near dawn she fell into a fitful sleep, and when she awoke, she was too weak to get out of bed to get to the water. She went back to sleep.

When she awoke again, there was a cool cloth pressed to her forehead.

"Be quiet now," whispered a soft voice.

Liana opened her eyes to see a woman with gray-flecked brown hair and eyes as gentle and kind as a doe's. "Who are you?"

The woman kept dampening the cloth and wiping away the sweat from Liana's face.

"Here, take this." She held a spoon to Liana's lips, then held her head so she could drink. "I am Jeanne Howard."

"You!" Liana said, choking on the herbal medicine. "Get away from me. You are a traitor, a liar, a demon from hell."

The woman gave a bit of a smile. "And you are a Peregrine. Could you eat some broth?"

"Not from you, I can't."

Jeanne contemplated Liana. "I imagine you are a good match for Rogan. Did you *really* set his bed on fire? Did you wear coins to his table? Were you actually locked in a room with him?"

"How do you know of these things?"

With a sigh, Jeanne rose and went to a table where a small iron pot sat. "Don't you know of the depth of the hatred between the Howards and the Peregrines? They know all there is to know about one another."

Liana, in spite of her fever and her weakness, was studying Jeanne. This was the woman who'd caused so much anger. She was an ordinary-looking woman, of medium height, with plain brown hair—

Hair! Liana thought, and put her hand on her own hair. In spite of herself, she began to cry.

Jeanne turned back to her, cup in hand, and looked in pity as Liana held the ends of her shorn hair. Then Jeanne's face changed and she sat down on the chair by the bed. "Here, eat this. You need the food. Your hair will grow back, and there are worse things."

Liana couldn't stop crying. "My hair was my only beautiful feature. Rogan will never love me now."

"*Love* you," Jeanne said in disgust. "Oliver will probably kill him, so what does it matter whether Rogan loves a woman or not?"

Liana managed enough strength to knock the cup

from Jeanne's hand and send it flying. "Get out of here! You have caused all of this. If you hadn't betrayed Rogan, he wouldn't be as he is now."

Tiredly, Jeanne retrieved the cup, put it on the table, then went to sit by Liana. "If I leave, no one else will come. Oliver has ordered that no one tend you. They dare not deny me entrance, though."

"Because Oliver will kill whoever thwarts the woman he loves?" Liana said nastily. "The woman who betrayed my husband?"

Jeanne stood and went to the window. When she looked back at Liana, her face looked many years older. "Yes, I betrayed him. And my only excuse is that I was a stupid, naïve girl. I was given to Rogan to marry when I was just a child. I had such dreams of my married life. I had been orphaned when I was a baby and I was a ward of the king, so I grew up with nuns, unloved, unwanted, unnoticed. I thought marriage was going to give me someone to love, that at last I'd have a real home."

She paused and slowed down. "You did not meet the older brothers. After Rogan and I were married, they made my life hell. To them, I was money— money for their war with the Howards—and nothing more. If I spoke, no one listened; if I ordered a servant, no one obeyed. Daily I lived in more filth than I had ever imagined."

Liana's anger was leaving her. There was too much truth in Jeanne's words.

"Rogan sometimes came to me in the night, other times he had other women." Jeanne stared at the wall beside Liana. "It was awful," she whispered. "I was less than an orphan to those odious, beautiful men; I was nothing. To them, I didn't exist. They talked to each other over my head. If I was standing where one of them wanted to be, he pushed me aside. And the violence!" She shivered in memory. "To get one another's attention, they threw axes at each other's heads. I never understood how any of them made it to manhood."

Jeanne looked down at Liana. "When I heard that you set his bed on fire, I knew you were right to do so. It was something Rogan would understand. No doubt you reminded him of his brothers when you did that."

Liana didn't know what to say. She knew that every word Jeanne said was true. She'd known how it felt not to exist. And, yes, she'd done the right thing with Rogan, but would it have been enough if she'd had his older brothers to contend with? She caught herself. She was *not* going to side with this traitorous woman. "And was all this"—she motioned toward the window and the vast estate—"worth your betrayal? Two brothers died trying to get you back. Were you glad to hear of their deaths?"

Jeanne's face turned angry. "Those men didn't die trying to get *me* back. They couldn't have picked me out of a crowd. They died fighting the Howards. All I ever heard when I was with the Peregrines was how vile the Howards were, and now all I hear is of the evilness of the Peregrines. When will this hideous feud stop?"

"You did not help with your betrayal," Liana said, and knew her energy was leaving her.

Jeanne calmed. "No, I did not, but Oliver was so kind to me, and this household . . ." She trailed off as she remembered. "There was music and laughter here, and bathtubs full of scented water, and servants who curtsied to me. And Oliver was so very attentive and—"

"So attentive you had his baby," Liana said.

"After Rogan's rough handling, Oliver was a joy to

bed," Jeanne shot back, then stood. "I'll leave you now and let you sleep. I'll return in the morning."

"Don't," Liana said. "I can do well enough on my own."

"As you wish," Jeanne said, then left the room. As Liana heard the bolt lowered, she fell asleep.

For three days Liana was left alone in the room. Her fever grew worse in the cold, unheated room. She neither ate nor drank, but lay in bed, half-asleep, half-awake, sometimes burning hot, sometimes freezing so that her teeth chattered.

On the third day, Jeanne returned and Liana looked up at her in a daze.

"I feared they were lying to me," Jeanne said. "I was told you were well and comfortable." She turned away, then went to bang on the door for the guard to open it. "Pick her up and carry her and follow me," Jeanne told the guard.

"Lord Oliver gave me orders that she was to remain here," the guard said.

"And I am countermanding his orders," Jeanne said. "Now, unless you want to be thrown into the road, pick her up."

Liana was vaguely aware of strong arms picking her up. "Rogan," she whispered. She slept while she was carried down the stairs, woke only a bit as the soft hands of Jeanne's ladies undressed her, bathed the sweat from her body, and placed her on a soft feather mattress.

For three days Liana saw only Jeanne Howard as Jeanne fed her broth, helped her to the chamber pot, bathed the sweat from her body, and sat beside her. Not once did Liana speak to Jeanne in that time. She was too aware that the woman had betrayed her husband.

But by the fourth day, Liana's resolve began to

crumble. Her fever was gone and now she was merely weak. "Is my baby all right?" she whispered, breaking her silence to Jeanne.

"Healthy and growing every day. It takes more than a little fever to harm a Peregrine."

"It takes a traitorous wife," Liana said.

Jeanne put down her needle, rose from her chair, and started for the door.

"Wait!" Liana called. "I apologize. You have been very kind to me."

Jeanne turned back, poured a liquid into a mug, and handed it to Liana. "Drink it. It tastes vile, but you need it."

Obediently, Liana gulped the awful-tasting herbal concoction. When she handed the mug back to Jeanne, she spoke. "What has happened since I was taken? Has Rogan attacked?"

Jeanne took her time in answering. "Rogan sent word that . . . that you were no wife of his, that Oliver could have you."

Liana could only gape.

"I'm afraid Oliver allowed his temper to get the best of him. He ordered your hair cut and sent it to Rogan."

Liana turned away from Jeanne's pitying stare. "I see. But even when they took my . . . hair"—she could barely bring herself to say the words—"it made no difference to him." She looked back at Jeanne. "What will your husband do now, send me back piecemeal to the Peregrines? A hand today? A foot tomorrow?"

"Of course not," Jeanne snapped. In truth, Oliver had threatened just what Liana mentioned, but Jeanne had known they were only words. She was furious with her husband for having taken Lady Liana, but now that she was here and Rogan refused to take the bait, Oliver wasn't sure what to do with her.

"What will you do with me?" Liana whispered, using her weak arms to push herself up. Jeanne handed her a velvet robe to put over her bare body.

Jeanne decided to be honest. "I don't know. Oliver talks of petitioning the king to annul your marriage and then marrying you to his younger brother."

Liana refused to cry. "It's good that Rogan hasn't risked his life and the life of his brothers to come for me."

"Since he has only one brother left, I can see his reluctance," Jeanne said, her tone sarcastic.

"If there were an attack, he'd no doubt have young Zared fight alongside the men."

Jeanne gave her a sharp look. "I doubt that. Even the Peregrines have some standards." She paused. "Did no one tell you Zared is a girl? Are they still dressing her as a boy?"

Liana blinked a few times. "Girl? Zared is a *girl?*" She remembered Zared smashing the head of the rat with his—her—fist. And Zared in her room in the middle of the night. Liana's eyes widened. Then she remembered being so angry because Zared had been in bed with three women. How Severn and Rogan had laughed when she'd raged at them!

"No," Liana said, her jaw clenched tight. "No one bothered to tell me Zared was a girl."

"She was only about five when I was there, and I think the brothers were embarrassed that their father had produced a female. They blamed it on the mewling, cowardly, but rich fourth wife of his. I tried to mother Zared. It was a mistake; she's as fierce as her brothers."

"And I am an even bigger fool, for I never guessed," Liana said. And they never bothered to enlighten me, she thought. They had kept her out of their lives. She had never been a Peregrine, and now they didn't want her back.

She looked at Jeanne. "There has been no response from the Peregrines since they received my . . . my hair?"

Jeanne frowned. "Rogan and Severn have been seen hawking and . . . and drinking together."

"Celebrating, you mean. I thought . . ." She didn't want to say what she thought. She thought that they had come to, if not love her, then need her. She thought Severn had locked her and Rogan in the room because Severn missed the things she had done for the entire castle.

Jeanne took Liana's hand and squeezed it. "They are Peregrines. They are like no other people. They care only for their own. To them, women are a means to get money and nothing else. I don't mean to be cruel, but you should hear this: The Peregrines have your money now, so why do they need you? I heard how you tried to clean their castle and give them better food, but those men won't appreciate such things. The rains last week have half-filled their moat and I hear that already three dead horses are floating in it."

Liana knew that what Jeanne said was true. How could she ever have believed that she meant anything to Rogan? No more would he have to put up with her interfering in his life. "And the Days?" Liana whispered.

"Already they are back," Jeanne answered.

Liana took a deep breath. "So what do you do with me now? My husband does not want me, nor do I think my stepmother would like having me back. I am afraid the joke is on your husband."

"Oliver has not decided yet."

"Rogan and Severn must be laughing heartily. They have gotten rid of me, kept my dowry, and saddled their enemy with a plain-looking, meddlesome shrew."

That seemed to be the gist of it, Jeanne thought, but said nothing. Her heart went out to Liana because she knew how she felt. Those first weeks, so many years ago, after Jeanne had been taken by Oliver Howard, she had been in agony. She had felt no love for her young husband or for his overbearing brothers, but she had suffered as she heard of the deaths that had occurred because of her. For a while it looked as if Rogan was going to die from Oliver's arrows, and when he recovered, he found out his brothers were dead.

Through all Jeanne's misery, there had been Oliver. He had never planned to love the young wife of his enemy, but Oliver's wife of a childless marriage had died over a year earlier and he was lonely, as was Jeanne, and they were drawn to each other. At first Jeanne had been defiant, standing up for a husband who had said very few kind words to her and never held her except during the sexual act. But in a very short time Oliver's quiet kindness made her soften. While outside the walls war raged and men died, inside Jeanne lay in Oliver's arms.

When Oliver knew Jeanne was carrying his child, he became furiously jealous. His hatred of the Peregrines increased because the woman he loved, the mother of his child, was someone else's wife. Jeanne begged him to allow her to go to Rogan and ask for an annulment, but Oliver became enraged at the idea. He was terrified that Jeanne would return to the Peregrines—or even that, upon seeing Jeanne and hearing the news, Rogan would murder her.

But, defying Oliver and endangering her life, she

went to Rogan. It had been an ordeal getting out of a castle that was under siege. On a black, moonless night, her ladies had helped her down the wall, a well-bribed man had rowed her across the inner moat, then she'd run, crouched, to the outer moat, where another boat awaited her. It had cost her much gold to bribe the guards on the parapets to look the other way, but she'd managed it.

Wearing a roughly woven cloak over her gown, she'd easily walked through Rogan's camp without one person recognizing her. If she had not been sure before, after seeing no recognition on the faces of people she'd lived with for months, she was sure. She walked past Severn and young Zared, and they didn't so much as glance at her. When she faced Rogan, there was no gladness at seeing her again, no joy that at last he could stop the siege. She asked him to walk away into the woods with her, and he had. As quickly as possible, she told him she had grown to love Oliver and now carried his child.

For a moment she thought he was going to kill her. Instead, he had taken her arm and told her she was a Peregrine and was staying with him, that he'd never release her to a Howard. She had forgotten what the Peregrines were like by half. At the thought of never seeing Oliver again and having to spend the rest of her life in filthy Moray Castle, she'd begun to cry. She didn't remember what she'd said, but she believed she remembered saying she'd kill herself if she had to live with Rogan.

Whatever she'd said, he'd released her arm and pushed her hard against a tree. "Go," he'd said. "Get out of my sight."

Jeanne had started running and hadn't stopped until she was safe inside a peasant's hut. That day the Peregrines had stopped the siege, and a month later

Jeanne heard that Rogan had petitioned the king for an annulment.

Jeanne was able to keep Oliver from learning of her visit to Rogan and so saved herself many jealous accusations. But in the years since, over their heads hung the fact that Jeanne had once been married to a Peregrine. For years Oliver looked at their oldest son askance, and once Jeanne saw him inspecting the boy's hair. "There is no red in it," she said, and moved past him. Oliver had been taught to hate the Peregrines from childhood, but now he hated them more. It seemed to him that the Peregrines had first claim to everything he owned: his castle and his wife.

So now, so many years later, Oliver had tried to get back at the Peregrines by yet again taking a wife of theirs. But this time Rogan wasn't going to fight. He wasn't going to risk losing another brother for a woman he'd never wanted in the first place.

Jeanne looked at Liana. "I do not know what happens now," she said honestly.

"Nor do I," Liana answered bleakly.

CHAPTER EIGHTEEN

Liana finished the last stitch on the embroidered dragon on her frame and snipped the thread. She had completed the entire pillow cover in just a few weeks. She'd forced herself to keep her hands busy because if her hands were busy, she thought less.

For five long weeks she had been a prisoner of the Howards. After she was well enough to move about, she had been given a pleasant, sunny guest room and all the sewing supplies she needed. Jeanne had shared two gowns with her.

Other than Jeanne, Liana saw no one but the servants who came to clean, and they were forbidden to speak to her. The first few days she had paced the room until her legs had grown tired, but then she began to sew, using the intricate stitching to take her mind off the news Jeanne brought her each evening.

The Howards kept close watch on the Peregrines, and they reported to Oliver. Rogan was seen every day. He trained with his men, rode with his brother, chased the peasant girls like a satyr.

Oliver renewed his threats to Rogan, saying Liana was in love with Oliver's brother. Rogan's reply had been to inquire if he was invited to the wedding.

Liana jabbed the needle into the tapestry and hit her thumb. Quick tears came to her eyes. Filthy beast, she thought. Daily she went over in her mind all the many terrible things Rogan had done to her. If she ever got away from the Howards, she hoped never to see a Peregrine again. She hoped all of them, including that boy-girl Zared, sank in their own mire and drowned.

At the beginning of the sixth week, Jeanne came to her with a frown on her face.

"What is it?" Liana asked.

"I don't know. Oliver is angry, more angry than I've ever seen him. He wants to force Rogan into a fight." Jeanne sat down heavily. "I can find out nothing, but I think Oliver may have issued a personal challenge to Rogan, a trial by combat."

"That will settle the feud once and for all. The winner will own this place."

Jeanne put her face in her hands. "You can afford to say that. Rogan is years younger than Oliver, and larger and stronger. Your husband will win and mine will die."

In the last weeks Jeanne had become very familiar to Liana, familiar almost to the point of friendship. Liana put a hand on her shoulder. "I know how you must feel. I once believed I loved my husband."

To the right was a clatter.

"What was that?" Jeanne asked, her head coming up.

"The man cleaning the toilet."

"I didn't know anyone was here."

"I forget them myself. They come and go so quietly," Liana said. "At home . . . I mean, at my husband's castle, the servants were inept, lazy, and had no idea how to clean anything."

Again came the clatter.

Liana went to the doorway of the garderobe. "Leave us," she ordered to the bent old man who'd been clumsily cleaning her room for the last three days.

"But I haven't finished, my lady," he whined.

"Go!" Liana ordered, and stood there while the old man hobbled out, one leg dragging behind him.

When they were alone, she turned back to Jeanne. "What did Rogan say to the challenge?"

"I don't believe it's been issued. Oliver could not think he could beat Rogan. Oh, Liana, this has to stop."

"Then release me," Liana said. "Help me get away. Once I am gone, Oliver's anger will cool."

"Will you go back to Rogan?"

Liana turned away. "I don't know. I have some property in my own right. Perhaps I'll go there. Surely I can find someplace where I belong, someplace where I'm not a burden."

Jeanne stood. "My first loyalty is to my husband. I cannot help you escape. He is not pleased that I see you every day as it is. No," she said firmly, "it would humiliate him if I betrayed him."

Betrayal, Liana thought. The history of the Howards and the Peregrines was rife with betrayal.

Abruptly, Jeanne left the room, as if she were afraid she'd change her mind if she remained with Liana.

The next day Liana was nervous, jumping at every sound. The door was unlocked and she looked up, hoping to see Jeanne and hear the news, but it was only the old cleaning man. Disappointed, she looked back down at the new piece of linen stretched on her embroidery frame. "Take the food tray away and get out," she said crossly.

"And where should I go?" said a voice that was so familiar to her that chills went up her spine. Very slowly, she looked up. Standing before the heavy door was Rogan, an eyepatch pushed up to his forehead, a padded hump on his back, a leg bandaged so that it looked as if it were crooked.

He was grinning at her in an infuriating way that Liana knew signaled he expected her to leap on him in joy.

Instead, she grabbed a goblet from her empty breakfast tray and threw it at his head. He ducked, and it went slamming against the door. "You bastard!" she said. "You randy satyr. You lying, cheating blackguard. I never want to see you again." One by one she threw items from the tray at him and then began on whatever she could grab in the room. "You left me here to rot. They cut my hair, but you didn't care. You didn't want me. You *never* wanted me. You never even told me Zared was a girl. You said Oliver Howard could have me for all you cared. You laughed while I was held prisoner. You went hawking with Severn while I was locked in this room. You—"

"It was Baudoin," Rogan said.

Having run out of ornaments to throw at him, Liana began to tear the blankets from the bed and threw them. They fluttered through the air, landing at his feet. There was now a large pile of ornaments, pillows, and dishes around him. "You deserve everything the Howards do to you," she yelled. "Your whole family is rotten to the core. I nearly died of a fever while you were enjoying yourself. I'm sure you won't care, but they tied me to a tree all night *in the rain*. I could have lost our baby. As if you'd care. You never—"

"It was Baudoin hawking. I was here," Rogan said. "That's just like a Peregrine: blame someone else.

That poor, innocent family man. *He* would care if someone cut off his wife's hair. He would—" She paused. There was nothing else left in the room to throw at him. "Here? You were here?" There was suspicion in her voice.

"I have been here searching for you for nearly three weeks. The location of your room has been a well-guarded secret."

Liana wasn't sure she believed him. "How could you be here and not be noticed? The Howards know you by sight."

"Not as well as they think. Their spies have seen Baudoin hawking and chasing the Days, not me. I have been here under disguise. I have cleaned things. I have whitewashed walls, swept floors—and listened."

Liana was beginning to hear him. Perhaps the news she had heard of his denials had been untrue. "*You* clean something?" she said. "I am to believe that? You wouldn't know which end of a broom to use."

"If I had one now, I'd know which end to use on your backside."

It was true. Oh God in heaven, it was true. He *had* been searching for her. Liana's knees weakened on her and she collapsed, sitting, on the bare feather mattress, put her face in her hands, and began to cry as if her heart would break.

Rogan didn't dare touch her. He stood where he was in the midst of the debris and stared at her. He hadn't thought ever to see her again.

The day she'd been taken, he'd rolled in stinging nettles and his skin was on fire. He'd imagined how his wife would have a tub of hot water prepared for him and she would ease his pain. But he'd bounded up the stairs to find a solar full of crying women. He couldn't get anything out of Liana's maids, but Gaby, between sobs, was able to tell him Liana had been taken by the Howards. Oliver Howard had sent a message that, for her return, he wanted the surrender of Moray Castle.

Rogan, without a word, had gone into their bedroom. He had meant to spend some time alone to plan his strategy, but the next thing he knew, Severn and Baudoin were on him, pinning him to the floor. The room was destroyed. In a rage so blind he still remembered none of it, he had taken an axe to the room and chopped up every piece of wood, iron, cloth. Candle wax mixed with cut sheets. Oak chair legs were crushed with a bent iron candle stand. Liana's fine crucifix was in splinters. Pieces of her clothing were everywhere. Red silk, blue brocade, cloth of gold, cloth of silver. Four of her headdresses lay broken, the padding spilling out of them.

The door had been chopped down by Severn and Baudoin as they went in to get their brother and keep him from injuring himself.

When Rogan came to his senses, he was calm—very, very calm. He was so calm that Severn's anger rose.

"We will attack," Severn said. "We have the money now. We'll hire mercenaries. We'll at long last rout the Howards from the Peregrine home."

Rogan looked at Severn and imagined his brother washed and laid out in a coffin—the way he'd seen Basil and James when they had fought to return Rogan's first wife. Rogan knew he must not do anything rash, that he must think clearly and calmly. He could not attack a place as vast as the Peregrine lands without a great deal of planning.

For days he worked long and hard, driving his men to exhaustion as he readied them for war. At night he stopped only when he could move no longer, then he fell into a heavy, dreamless sleep.

But even with all his work, he still missed her. She was the only person in his life who'd ever made him laugh. Neither his father nor his older brothers had ever laughed when they were alive. But then he'd married this girl for her money and nothing had been the same since. She was the only woman who dared to criticize him. Other women were too afraid of him to complain of his treatment. Other women didn't tell him what he did wrong. Other women had no courage, he thought. They didn't set beds on fire, didn't wear coins to dinner, didn't dare ask him about his first wife.

He was supervising the packing of war machines on to wagons when a Peregrine knight came with a package from the Howards. The little oak chest had been catapulted over the wall with a message that it be given to Rogan.

He wrenched the lock off with a steel pick and took out the cloth-wrapped bundle to see Liana's hair inside. Somehow, he managed to remain calm. With her hair, her beautiful, silky hair, clutched in his hand, he started toward the tower.

Severn caught up with him. "Where are you going?" he demanded.

"This is between Oliver Howard and me," Rogan said quietly. "I go to kill him."

Severn swung Rogan around. "Do you think Howard will fight you one on one? That he will fight you fairly? He's an old man."

Rogan felt the hair in his hand. "He has harmed her; I will kill him for it."

"Think what you're doing," Severn pleaded. "If you so much as ride up to Howard's gate, he'll have that thick hide of yours filled with arrows. Then where will your wife be? Come, help us prepare for war. We'll attack Howard properly."

"Properly!" Rogan said, half sneering. "As we did in 'thirty-five? There were five Peregrine brothers then and still the Howards beat us. How can we, as poor as we are, hope to battle the Howards? We will take our tiny force and lay siege and Howard will laugh at us from atop his walls."

"Yet you think that you, one mere man, can do what all our men cannot?"

Rogan had no answer for him. Instead, he went to his brooding chamber, locked the door, and did not come out for twenty-four hours. By then he knew what he was going to do. When he and Liana had gone to the fair, he had seen how easily the peasants walked in and out of Moray Castle. He had always seen them, of course, with their baskets of squawking chickens, their three-wheeled handcarts loaded with crude goods, men with tools strapped to their bodies as they came to do repair work, but he'd never noticed them. Only when he was wearing peasants' clothing did he see the freedom of access these people had, the way they went through the gates without a question asked. Yet if a man in armor on horseback had come within ten miles of Moray Castle, he would have been greeted by armed men.

Rogan called his two brothers into his brooding chamber, for the first time including Baudoin as family. Liana did that, he thought. She had given him that most precious of gifts: another brother. Rogan told his two brothers he planned to dress as a peasant and go alone into the Howard fortress.

Severn's shout of protest made the pigeons fly off the roof. He yelled, he raged, he threatened, but he couldn't sway Rogan.

Baudoin, who had been quiet through Severn's storming, finally spoke. "You will need a good disguise. You're too tall, too easily recognized. Gaby will make you a disguise that not even Lady Liana will see through."

That day Rogan and Gaby and Baudoin had worked on turning him into a one-eyed, humpbacked, crippled old man. Severn had been so angry he'd refused to participate, but Rogan had gone to him and asked for his help. Rogan knew that Howard spies watched them, and he wanted Severn to make them think Rogan was still at Moray Castle. Severn and Baudoin were to make the Howards think that Baudoin was Rogan.

Alone, Rogan had gone to the Howard fortress. As he and Severn had parted in the forest, Severn had clasped his brother to him, a rare gesture between Peregrine men that would not have happened before Liana came and softened them.

"Bring her back to us," Severn said softly. "And . . . I don't want to lose more brothers."

"I will find her." He gave Severn one last look. "Take care of Zared."

Severn nodded, then Rogan was gone.

Rogan found that his stooped, leg-dragging stance made his back ache, and the Howard men who ordered him about often punctuated their orders with kicks and shoves. He made note of their faces and hoped someday to see them on a battlefield.

He skulked about the castle, hauling swill, doing whatever he could to be near people who were talking. The castle was abuzz with gossip about the treachery of the Peregrines, how they were trying to steal what rightfully belonged to the Howards. The people speculated on Liana and said she wasn't good enough for Oliver's young brother. Rogan snapped a broom handle in half at that, which caused a cook to beat him with a leg of mutton.

He ate what he could steal, and since the Howards,

on the Peregrine family's estates, were so wealthy, they never missed the food. He slept in a corner of the stables or in the mews with the birds.

He worked and he listened, keeping his uncovered eye open for anyone who looked as if he might know something.

It was in the third week, when he was about to give up hope, that a man kicked him in the small of his back and sent Rogan sprawling in the dirt. "Come with me, old man," he said.

Rogan picked himself up and followed the man, planning his death as they climbed the stairs. The man handed Rogan a broom. "Go in and clean," he'd said, and unbolted a thick, iron-clad door.

Inside the room, Rogan stood for a moment blinking, for there was Liana, her lovely face bent over a tapestry frame, her hair covered with a cap of white linen. He couldn't move, but just stood there and stared at her.

She looked up. "Well, go on," she said. "You have better things to do than gawk at the Howard prisoner."

He'd opened his mouth to tell her who he was, but then the door was opened behind him. Rogan had scurried into the garderobe, staying by the doorway to listen. He'd breathed a sigh of relief when he heard a woman's voice, but as he continued to listen, he heard Liana call the woman Jeanne. Was this the Jeanne he'd once been married to?

He left the garderobe and began moving about the chamber. Neither woman paid him the least mind. He looked at the woman Jeanne and he thought she was his first wife, but he wasn't sure. Their marriage had been brief and over with a long time ago, and besides, she hadn't been very memorable as a wife.

He listened to the two women and heard stories of

his own indifference, how he was drinking and hawking and couldn't care less about his wife being held prisoner. He smiled when he heard mention of the baby Liana was carrying. But he lost his smile when he saw that Liana believed every word Jeanne was saying. Did women have no loyalty? What had he ever done to deserve his wife's distrust? He had given her a roof over her head, food in her belly—as well as a brat—and he had even given up his women for her. And he had come to save her from the Howards.

He was so disgusted by her disloyal behavior that while he made arrangements, bribing guards and retainers with money that was needed elsewhere, and went to her room every day, he didn't reveal himself to her.

So now he was here, and after all he'd gone through to find her, she wasn't even grateful.

"What were you doing outside the castle walls?" he asked, frowning. "I gave you orders not to leave the grounds." The little cap over her head was so fine it was nearly transparent and he could see how little was left of her hair. If he ever got his hands on Oliver Howard, the man's death would be long and painful.

"I was going to get herbs to soothe the nettles. Gaby said you rolled in them." She was sniffing loudly.

"Nettles!" he said under his breath. "You caused all of this because you went to get herbs for nettles?"

Liana was beginning to realize that he *had* come for her, that all the reports she'd heard of his indifference were false. She leaped off the bed in a flurry of silk and flung her arms about his neck and accurately planted her mouth on his.

He held her so tightly her ribs nearly broke. "Liana," he whispered against her neck.

She stroked his hair, and more tears came to her eyes. "You did not forget me," she whispered.

"Never again," he said, then his voice changed. "I can't stay longer. Tonight there is no moon. I'll come for you and we'll leave here."

"How?" She pulled away to look at him. It seemed that she forgot from one moment to the next how splendidly handsome he was. Even under weeks' worth of ashes and dirt, his face was—

"Are you listening to me?"

"Intimately," she answered, snuggling her hips against his.

"Behave, and listen to me. Do not trust Jeanne Howard."

"But she has helped me. She may have saved my life. I was burning up with fever and—"

"Swear to me," Rogan said fiercely. "Swear to me you won't trust her. Don't confide in her, don't tell her I've been here. She's betrayed my family once, and if she betrayed me again, I would not live. I could not fight off Howard men alone as I am now. Swear to me."

"Yes," Liana whispered. "I swear."

He had his hands on her shoulders, and he gave her one last long look. "I must go now, but tonight I will come to you. Wait for me, and for once, give your loyalty to me." He smiled just a bit. "And clean up this room. I've learned to like cleanliness."

He kissed her once, hard and fiercely, and then he was gone.

For a long while Liana leaned against the door. He had come for her. He hadn't been drinking and hawking while she was held prisoner. Instead, he had risked his life by entering the Howards' domain alone. He hadn't said that he didn't want her.

Dreamily, she began to pick up all the things she'd thrown at him. She didn't want Jeanne to see the mess and ask questions.

Tonight, she thought, he was coming for her tonight. As she began to think less romantically about his coming for her and more realistically, she began to be afraid. What if he were caught? Oliver Howard would kill Rogan. She sat down on the bed, her hands clasped tightly, and the fear beginning to course through her body made her rigid.

As the sun began to set, Liana's fear settled into her bones until she felt as if she were seeing herself from a distance. Slowly, she rose, removed the silk gown Jeanne had loaned her, and put on the peasants' clothes she had been wearing when she had been taken. She put the silk gown back on over the peasants' garb, then sat down to wait.

Every muscle in her body was tense as she sat still and stared at the closed door. She heard the castle grounds quieten as the workers went off to their beds. A servant brought her supper on a tray and lit a candle, but Liana didn't touch the food. Instead, she waited for the night to bring Rogan.

At about midnight, very slowly, the door opened and Liana stood up, her eyes wide.

Jeanne stepped into the room, her eyes on the bed, then, startled, she saw Liana. "I thought you'd be asleep."

"What's wrong?" Liana whispered.

"I don't know. Oliver is very angry and he's been drinking. I overheard . . ." She looked at Liana. She didn't want to say what she'd overheard. In all areas except one her husband was a sensible man, but when it came to the Peregrines, he lost all sense of proportion, of honesty, of sensibility. Today she'd overheard Oliver saying he meant to kill Liana and deliver her body to Rogan. "You must come with me," Jeanne said. "I have to hide you."

"I cannot," Liana said. "I must wait here for—"

"Wait for what?" Jeanne asked. "Or do you wait for someone?"

"No one," Liana said quickly. "No one knows I'm here, do they? How could I be waiting for someone? I was just sitting here, that's all." She closed her mouth. She couldn't tell Jeanne that Rogan was coming for her. Jeanne could tell Oliver. But if she moved, how would Rogan find her? "This room is so nice," Liana said. "I'd rather stay here than move to another. I don't think I could bear a cold room."

"Now is no time to think of luxury. I am concerned for your life. If you wish yourself and your child to live, come with me now."

Liana knew she had no choice. With a heavy heart she followed Jeanne down the torch-lit stairs. She followed her out of the tower, across the dark inner ward, and at last down steep stone steps into the cellar of one of the gate towers. Here were huge bags of grain, in places piled almost to the ceiling. It was a dank, dark, moldy-smelling place, the only window an arrow slit high above her head.

"You cannot mean for me to stay here," Liana whispered.

"It's the only place I could find where no one will look. This grain won't be needed until spring, so no one will come in here. I have put wool blankets there, and there's a chamber pot in the corner."

"Who will empty it?" Liana asked. "The old man who comes to my room seems stupid enough to be safe."

"Not this time. I will come tomorrow night. I trust no one but myself." She feared that when Oliver found Liana gone, he'd offer a reward for her, and if he did, anyone was likely to turn her in. "I am sorry. This is a hideous place, but it's the only safe place. Try to sleep. I will come tomorrow."

When Jeanne left and bolted the door behind her, the sound echoed in the round stone room with its vaulted ceiling. It was absolutely dark and cold as only stone that had never been heated could be. Liana struggled forward, stumbling over bags of grain to find the blankets Jeanne had left. When she found them, she tried to make a bed on the lumpy bags, but there was no way to make them comfortable.

At last, settled with the hard, dusty bags under her and two inadequate blankets over her, she began to cry. Somewhere outside, her beloved Rogan was risking his life to find her. She prayed that he would not do something foolish when he found she was gone. But even if he kept silent, he would never find her in this cellar, for no guards or servants knew where she was now. Only Jeanne Howard knew where Liana was.

Jeanne did not come the next day. Liana had no food, no water, no light, no warmth. And as the day grew into night, she had no hope. Rogan had been right about Jeanne: She could not be trusted. Liana began to remember that it was Jeanne who had told her of Rogan's not caring that she was held prisoner. It was Jeanne who had made her believe in Rogan's treachery.

Jeanne came on the night of the second day. Quietly, she opened the door and stepped into the cold, dark cellar. "Liana," she called.

Liana was too weary and full of anger to answer.

Stumbling over grain bags, Jeanne began to feel her way about the room, gasping when she touched Liana. "I have brought you food and water and another blanket." She lifted her skirt and began untying bundles. She held a gourd of water to Liana's lips, and she drank greedily, then Jeanne handed Liana cold beef, bread, and cheese.

"I could not come yesterday. Oliver suspects that I

have had something to do with your escape. He has set everyone to spying on everyone else. I'm afraid of even my own ladies. I had to plead illness and have my food brought to me in my room in order to get you something to eat."

"I am to believe you gave up your own meal for me?" Liana asked, her mouth full.

It was dark and she couldn't see Jeanne's face, but there was a pause before she spoke. "Something has happened," Jeanne said. "What is it?"

"I have no idea what you mean. I have been here alone in this freezing place. No one has come or gone for two days."

"And it has no doubt saved your life," Jeanne snapped. "You are the wife of my husband's enemy, and I have risked much to keep you healthy and safe."

"What risk? Your lies?" Liana wished she hadn't spoken.

"What lies? Liana, what has happened? What have you heard? *How* have you heard anything?"

"Nothing," Liana said. "I have been held in close confinement. I could not have heard anything."

Jeanne walked away from her. Her eyes were beginning to adjust to the blackness and she could see shadows of the grain bags and the darker outline of Liana. She took a deep breath and looked at Liana. "I have decided to tell you the truth, all of the truth. My husband means to kill you. That's what I overheard when I took you from the tower room. He has no use for you. He never meant to take you, you just appeared, so to speak, and he took you on impulse. He hoped to force Rogan to surrender Moray Castle to him. What he actually wants is to take every blade of grass the Peregrines own." There was bitterness in her voice.

Jeanne continued. "I don't know what to do with

299

you now. I can trust no one. Oliver has issued a death threat to anyone seen helping you. He knows you're still in the castle, because since he took you, he has had the guards look at the face of every peasant who enters or leaves the walls. His men are even now combing the woods outside the walls."

Jeanne paused. "Damn that Rogan! Why hasn't he tried for your return? I never thought he'd be content to let one of his own rot."

"He hasn't!" Liana said, then bit her tongue.

"You *do* know something." Jeanne grabbed Liana's shoulders. "Help me save your life. It's only a matter of time before Oliver's men search this cellar. I cannot save you if you're found."

Liana refused to speak. Rogan had made her swear not to trust Jeanne, and she was going to keep her word.

"All right," Jeanne said tiredly. "Have it your way. I'll do the best I can to get you out of here as soon as possible. Can you swim?"

"No," Liana answered.

Jeanne sighed. "I will do my best," she whispered, then slipped out the door.

Liana spent a restless night on the bags of grain. She could *not* tell Jeanne that Rogan was within the grounds and that he would help her escape. If she told Jeanne of Rogan's disguise, Jeanne could tell Oliver.

On the other hand, what if Jeanne were telling the truth? It was indeed only a matter of time until she was found. And if they took her, would Rogan stand aside in his beggar's dress and silently watch her be put to death? No, Rogan would not remain silent and Oliver Howard would take both of them.

In the morning, Liana heard noise coming through the arrow slit high in the wall. It took her a long while, but she managed to drag the one-hundred-pound bags of grain around until she formed a pyramid that she could climb on. Climbing up, she was able to see out the bottom of the long slit.

The castle grounds were alive with activity, men and women running and shouting, doors being thrown open, horses taken out of the stables, carts filled with goods being unloaded. She knew they were searching for her.

As she strained up on her toes to see out, far across the grounds she saw an old, crippled beggar man, a hump on his back, one leg dragging behind him. "Rogan," Liana whispered, and stared at the man with all her might, urging him to come to her. As if he sensed her message, he came slowly toward her.

Her heart was pounding in her throat as he drew near. The window wasn't far above the outside ground level, and if he came close enough, she'd be able to call out to him. As he came nearer, she held her breath. She opened her mouth to call to him.

"Here! You!" a Howard knight shouted at Rogan. "You have two good arms. Drive this wagon out of here."

Tears came to Liana's eyes as she saw Rogan awkwardly pull himself up to the wagon seat and drive the horses away. She sat down on the grain sacks and began to cry. What Jeanne had told her was true. Oliver Howard was tearing the place apart to search for her, and if not today, tomorrow he would find her.

A voice inside her head said she had to trust Jeanne, that her only chance for living was to tell Jeanne that Rogan was near and that he had a plan for escape. If she did not trust Jeanne, she was sure to die. If she did trust her, there was a possibility both she and Rogan might live.

By the time Jeanne came that night, Liana's head was pounding from her agony of indecision.

"I have arranged something," Jeanne said. "It is the best I could do, but I do not know if it will work. I have not dared trust any of my husband's men. I fear that one of my ladies is telling my husband everything. Come with me now. There is no time to lose."

"Rogan is here," Liana blurted.

"Here? In this room?" Jeanne's voice was full of fear.

"No. He is in the ward. He came to me in the tower room. He said he had a plan and meant to take me away the night you brought me here."

"Where is he? Quick! People are waiting to help you, and we desperately need your husband's help."

Liana dug her fingers into Jeanne's arm. "If you betray us, I swear before God that I will haunt all the days of your life."

Jeanne crossed herself. "If you are caught, it will be because you have used valuable time threatening me. Where is he?"

Liana described how Rogan was disguised.

"I have seen him. He must care for you to risk coming here alone. Wait, I will return for you."

Liana sat down with a thud on a pile of grain bags. Now was when she'd know if she'd made the right decision. If her decision was wrong, she was as good as dead.

CHAPTER
NINETEEN

Jeanne barged into the Great Hall, two silk-clad ladies behind her, in a fury of temper. The floors were covered with straw pallets where men and dogs were sleeping. Other people tossed dice in a corner; one man fondled a maid in another.

"The drains in my garderobe are clogged," she announced. "I want someone to clean them. Now."

Those who were awake snapped to attention at the sight of her ladyship, but no one volunteered for the smelly task.

"I will send someone—" one knight began.

Jeanne saw Rogan in his filthy clothes sitting against a wall. She could feel his eyes on her. "That one will do. Come with me." She turned, hoping he would follow her. He did, and she waited until they were in the deep shadow of a building. She signaled her two ladies to leave her, then turned to Rogan.

Before he could step back, she reached out and flipped up his eyepatch. "It is you," she whispered. "I did not believe what Liana told me could be true. I didn't believe a Peregrine could care whether a woman lived or not."

Rogan's hand caught her wrist, crushing it painfully. "Where is she, bitch? If she's harmed, I'll do to you what I should have done years ago."

"Release me or you'll never see her again."

Rogan had no choice but to obey her. "What did you do to her to make her tell you of me? I'll take pleasure in killing you if—"

"You can give me your sweet words later," Jeanne snapped. "She is hidden now and I mean to get her out, but I need help. She can't swim, so she has to take a boat across both moats. You must row her. Go now to the wall this side of the northeast tower. There is a rope hanging down. Go across the outer ward to the northwest. There will be another rope down that wall, and a boat will be waiting below. Wait for her in the boat. I will help her to the outer wall, then it's up to you to get her across the bank and the outer moat."

"Am I to believe you? Howard's men will no doubt be waiting for me."

"My women are going to divert the guards atop the walls. You *have* to believe me. There is no one else."

"If you betray me again, I will—"

"Go!" Jeanne commanded. "You are losing precious moments."

Rogan left her, rushing, but dragging his leg in case anyone watched. He had never felt so naked in his life. His life and Liana's were in the hands of a lying traitor. Part of him was sure that he was going to reach the northeast tower and find twenty men waiting to murder him. But another part of him knew this was his only chance. He'd been searching in vain for Liana for days and had had no more luck than Howard's men had.

There were no men waiting at the tower. Instead, in

the darkness, a rope hung down from the top of the wall. He threw off his eyepatch, pulled the stuffing that formed a hump from his back, and untied his leg. He took a knife from inside his dirty shirt, put it in his mouth, and began to climb.

He expected men to be waiting for him at the top of the rope, but none were. Silently, he lowered himself down a rope on the other side of the wall.

Once he was on land again, he ran, crouching, across the middle ward. He melted his body into the dark stone of the outer wall as he heard laughter. Two guards walked by, never noticing Rogan a few feet from them or the rope hanging in the shadows down the wall to their right.

Rogan had one more wall to climb before he reached the moat. It took him precious minutes of searching to find the rope and then to start climbing. At the top, he had to pause because he heard a man's voice followed by a woman's giggle. Rogan waited until they were gone, then he heaved himself onto the wide, flat parapets.

The next rope was farther down the wall and Rogan climbed down it swiftly. In the shadows, hidden in tall reeds, was a tiny boat with two oars. He got in it, crouched down, and waited. He kept his eyes on the wall above him, watching so hard that he rarely blinked.

It was a long while before he saw the dark shadows of the heads near the top of the wall where the rope hung. He had begun to give up hope. The Howard bitch had indeed left the ropes and the boat, but would she bring Liana?

Rogan held his breath as he watched the two heads. They seemed to be *talking*. Women! he thought. They must put everything into words. Words were everything to them. They talked when a man tried to bed them. They talked when a man gave them a gift—they wanted him to *explain* why he gave them a gift. But worst of all, they talked when they were on top of a wall surrounded by armed men.

Then everything happened at once. One of the women's hands went into the air as if she meant to strike the other one. Rogan was on his feet and running toward the wall. There was a woman's cry above his head, then the sound of men running along the wall. Rogan had his hands on the rope, ready to climb up, when Jeanne shouted down at him.

"No!" she called to Rogan. "Save yourself. Liana is dead. You cannot save her."

Rogan started up the rope and was six feet off the ground when it fell away and he hit the earth. Someone above had chopped the rope off.

"Go, you fool," he heard Jeanne scream, then her voice was muffled as if someone had put a hand over her mouth.

Rogan didn't give himself time to think, for arrows were beginning to rain down on him. He ran for the boat, but two arrows had hit it and it was sinking. He plunged into the cold water of the moat and began to swim, arrows whizzing past his head.

He reached the bank, then ran, crouching, across the northern bank, just outside the walls of the western bailey. Sleepy guards, hearing the commotion across the moat, were coming awake and looking down the walls at the steep bit of land between the inner and outer moats. When they saw movement, they shot arrows.

Rogan reached the outer moat just as an arrow scraped across his back, searing his skin. He jumped and began to swim northward, away from the walls but into the north lake, which fed the two moats. He was a strong swimmer, but he was losing blood. When he reached the shore, he had to pull himself onto the land, where he lay in the reeds for a moment, coughing water from his lungs, his sides heaving with exertion, blood covering his back.

When at last he could walk, he made for the forest, hearing the hooves of Howard's men on horses not far behind him. He and Howard's men played cat-and-mouse the rest of the night and most of the next day as Rogan hid from them, then they circled back and he hid again.

At dusk he jumped on a Howard knight, slit his throat, and stole his horse. The men chased him, but Rogan whipped the horse until it bled and he outran them. At dawn the horse stopped, refusing to go further. He dismounted and began to walk.

The sun was high in the sky when he saw the outline of Moray Castle. He kept walking, stumbling over rocks, his muscles at last giving out after weeks of abuse.

One of the men on the parapets saw him, and within minutes, Severn was riding furiously toward him. Severn leaped off his horse before it stopped and clasped Rogan to him just as Rogan collapsed.

Severn was sure his brother was dying when he saw blood on his hands from Rogan's back. He started to pull Rogan toward the horse.

"No," Rogan said, pulling away. "Leave me."

"Leave you? By all that's holy, you have put us through hell. We heard Howard had killed you last night."

"He *did* kill me," Rogan whispered, turning away.

Severn saw the wound on his brother's back. It was still bloody and deep, but it was not enough to kill a man. "Where is she?"

"Liana?" Rogan asked. "Liana is dead."

Severn frowned. He had just been beginning to like

that woman. She was a great deal of trouble, like all women, but she wasn't a coward. He put his arm around Rogan's shoulders, "We'll find you another wife. We'll find you a beautiful one this time, and if you want one that'll set your bed on fire, we'll find her. As soon as—"

Severn wasn't prepared when Rogan whirled on him, slammed his fist in his jaw, and knocked him to the ground.

"You stupid bastard," Rogan said, straddling his brother's legs and glaring down at him. "You never understood anything. You with your high-born slut locked away, you fought her all the time. You made her life hell."

"Me?" Severn put his hand to his bloody nose. He started to rise, but one look at Rogan's face made him decide to stay where he was. "I wasn't the one who slept with other women. I didn't—" He stopped because the anger had left Rogan's face. He turned away and walked into the forest.

Severn got up and went to stand behind his brother. "I didn't mean to insult her memory. I liked her, but she's gone now and there are other women. At least she didn't betray you with Oliver Howard as your first wife did. Or did she? Is that why you're so angry?"

Rogan turned to his brother and, to Severn's horror and disbelief, there were tears that were beginning to roll down Rogan's cheeks. Severn could not speak. Rogan had not shed tears at the death of his father or any of his brothers.

"I loved her," Rogan whispered. "I loved her."

Severn was too embarrassed to watch this. He could not bear to see his brother cry. He backed away. "I'll leave the horse," he mumbled. "Come back when you're ready." He left very quickly.

Rogan collapsed to sit on a rock, his face buried in

his hands, and began to cry in earnest. He had loved her. He had loved her smiles, her laughter, her temper, the pleasure she received from the smallest things. She had brought laughter to him after a lifetime of hatred. She had given him clothes without lice or fleas, food that didn't grind his teeth down. She'd brought that arrogant bitch Iolanthe out of hiding, and she didn't know it but she'd made Zared ask Rogan to buy her some women's clothes.

And now she was gone. Killed in the feud with the Howards.

Perhaps her death should increase his hatred of the Howards, but it didn't. What did he care for the Howards? He wanted Liana back, his soft, sweet Liana who threw things when she was angry and kissed him when she was pleased.

"Liana," he whispered, and cried harder.

He didn't hear the footsteps in the soft bracken, and his grief was so deep that he didn't move when the soft hand touched his cheek.

Liana knelt before him and pulled his hands away from his face. She looked at his tear-stained face and tears came to her own eyes. "I am here, my love," she whispered, and kissed his hot eyelids, then his cheeks. "I am safe."

Rogan could only gape at her.

Liana smiled at him. "Have you nothing to say to me?"

He caught her and pulled her into his lap, then went rolling with her to the forest floor. His tears turned to laughter as he rolled over and over with her in his arms, his hands running up and down her body as if to reassure himself she was real.

At last he stopped and lay on his back, Liana on top of him, holding her so close she could barely breathe.

"How?" he whispered. "The Howard bitch—"

She put her fingertips to his lips. *"Jeanne,"* she said pointedly, "saved our lives. She knew one of her women was a traitor, and moments before she came to me, she overheard something that made her believe she knew which one it was. She sent me one way and took her traitorous maid the way you went. The woman thought Jeanne, shrouded in a cloak, was me and tried to stab her. Jeanne killed the woman while I was safe further down the wall. She had to tell you I was dead because she knew that otherwise you'd never leave the grounds."

She caressed Rogan's cheek. "I saw you swimming. If the Howard men hadn't been so interested in you, they would have seen me. Jeanne had horses waiting, so I was never far behind you, but you traveled so fast I could not catch you."

Her peasant's hood had fallen away in their tumbling and her hair had come down. It lay softly on her shoulders. Rogan touched it. "Do you find it ugly?" she whispered.

He looked back at her, love in his eyes. "There is *nothing* ugly about you. You are the most beautiful woman in the world and I love you, Liana. I love you with all my heart and soul."

She smiled at him. "Will you let me judge the courts? Can we add on to Moray? Will you stop fighting with the Howards? What should we name our son, my love?"

Rogan's anger began to rise, then he laughed and hugged her to him. "The courts are men's business, I'm not adding on to that heap of stone, Peregrines will always fight Howards, and I shall name my son John, after my father."

"Gilbert, after my father."

"So he can grow up to be lazy?"

"You'd rather he spent his life impregnating the

peasant girls and teaching his children to hate the Howards?"

"Yes," Rogan answered, holding her and looking up at the sky. "We may disagree on most things, but there is one we seem to agree on. Take off your clothes, wench."

She lifted her head and looked at him. "I am always obedient."

He started to speak, but she kissed him and he didn't say another word for hours.

A Captivating New Novel of Passion and Pride in the
Bestselling Tradition of *A Knight In Shining Armor*

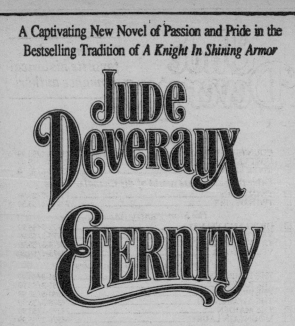

JUDE DEVERAUX

ETERNITY

The saga of the Montgomery family continues in
the stunning new novel from the *New York Times*
bestselling author Jude Deveraux.

Carrie Montgomery had never had to fight for
anything—until she met the most wonderful, most
exasperating man. Savor the romance and
adventure as they discover if their love can last for
all ETERNITY.